NIGHT
SHE

minds o... ...-stopping twist!'
Kathryn Croft, author of *The Girl With No Past*

'Deep, dark and disturbing . . . *The Foster Child* is a book that will
stay with me. I loved it' Liz Lawler, author of *Don't Wake Up*

'A perfect blend of psychological intrigue and downright creepiness.
I was thrilled, chilled, terrified and enthralled. This deserves to be
a huge hit' SJI Holliday, author of *Black Wood*

'Completely engrossed, I devoured this in two sittings and couldn't turn the pages fast enough. An exhilarating read' Nina Pottell

Praise for **Before I Let You In**:

'An unnerving psychological thriller with a stonking final twist' *Sunday Mirror*

'Compelling, disturbing and thoroughly enjoyable' Sharon Bolton, author of *Little Black Lies*

'I loved it. Jenny is an evil genius' Lisa Hall, author of *Between You and Me*

'An outstanding and original thriller with . . . an explosive conclusion' B A Paris, author of *Behind Closed Doors*

'[A] captivating, twisty and satisfying tale . . . I can't wait to see what Blackhurst comes up with next' S.J.I. Holliday, author of *The Damsel Fly*

'Gripping and relatable. I loved it' Helen Fitzgerald, author of *The Cry*

'A gripping, clever book. I loved it and didn't want it to end' Claire Douglas, author of *Local Girl Missing*

'Such a clever twist, I really enjoyed it' Claire McGowan, author of *Blood Tide*

'A superb thriller. Compelling and thoroughly gripping. Highly recommended' Luca Veste, author of *Dead Gone*

'Brilliant. A dark psychological thriller that will have you looking suspiciously at your own friends' Mason Cross, author of *The Killing Season*

1

Rebecca

The night of the wedding

The remaining wedding guests gather on the lawn, sobered by shock, stunned into silence by their grief. A woman, Evelyn's Great Aunt Beth, sobs quietly into a handkerchief handed to her by her husband, a slip of a man, weak-chested and weak-willed. Only three hours ago he had frowned and nodded in all the right places while Beth had complained about everything from the 'bohemian' ceremony, music, décor and the 'downright hippy' friends Evelyn had made herself. How her late niece, Evelyn's mother, would be turning in her still-fresh grave to see her friends and family associating with such classlessness. Now silence prevails as it seems her daughter will be joining her.

My heart thuds as I stand outside the hotel door, listening to muted voices interspersed with furious outbursts. Richard.

I brace myself to go in, but falter as Richard begins to shout again, screaming that he should be out searching, that his wife would not have done this to him. This is my cue – I know that as Evie's best friend and maid of honour I have my part to play – but suddenly I don't want to open that door. I don't want to see the look on Richard's face or watch his heart breaking.

Footsteps the other side of the door shock me into action and I slam my fist against it.

'Richard!' It opens almost immediately, and behind it stands one of the police officers I'd seen lead Richard away twenty minutes before. The longest twenty minutes of my life. 'I need to speak to Richard.'

'I'm sorry,' he begins, but a voice from inside cuts him off.

'Let her in,' Richard says, and the sigh of resignation tells me what I need to know. 'She's Evie's best friend, she deserves to hear this.'

The police officer steps to one side and I barrel past him into the small hotel room, with its whitewashed walls and near-perfect view of the cliffs. The same cliffs Richard Bradley's wife has just thrown herself from.

'Richard!' I hurl myself at him, grasping his forearms. 'Where's Evie? They're saying downstairs that she jumped off the cliff, but that's crazy. Where is she?'

When he doesn't speak I shake him, but he still can't say the words. One of the police officers, the woman, looks as though she wants to cry as she steps forward and places a hand on my arm and gently but firmly guides me away.

'My name is Detective Michelle Green, this is Detective Thomas.'

First-name Michelle's voice is slow and kind, Detective Thomas just stands there looking brooding. He is tall and broad, olive skin and dark hair. He looks like a TV cop – but so far it's a non-speaking part. Every now and then he gives me an appraising look, one that makes me feel guilty, like I'm doing something wrong for being here. He's just watching, waiting. What for?

'We've had reports of a woman fitting Evelyn's description seen entering the water around forty minutes ago. Have you seen Mrs Bradley in the last hour?'

I picture my best friend the last time I saw her, forty-five minutes ago. She is walking towards the edge of the marquee when she turns back. She seeks me out, and as our eyes meet she gives me a reassuring smile. She doesn't look afraid, as I am, she is unflinching and unhesitant. She turns away and disappears into the darkness and for a split second I want to run after her, grab her and not let go. But my feet don't move, and the moment is gone. *She* is gone.

'No,' I say. 'I haven't seen her.'

I've sobbed until my eyes are raw and tight, real tears that take me by surprise. *That's it then*, a voice in my mind says. *She's gone. You're on your own.* And the thought is almost too much to bear.

Richard is still talking to the police, and I get the impression they are keeping him here so he won't go to the clifftop, so he won't do anything stupid. I am staring out of the window at where torches are panning the area, and where the white lights of the search and rescue helicopter light up the sky.

'They have a helicopter,' I say, and my voice sounds as though it belongs to someone else. I wish it did, then those lights would be seeking out someone else's best friend in the darkness.

'Which is only just arriving. It's been nearly a fucking hour,' Richard blasts. He walks to the window then immediately back, chewing at the loose skin on his top lip – an annoying habit that pops up when he's anxious. 'She'll be freezing. And why are they concentrating on below the cliffs? She could have swum halfway back to London by now.'

Because they aren't looking for a woman swimming. I don't want to say the words, and neither do the police. Richard has to come to the obvious conclusion himself. That tonight his wife, my best friend, jumped into the sea to die. And I'm the only person who knows why.

2

Rebecca

I remember the first time I met Evie White, although I had no idea then of the darkness she would bring into my life. I was eighteen years old and head over heels in love with a bass guitarist called Steve, who was, of course, a complete idiot, and who I genuinely believed would be my ticket into social acceptance at the University of London. I'd been there almost a year and managed to amass a grand total of three friends: Sandra, an overweight History student whose idea of a wild night out was a Nando's after debate society; Christopher – not Chris, never Chris – who turned bright red when anyone talked to him and had only become my friend when he'd been forced to work with me in the café; and Sunny, a Chinese exchange student who I had bonded with over our mutual appreciation of *Twilight*. This was not how I had pictured my first year – the year where I was supposed to shake off my geeky senior school persona and walk head high among my people.

Steve and I met on a business course. I was there because I thought that I was destined to be the next Karren Brady; he was there because his dad had told him if he wanted to continue to be funded he'd better get himself a bloody degree.

I think Steve realised pretty quickly that there was no way he was going to pass the course on his own (so maybe not a total idiot), and his best chance lay with the plain, shy, but not totally unfortunate-looking female sitting at the back of the room on her own. Me. I'd had no idea what to do with myself when he sat down next to me and whispered, 'Hi.'

'Hi me?'

Even his smile was lazy and feckless. His eyes were barely visible under his mop of sandy brown curls, which he pushed from his face every few minutes.

'Yeah, hi you. You wanna buddy up for this project?'

I groaned. 'You mean, do I want to do the project for both of us?'

To his credit, his expression remained unchanged. It wasn't until later I'd realise he only had that one docile expression.

'I'm hurt.'

'Come on. What's in this for me?'

'Okay fine,' hair push. 'I happened to notice that you have managed to do every single project on your own so far. No one meets you from class and the only person I've seen you with in the Union is that fat chick.'

I opened my mouth to defend Sandra but he didn't give me the chance.

'So, I figured, I get to pass a project with a decent mark for once, and you get to hang around with someone who doesn't smell like they ran a marathon when they just went to get a Coke.'

'That's really mean.'

He smiled then, a killer shot-to-the-heart smile, and I knew there was no way I was saying no.

'Do we have a deal?'

'Fine, deal.'

A week later we were sleeping together. Two weeks later

he referred to me as his 'girlfriend' at a party in front of his friends. Okay, so he was drunk and stoned but as far as I was concerned it still counted. In two weeks, my evenings had gone from reading about other people's lives to actually living mine. Steve's apartment was rarely ever empty, there was always someone over for a few drinks, the band practising until all hours in the morning, or people just dossing over after a night in the city. It was great fun but at some point it became a bit too much for a straight-laced A-grade business student like me.

'I'm going to stay at mine tonight, babe.'

Steve propped himself up on his elbow in bed next to me. 'What's up? You tired of me already?'

I smiled. Nothing could be further from the truth. 'Don't be stupid. I just need to get some sleep, I've missed the last three morning classes in a row. I'll pop over after Economics.'

'Okay, gorgeous, take notes for me, yeah?'

'Always do.'

The next morning, freshly showered with a full night's sleep and real food in the morning, I'd felt amazing and I'd paid attention during my lecture for the first time in two weeks, making detailed notes to share with my new boyfriend. On the way round to his flat I'd picked up coffee and bacon sandwiches, a gesture I knew he'd appreciate after the night of drinking he'd no doubt had. God he was lucky to have me.

We hadn't got to the spare key stage so I knocked on the door of his flat and prepared myself for the twenty-minute wait it usually took him to get himself up. More surprising than the fact that the door opened after only a couple of minutes was the half-naked girl who stood in the empty frame.

She was Amazonian tall, with tanned legs that seemed to go on forever. Her feet were bare, as was the rest of her bottom half, save for a grey thong that at some point before the student-style one-load-fits-all washing had surely been white. On her top half she wore a short, baggy grey T-shirt that clearly had nothing underneath. Her face was as tanned as her legs, with a smattering of freckles that suggested her colouring wasn't bottled. Her hair was dark blonde and tousled and she had the tired but relaxed demeanour of someone who had spent the night having sex. With my boyfriend.

'I'm looking for Steve,' I managed stupidly.

'Shower.' She opened the door wider to let me in and disappeared inside without even asking who I was.

When I mustered the courage to walk inside she was sitting on the sofa, rolling a joint. I sat down on the chair opposite her, self-consciously hugging the bag with the rolls in my lap.

'Um, who are you?'

The girl studied me intently. Here she was, a thing of pure beauty, and yet she looked at me as though I was a rare butterfly under a microscope. Her eyes were the colour of mint ice cream. She lit up the joint and took a long drag.

'Evie.' Her voice was smooth, melodic. 'Want some?' She held it out, blowing smoke through lazily opened lips.

'No, thanks.'

She lay back on the sofa and shrugged. I shifted in my seat.

'Actually, yes, please.'

The look on Steve's face when he came out of the shower was priceless. Clearly, he had no concept of the time, having spent the night screwing the goddess who was now lying on his sofa, and managed to splutter his way through an apology neither of us were really listening to. Evie was talking about cultural stereotypes in advertising with such passion on her face that my relationship with Steve was dead before the

10

joint the three of us shared. At the time he thought he'd dodged a real bullet, me not freaking out and just stepping gracefully aside to let the beautiful Evie White take my place.

'What are you studying, Evie?' I asked while Steve threw bemused looks at me.

'Photography. You can find the mind's construction in the face.' She leaned over the side of the sofa and picked up a fancy-looking long-lens camera, revealing more tanned flesh as she lifted the hem of her T-shirt to dust it off. Resting her elbows on her knees, she peered into the viewfinder. 'They say that every time someone takes your photo they take a part of your soul.'

She pressed down on the shutter and the camera whirred.

'There you go, now I have your soul.'

3

Rebecca

'What the fuck is going on here?'

That thick French accent, the demanding tone – Evie's father has arrived. Dominic Rousseau charges past Detective Thomas into the room and I cringe at the despair on his handsome face. The man who has had women falling at his feet over the years, such a dominating force in the business world, looks utterly broken. Michelle visibly shrinks back at his voice. After a few seconds Richard steps forward.

'Dominic, they're saying she jumped—' Dominic rounds on him and Thomas takes a step forward, ready to step in if things take a turn for the worse – as if this night could get any worse.

'Impossible! Today is Evelyn's wedding day! Why the hell would she try to kill herself on what is *supposed* to be the happiest day of her life?'

'She was seen, sir,' Michelle stutters. 'Two witnesses on the cliffs opposite called the police when they saw a woman in a wedding dress enter the sea. We're doing everything we can to find her.'

'Clearly that's not enough. You,' he turns to me. 'Did she say anything about this to you? Was she upset about anything?'

'I, no sir, she seemed fine the last time I saw her.'

In a way, it is harder to lie to Dominic than it is to Richard or the police. I feel like he can see right through me, into my thoughts, like a human lie detector.

'What did you do to her?' The treacherous coward inside me breathes a sigh of relief when he turns back on Richard.

'What do you mean, *do* to her?' Richard finds his voice and it's a furious one. 'I didn't do anything to her! I love her. We just got married.'

'Well you must have done something to make my daughter so miserable she would pull this stunt on her wedding day!'

'Evie never gave anyone responsibility for her happiness, you of all people should know *that*.'

'What do you mean, *me of all people?* What's that supposed to mean? I wasn't even here!'

For a fleeting moment, it crosses my mind that this is exactly what Evie would have wanted. She couldn't have planned it better if she'd been here to throw the bait. The two men in her life fighting over who had loved her more, even as her body smashes against the rocks, even as her soul drifts out to sea, she is still the most imposing figure in any room. *There you go, now I've got your soul.*

And she had. For the next seven years Evie White had had my soul, and now she's given it back and I don't know what to do with it any more. She'd been the most important thing in my life, deciding where we'd go and what we'd wear so often that I no longer have any idea who I am without her. What films will I watch now I have to choose them alone? What music do I like? Every CD I own was recommended to me by my other half with her infectious enthusiasm. *Try this, Becky, you'll* adore *it. This would smell* wonderful *on you. Blue is* absolutely *your colour.* What do I do now?

'That's exactly my point,' Richard snaps. 'Perhaps if you'd *been* here for the happiest day of her life. . .'

I suck air between my teeth, waiting for an explosion that doesn't come. Instead Dominic looks weary, rubs a hand across his face and turns to Michelle.

'What is being done? Is someone out there looking for her? Every second you wait is a second my daughter is on her own, in the darkness. She will freeze to death.'

'There are helicopters scanning the area now, sir.'

'Well they don't seem to be doing enough.' Michelle goes to speak but he holds up a hand and her mouth closes like a fish. 'I don't want to hear your empty platitudes. Have your superiors contact me in my room immediately. I want to know how they plan to find my daughter.'

And with that, he left, not even glancing at Richard or I on the way out.

One month later

4

Rebecca

The child behind me in the heaving queue grasps the corner of my bag of pasta and yanks. I realise too late – despite this being the thirteen hundredth time he's done it – and he breaks into hysterical laughter as my conchiglie crashes to the floor. His mother doesn't look up from where she's thumbing the screen of her phone frantically as if she's one of the Bletchley Girls. As I bend down to retrieve my food he throws his plastic figure at me, so close that I feel it snag my hair. He laughs and holds out his hand for me to pass it back to him. With a swift kick I send it skidding under the checkout – small victories.

I heave the 5p bags into the boot of the car and slam it shut with a satisfying click. I seem to spend half my life at one supermarket or another lately, keeping my own house running as well as making sure Richard is fed. Because if I didn't do it, let's face it, he'd probably forget to eat altogether.

It's been four weeks since the wedding, four weeks with no body, and no answers. We – Richard and I – spent the first week in the hotel, mainly sitting in his room trying not to look out of the window, waiting for the phone call to come.

It was Michelle who quietly suggested that Richard went back to Kensington and tried to resume some kind of normality – promising to call him at the slightest bit of news.

That was three weeks ago, and she kept to her promise, calling him every day at first, just to check how he was getting on. Then the calls slowed to every other day. I'm not sure he's even had one this week.

No body equals no closure and we've returned back to London. I work from home as an online PA so at least I can keep a close eye on Richard. Until Evie is found, he can't even begin to move on, stuck in some awful limbo circle of confusion, hope and guilt. How do you desperately hope for confirmation your wife is dead without feeling guilty? And yet while there is still hope there is no chance of moving past the denial stage of grief. He wants answers – the main question being, *why?*

He's been snappy and surly, so much so that two weeks after we came home I was ready to ditch him altogether, let him ferment in filthy underwear and suffocating self-pity, but it was Evie's voice that forced me to stay. *We did this to him*, I heard her whisper in my ear. *Now you have to help him through it.*

And slowly, there have been signs of change. He's started to get dressed before I even turn up in the mornings now, and bit by bit I can sense the old Richard, with his dry wit and his infinite eighties cult movie references, beginning to surface. Every now and then, though, I catch him asking that same question in his mind. *Why?*

'Maybe she was ill,' he'd suggested to me just last night, as we'd watched one of the soaps that neither of us ever liked but Evie never missed. An old man on the screen was clasping the hand of a young woman – his daughter, I think – asking her to help him, when the time came. 'Maybe she was like this guy, maybe she had cancer and she didn't want any of us to suffer. That would be just like her.'

'Maybe,' I'd mused. 'But it would be more like her to want us all to know about it first.'

'Still, I'll ask my solicitor about getting access to her medical records.'

Tonight I'm cooking spaghetti carbonara, fully aware that Richard will probably push his portion around the plate, take a couple of bites and make the obligatory yummy noises before scraping the lot into the bin.

Shoving the car into reverse, I'm about to negotiate my way out of the car park when my phone buzzes in the centre console. Cursing under my breath I swipe the screen, hoping it's not Richard asking me to go back in; knowing I will if he asks. *Grow a backbone, Rebecca, or are you going to let him walk all over you now?* Unfair – his wife is missing presumed dead, he's entitled to ask me to pick up some chocolate chip cookies, or whatever he wants now.

It's not a text message, it's a Facebook notification.

Evelyn Bradley sent you a friend request!

5

Evie

'Papa! Papa! *Mère est morte!*' the five-year-old girl threw herself through the door of her father's work room. *'Morte!'*

'Calm down, Evelyn,' her father spoke slowly and in perfect English. He loved his native language but since moving to England he had acquiesced to her mother's request that they spoke only English at home. *We don't want her growing up here as the French girl, Dominic. Girls around here, it's important that they fit in.* 'Your mother is not dead. I just spoke with her half hour before. What is this silliness? *English please.'*

'On the sofa. . . *morte! Elle a.* . . um, she has, she has eaten the sleepy pills and she won't move.' Evie collapsed against her father's chest, tears spilling down her cheeks. *'S'il te plaît, viens!* Please come!'

Evie's father sighed and laid down his pen. He lifted his daughter up under her arms and placed a kiss on a forehead besieged by messy blonde curls.

'Your mother is very much alive, Evelyn Rousseau, and just to prove it I shall go and throw a cup of water on her silly face.'

Evelyn's eyes widened. She was so very sure that her mother was dead, but it was still a risky plan.

'If you do that, Papa, you had better hope Mama is dead,' she warned him, her face full of seriousness.

Her father laughed. It was his true laugh, the one he laughed with her (although she didn't always know why) and Emily, the English tutor he had bought for her before Mama had sent her away, but never with the businessmen that came, and not even Mama any more. They got the fake laugh, the bastard laugh. Evelyn called it that because when Papa was with these people he was a bastard, pretending they were funny and interesting and completely ignoring her. Touching the women when Mama wasn't looking, or when she was unwell in her bedroom, thinking Evelyn was too young to realise what was happening when he leant in close to them and whispered in their ears, or when they put a hand on his chest, lowered their eyes and smiled. She knew what those dirty hors wanted. That's what Mama called them, Daddy's Dirty Hors and those Bastard Men.

And now, Papa marched her to the big house, and carried her into the kitchen where he put her on the floor and filled a glass of water.

'Come, Evie.'

She hung back and shook her head. Mama was dead and Evie didn't want to see her being dead again. It had been a heck of a shock the first time, her mouth hanging open and her fat pink tongue flopping out of the side of it.

'Okay, sweetie, you wait there.'

She heard her father move into the drawing room where she knew Mama was dead. She heard him say one of the worst cuss words and heard the splash of the water hitting her mother's face and her mother's scream, then equally-as-damning cuss words.

She's alive! So why is Papa shouting? Why is he so mad, Mama is alive, thank the Lord!

'You stupid bitch! What are you trying to do to that poor girl? Do you want her to be as fucked up as you?'

'If I'm fucked up, Dominic, it's because of you! You and your dirty whores. You drive me to this, you know that? If I kill myself my blood will be on your hands. I'd rather die than lose you.'

Evie shuddered. Even at five years old she knew this wasn't how love was supposed to be. And one thing she knew for certain – she would never let herself love someone enough that they made her want to die.

6

Rebecca

Sitting in the supermarket car park staring at the friend request on my phone, my first thought – as stupid as it seems – is that it's her. *It's really her.* She's alive!

As quickly as my heart starts thumping in my chest, the normal, rational side of me kicks in.

Idiot. If Evie were alive she would not be contacting you via a Facebook profile you've never seen before. This was not part of any plan.

I click on the profile picture – it's from a distance but there she stands, on the edge of a cliff in her wedding dress. Her wedding day; the night she died. There's no way Evie could have taken this photo herself.

The only way to find out is to click 'accept'. I know how weird it's going to look if any of our friends see on my timeline 'Rebecca Thompson is now friends with Evelyn Bradley' but does it matter? If anyone asks I can tell them the truth – some weird troll has created a Facebook profile and I accepted the request to find out who it was.

I scroll down the profile. I am Evelyn Bradley's only friend and the irony doesn't escape me. Despite how everyone she met fell in love with her charm, her beauty and her wit,

Evie trusted very few people with her love in return. There were a couple of girls in high school back in Wareham, posh totty types who had squealed and hopped up and down at the sight of Evie in her wedding dress, but for all of my best friend's popularity, the number of people who really knew her could be counted on one hand. And Richard wasn't one of them.

The profile is empty save from the picture of Evie on the clifftop and it doesn't seem to have any real purpose. The caption reads: 'When fair is foul, and foul is fair.'

Then, as I think I'd known it would ever since I saw the friend request, the phone buzzes and a circle pops up with Evie's profile picture in it. A message. As I click on it an image of Evie emerging from the sea flashes into my mind. Her skin is encrusted with barnacles, chunks of flesh have been peeled away by birds and other scavengers. One eye protrudes from the socket. I think I might throw up. Four whole weeks of waiting for my best friend's body to be dragged from the sea has taken its toll. For one brief moment I pray that this person is really her, that she's alive and playing one of her silly games.

Long time no see, bestie. What's up? You look like you've seen a ghost LOLOLOLOLOLOLOLOL

I let out the breath I was holding in, a mixture of disappointment and relief. It isn't her.

7

Rebecca

I scan the other cars in the car park. Sunlight reflects off the windscreens; they could all be empty, or any one of them could be masking an axe-wielding maniac. Scenes from countless horror movies run through my mind and I sneak a look over my shoulder into the back seat. Empty. I used to scoff cynically at the stupid girls running up the stairs screaming – usually with their heaving bosoms spilling from their teeny vest tops – and waiting to be saved by a heroic man. Evie would be cheering on the faceless killer and pointing out all of the ways that they could be more successful in their murderous rampages. Now I wish she was here to tell me I was being ridiculous, jumping at text messages – no killer ever struck in the middle of the day in a supermarket car park.

The woman from behind me in the supermarket queue struggles to get her tiny psychopath into his car seat and an old guy sits in an Audi wearing a crumpled suit jacket and looking like he might have fallen asleep waiting for his wife to do the shopping. There's no one else around me.

COLD

IM NOT IN A CAR

My thumb freezes over my phone screen. I glance at the mirrored windows of the supermarket café. Are they inside? I picture myself going into the café and confronting whoever it might be, but the image of me ripping the phone from someone's hands to find out they are texting their mum stops me. *Stop being so paranoid. No one is watching you.*

I type back:

Who is this?

And wait.

I don't have to wait long, 'Evelyn' replies almost instantly.

YOU KNOW.

Still with the sickening sense someone is watching me, I toss my phone onto the passenger seat, put the car into reverse and start to pull out. Right on cue my head unit starts to ring with a call from a private number. When I punch 'accept' the call cuts off and my phone buzzes again. I slam on the brakes.

DON'T IGNORE ME

Someone walks in front of the car, making me jump. Just a posh-looking middle-aged woman in a quilted jacket who scowls at me for no apparent reason.

I don't know who this is but you're sick. We are grieving for my best friend. Leave me alone and delete this profile or I will call the police.

The bitch with the devil child pulls up behind me and taps the horn, forcing me to pull off with the phone still in my lap. I'm turning onto the main road when the head unit rings again, loud and persistent, only to cut off when I press 'accept'. I pick up my phone and wedge it between my knees, trying to read the string of messages and not lose control of the car.

SHAME YOU HAD TO GO. I WAS ENJOYING THAT.
WHY DO YOU MAKE SUCH FACES? WHEN ALLS DONE,
YOU LOOK BUT ON A STOOL.
WHY THE LONG FACE, BECKY?
WHY ARE YOU IGNORING ME?
WHY ARE YOU IGNORING ME?

Letting out a growl of frustration I chuck the phone into the back seat and hit the Bluetooth button to disconnect from the car. I can hear it buzzing all the way back to Richard and Evie's house and when I pull up outside there are fourteen missed calls from private numbers and two more messages.

YOU CAN'T IGNORE ME FOREVER.

My hands are shaking as I reverse onto the drive. I should just start up the car and drive to the police station, but I'm certain they won't do anything but take a report and tell me to block the bastard, which is exactly what I'm going to do.

I type back Who is this? What do you want? in a last-ditch attempt to find out who is behind the profile but I'm not expecting the troll to come clean and give me their name and address. They reply instantly.

YOU COULD HAVE SAVED ME

Me? As in Evie?

YOUCOULDHAVESAVEDMEYOUCOULDHAVESAVEDME-
YOUCOULDHAVESAVEDMEYOUCOULDHAVESAVEDME-
YOUCOULDHAVESAVEDMEYOUCOULDHAVESAVEDME-
YOUCOULDHAVESAVEDMEYOUCOULDHAVESAVEDME-
YOUCOULDHAVESAVEDMEYOUCOULDHAVESAVEDME

Over and over it continues until I pull up the Evie profile and click 'block'.

8

Evie

Piano music drifted into Evie's bedroom from the reception hall downstairs. The party had begun. This was Evie's favourite part of Mama and Papa's parties, the part where the guests arrived in all of their finery, the women looking like shimmering angels and the men looking handsome in their fine suits. As the evening wore on inevitably the flowers would wilt, the swans beginning to look more like ducklings as make-up faded and eyes glassed over. Voices would become louder and everyone would seem that little bit more real and oh so slightly less appealing. For now, until the masks slipped, they would be ethereal.

She had found, after years of spying on her parents' parties, that if she lay on her bedroom floor and opened her bedroom door just a crack, Evie could see the guests as they were escorted from the sweeping reception hallway to the entertaining room. Faces she recognised from the television and newspapers were greeted by Papa like old friends and Evie longed to be by his side, in her best party dress to be kissed on the cheek and congratulated on being the prettiest girl in the room. But she must wait a while, until Papa was engaged with his 'guests' before she could sneak downstairs for a peek. So for now she was lying flat on her stomach watching the guests arrive, waiting for her chance to sneak down and look around.

Her mother said the word 'guests' as though it were a cuss word, like it tasted nasty in her mouth, but Evie thought she must have imagined it because they liked the guests, didn't they? Otherwise why would they be inviting them to a party? Unless maybe it was like her birthday party, when she had invited the whole class because even though some of the boys were a bit mean and rude she couldn't bear to have left any of them out – not when the rest of the class would be talking about it for weeks. So maybe Mama secretly didn't like some of the guests but she just didn't want them to feel left out.

When she was certain the party was full enough for her not to be seen, Evie slipped into the ballroom, looking around immediately for signs of Papa. She couldn't see him anywhere; he was always so busy at these parties that she was bound to be able to stay out of his sight.

Finally, she had a chance to look at the ballroom. It was magical. In the daytime the ballroom was too big and empty to be any fun. Her voice echoed around it and there was always a chill in the air. There was no such chill tonight. Everything was shimmering, bathed in a golden light. Tables and chairs adorned with cream silk and golden bows, feathered centre-pieces, mirrors and pearls. The grand piano in the corner was being played by a man Evie recognised as Serge, who had come all the way from France. She had met him several times before and at first found him a little scary, with his wild curly hair and features too large for his face, always puffing on an awful cigarette. But he had been playful and kind to her, rubbing her hair and singing to her, and now she always looked forward to his visits to the house. Although Mama didn't feel the same, she always seemed to regard Serge with exasperation.

THE NIGHT SHE DIED

Evie had heard her refer to him as a 'bloody liability' to Papa who had only smiled and replied, 'You know why he does these things, Monique. And it works, the whole world knows his name.' Evie longed to go and see him now but Papa would certainly throw her out of the party if she went to join the musician, who had a woman on his lap already and a cigar the size of a rolled-up newspaper hanging from his upper lip.

Evie slipped through the crowd, mostly unseen in a sea of champagne drinkers, some swaying slightly to the music, others engaged in loud, lively conversation, swilling drink from their glasses so vehemently that it sloshed over the sides and splashed onto the shiny parquet floor where it would leave sticky marks for the cleaners who would be drafted in to restore order in the morning. Outside on the veranda more people gathered to smoke cigarettes and cigars under the watchful eye of the moon.

At the near side of the garden a young boy, maybe a couple of years older than Evie herself, played quietly under the oak tree. He was dressed in beige chinos and a white linen shirt and his gaze focused intently on the model of a soldier he held in his hand. Dark curls fell forwards into his eyes; Evie couldn't see the colour but she imagined they were a vivid green, the exact same shade as hers. His face was tanned and set in a slight frown of concentration. Aside from her father, Evie thought he was the most beautiful boy she had ever seen.

The boy looked up, catching her off guard, and she didn't have time to look away. He spotted Evie and lifted a hand in a half wave. Her head thought about waving back but her hand didn't move. He gestured for her to come closer, to join him under the tree, and she forced her legs to propel her forwards, her heart hammering in her chest. How would she speak to him? What if she said something stupid and he laughed at her?

Evelyn Rousseau, if someone laughs at you they are not the kind of person whose opinion you should court, Papa's voice spoke in her mind. And yet she did care if this boy laughed, she cared very much, it seemed.

'Hello,' the boy said as she approached. 'Who are you?'

Evie saw that his eyes were not the exact same shade of green as hers, but a clear cornflower blue, like the ocean on a calm day. She almost forgot to answer.

'Evie,' she said eventually. 'Who are you?'

'James Preston-Addlington Jr,' he said, with the air of someone who introduced himself by full name on a daily basis. 'My father is James Addlington and my mother is Daphne Preston. Who are your parents? Why are you wearing your pyjamas?'

Evie hesitated. She knew that telling the truth would likely impress the boy very much; after all it was her party he was at, her tree he was playing under. But Papa had told her very firmly that she was not to come to the party. If this boy tattled on her she would be in big trouble.

'My mother is working in the kitchens,' she lied quite easily. She had watched Mama do this for as long as she could remember; as long as you were confident in what you said most people would believe anything. And if there were difficult questions, a very simple 'Oh darling, what does it really matter?' would usually suffice.

'Are you supposed to be out here with the guests?' His tone was somewhat rude. Evie felt her chin lift defiantly, despite her best intentions to make a good impression.

'Why shouldn't I be?'

The boy looked wrong-footed, as though he hadn't expected to be challenged, or maybe because the answer was so obvious.

'Well, because you're with the help,' he shrugged. 'You shouldn't be out here with the proper guests. You should be in the kitchen.'

32

'I don't see why,' Evie replied, affronted. She had almost forgotten that her guise of a kitchen maid's daughter was a lie. '*I'm* not working.'

'Look,' the boy smiled in an affable way. Five minutes ago Evie would have said it made him even more beautiful. Now she thought it an arrogant smile that she would very much like to wipe off his exquisite – no, *conceited* – face. 'I'm not trying to be rude. I'm just letting you know, in case you didn't, that there are certain social conventions at something like this. The guests stay out here, and the help, they stay in there,' he gestured to the house. 'In the kitchen, out of sight. Unless they are bringing drinks and things but even then they have to look smart, not in their *pyjamas*, and they shouldn't really talk to the guests. I'm just trying to help you.'

At seven years old Evie had been brought up well enough to know what social conventions were. They were things like always saying please and thank you, not wiping your nose on your sleeve in company, smiling if someone thought they were making a joke, even if it wasn't funny, and never, *ever*, saying bloody hell in front of grown-ups. She'd never once heard Mama or Papa saying that the kitchen staff should stay in the kitchen, or that they weren't to talk to the guests. Goodness, Yasmin was like a part of the family!

'But, but the kitchen staff are just normal people, like you and me.'

James Preston-Addlington Jr smiled again and this time Evie had to hold one hand in the other to stop it slapping his face.

'Of course, they are. I'm not saying they aren't. They just have to know their place, like everyone else. I know mine, and you must know yours. Everyone can't be equal, can they? Some people just have to be better. I'm not being rude.'

'Well you bloody are!' Evie exclaimed, forgetting both the rule about cuss words and the rule about raising one's voice. 'You are being, being,' she struggled for a word strong enough, 'a bastard!'

The boy raised his hand to his cheek as though he had been slapped. Then, recovering quickly, he gave a curt nod.

'See what I mean? Kitchen staff aren't fit for decent company. You'd better get lost before I have your mother fired for what you just said to me.'

Evie could barely speak through her anger. She was desperate to let this horrid boy call his father, have them realise who she was and get him thrown out of her house. But then, she realised miserably, what would that prove? That she was a worthy person, not because she was a kitchen maid's daughter, but because her father was Dominic Rousseau. The party ruined, Evie turned on her heels, stormed back into the house and upstairs to her room without stopping for her hot milk.

She sobbed hot angry tears until the lightest of knocks on her bedroom door.

'You were at the party tonight, Evelyn Rousseau?'

Evie's eyes widened and then dropped to the floor. So, the dog was out of the bag. She nodded and waited for the yelling to start.

Her father placed a finger under her chin and lifted her face so their eyes met.

'What am I to expect? I raised a strong independent young lady, I shouldn't be surprised when she uses that strength to disobey me.'

Evie thought of the party, of that awful boy who had made her feel so bad, and began to sob again. Papa, a shocked look on his handsome face, pulled her quickly to his chest.

'Oh Evie, sweetheart, what is it? What did I say now? You

must ignore me, I am a silly old goat who clearly knows nothing of the sensitivities of women. Ask your mother, I'm sure she has a folder detailing all the stupid things I have said to her.'

'It's not you, Papa,' Evie sniffed between sobs. 'At the party, there was a boy.'

'Ouch. Boys already?' Dominic Rousseau held his daughter at arm's length. 'I must admit I thought I had a few more years before negotiating this particular obstacle. So tell me, my love, what is the name of the boy I am to have killed?'

Evie smiled and wiped her tears onto a now grubby sleeve. 'Papa.'

'Okay fine, I'll just have Phillip rough him up a bit. No?' he widened his eyes and Evie laughed. 'So tell me, what a father is to do when a boy makes his little princess cry? What did he do to you, angel Evie?'

'He said mean things.'

'About the most beautiful girl in the world? What could he possibly say?'

'It wasn't about me, Papa,' Evie sighed impatiently. 'He thought I was one of the service lady's daughters.'

'And why did he think that?'

'Because I told him I was,' Evie mumbled. She set her jaw defiantly. 'And he said I had no place being with, with. . .' she struggled to remember the words. 'With the high classes. With *important people.*'

Dominic's lip curled in amusement. 'So why does this make you so sad, Evie? You know that you are not the daughter of the service lady. You know who you are.'

'But Papa, what he said. . . do you believe it's true? Do you believe that I would be less important if you and Mama worked on service? Would I be less worthy?'

Now her papa was smiling properly and Evie felt a swell of anger at him now, as well as the boy.

'You should take me seriously, Papa.'

'Oh Evie, I do.' He rearranged his face into a sombre expression. 'My child, I am smiling because you speak with the wisdom of someone five times your seven years. There are those within our circles who believe that people with money and status are worth more than those without. Ah, wait a minute,' he held up a finger at her indignant expression. 'I didn't say I was one of them. Your outrage shows me what kind of heart you have, Evelyn, and the boy's words, well they may not be a sign of his heart but more a product of his upbringing. Remember, a child will be soaking in opinions and ideas from their parents since they were a very small baby. You cannot hope to change these in one party.'

'Then how do I change them, Papa?'

'You must find a way to make people see the world from behind your eyes. And don't ever let the world change what you see. We love who we love, Evelyn, without class or status, creed or colour and without fear. And when they are stripped back, the heart of a person who holds a tray is equal to that of those who eat from it. Don't ever let anyone tell you what you are worth. You must discover that for yourself.'

9

Rebecca

My hands still feel slightly shaky as I knock on Richard's front door, still reeling from the messages.

You could have saved me.

Who was trying to blame me for what happened to Evie?

When Richard opens the door he grins.

'Finally – the food delivery. I ordered it hours ago,' he jokes, then looks down at my empty hands. 'Where's the food?'

'Erm,' I look down stupidly. 'I left it in the boot.'

'Okaaay,' he says, his eyebrows furrowing and concern filling his brown eyes. 'Do you want a hand with it?'

'Oh, um, yes please.'

He turns to put something down and it's not until we are returning with the bags of shopping that I see what it was. It explains his good mood at least – a bottle of beer.

'Have you been drinking?'

Richard glances back guiltily. 'Just a couple.'

'Richard, it's one in the afternoon. I thought things were getting better. I thought you were—'

He lifts the shopping bags from the boot and turns to me.

'Well I thought I was entitled to a drink, considering I am on my honeymoon.'

Instantly I feel terrible. Today was supposed to be Evie and Richard's honeymoon, of course it was. They had deferred the trip because of Richard's work, so instead of heading off straight after the wedding they'd had to book for a month or so later. Today, it appeared. I sigh.

'God, I'm sorry. I completely forgot. Do you want me to go?'

Richard shrugs, as though he couldn't care less, which stings a bit. I don't know many of his other friends who would basically take on the task of keeping him alive while he drowned in his grief. No pun intended.

'If you're going to stay, at least have a drink. It's not the Maldives, I'm afraid, but then. . .'

He stops short of saying, 'But then you're not Evie.'

'I asked my solicitor about getting access to her medical records.' Richard emerges from the patio doors onto the veranda holding a couple of beers in one hand and a blanket in the other. He throws the blanket at me and switches on the patio heater for good measure.

I'd managed to convince him to hold off on his drinking until he'd eaten some lunch – if I couldn't stop him getting tanked the least I could do was line his stomach first. As I washed salad and grilled chicken, I checked my phone every few minutes but there were no more friend requests or messages. When Richard went to use the bathroom I had a few minutes to get into his computer, but Facebook doesn't figure in Richard's life for the last four weeks. Unless he's wiped his history, he's not responsible for the messages I received this morning.

'What did he say?' I ask, trying to sound casual.

'He asked if I'd spoken to Dominic,' Richard scowls.

'Despite the fact that Evie was. . .' he looks pained, '*is* a grown woman. But what I did get out of him was that once a person is deceased their records are no longer covered under the Data Protection Act. Without a. . . a body, Evie isn't legally deceased but he's going to look into it. He's not sure we have justifiable cause to ask to view her records.'

'That sucks.'

'Well, Dominic doesn't pay him a fortune for no reason. Evie said once that he has ways of getting information that others might not, so we'll just have to wait and see if he comes up with anything.'

I know he won't. Evie didn't have cancer, she wasn't dying. But for now Richard is holding onto whatever he can, and I'm happy to let him. Besides, Richard's solicitor is also Dominic Rousseau's solicitor; it's unlikely he'd tell Richard anything without her father's say-so anyway.

From the little she told me about her parents, and from overhearing the odd conversation, I'd built a picture of what life was like for her at home. I'd see her get excited over the smallest thing her father would send her – like some clip for her camera that I never really understood the purpose of – and I'd watch her discard designer dresses and jewellery that cost more than my tuition with a look of disgust. Most of the time these items fell to me, and I wasn't too proud to accept them, but the thoughtful ones, however little they cost, she always kept.

Dominic Rousseau, I came to understand, was a formidable businessman who was adored by all of the women in his life. Originally from France, the Rousseaus had moved to the English countryside when Evie was young. She grew up in one of the most magnificent houses I'd laid my eyes on, although I only ever saw it in photos – she stalwartly refused to take me anywhere near her childhood home. At the age of eleven she had been sent to an all-girls boarding school with some of the country's richest offspring. Her mother, Monique Rousseau, née White, was an absolute beauty and – from what little I could glean – suffered from severe bipolar disorder. Evie would check in with Yasmin every evening to see how her mother was coping while she was away and I could usually tell what mood she was in by the look on Evie's face after she'd taken the call. More than once I'd heard Evie follow up with a call to her father; these would be louder, a chorus of 'how could you' and 'you promised no more, Papa!' followed by a furious diatribe in French of which I could usually only make out very English words like 'whore' and 'bastard'.

It wasn't a stretch to imagine the handsome Frenchman I had seen in the photographs in Evie's apartment stepping out on his adoring wife, knowing she would remain by his side for official engagements while dying quietly inside. I could never push Evie too much on the subject but I often wondered what it must have been like for her growing up in that environment, spoiled, adored and ignored; a mother who locked herself away for days at a time and a father who showered them with love and gifts only to cruelly rip his attention away and shine his gaze on other women. And for Monique, the humiliation of all their high society friends knowing exactly what he was like, wanting to believe the promises that it would never happen again but knowing that it was still going on, even as he said the words. It was a far cry from my council estate upbringing, a world I could only dream about inhabiting, and as out of reach to me as Narnia.

I glance down at the phone in my lap. No more messages from 'Evie' or anyone else.

'Do you remember when she bought you that Mr Frosty?' Richard asks, smiling. He leans forwards and takes a sip of his beer.

Of course I remember. As obsessed as I became with

learning more about Evie White, trying to unpick her past and use it to fit her neatly into boxes created by Freud and Jung, she was similarly intrigued by me. I would never have imagined that someone who had led such a glamorous life-style, surrounded by people ripped from glossy magazines, would be so eager to hear about my life growing up as one of four children in a three-bed mid-terrace in Yorkshire, but she devoured my stories as though they were heroin and she needed a fix. She would listen delighted as I recounted the afternoon I spent digging up the garden after my brothers told me the lost treasure of Captain Ditio was buried under Mum's favourite plants, or how they convinced me my favourite sweets were really made of poo so they could have my share, and how the only thing I ever wanted in life was a Mr Frosty and when I finally got one my eldest brother stole it to make vodka slushies for his friends.

Life with Evie alongside me wasn't all falling in and out of parties in the West End – although most of my memories are of watching her through a haze of smoke tinged with the smell of incense and weed. We would peruse charity shops and independent ornament or jewellery shops for hours, tasked with finding the most perfect present to send back to Yasmin, or wander Portobello Market – the traders seemed to know Evie by name and we would always leave with perfectly wrapped gifts that they had put aside because they knew she would love them. Wherever we went people were happy to see us – to see her – and she would treat everyone she met as though they were the most important person she would see that day.

And yet it was almost always as though Evie's life was one big act. Like her entire existence was a stage play and she was having the time of her life playing the main char-acter. And when the curtain was down, when the effort of being dazzling became too much, we would gate-crash another party in another run-down Victorian terrace and she would sink into the background – still shining slightly brighter than those around her, but for the most part just *being*. It was then that I realised that this was the way she had always been – she knew no different. Put on a face for the important people, Evie, smile and show them how charming the daughter of Dominic Rousseau is – isn't she beautiful! Yet the only time I ever saw her relax was when she was no one in particular.

Christmas Day, our first one as friends, I received a package. It had turned up the day before – even expensive couriers take Christmas Day off – but my mother had kept it hidden from me, as per the very polite instructions that had accompanied it. There was no name, but I didn't need one – I only really had Evie. Please, don't get out the violins – I had other friends, they just weren't present-giving close. My other friends were more 'buy you a drink when I see you' passing acquaintances.

I ripped off the paper, closely watched by my family who were all keen to see what Becky-no-mates (their endearing nickname for me) had been sent by DPD. The look on their faces when I pulled out a child's toy from the nineties was classic. My very own Mr Frosty, complete with bottle of vodka.

'I can't believe she remembered.'

'She's like that though, isn't she?' Richard is sitting opposite me on the cushioned garden furniture his wife made from old pallets. Although the afternoon is a warm one – warm enough for him to suggest we take our drinks outside – I'm freezing cold and pull the blanket he brought me up over my knees. *Was*, I think. She *was* so like that.

'She listened to everything – I'd say she knows more about us than we'll ever know about her.'

'Do you want another drink?' he asks, and I look down to realise I've drunk my beer in just a few gulps.

There seems little point in pacing myself now so I just nod.

'Why don't you just bring the pack out?'

Richard goes back inside to retrieve the rest of the beers and I pull out my phone. I've had it on silent since the supermarket, although I've been checking it constantly. When I look down there's a message received just seconds ago.

Don't you want to be my friend?

It's a text message, not through Facebook this time. The calls this morning had come through Messenger and I'd convinced myself it could have been any old troll – Evie's death had been in all the local papers after all and I'd heard of people doing this sort of thing all the time. Bored teenagers cooped up in their bedrooms with nothing better to do than taunt people who had lost loved ones. But then my mind goes to the profile picture, the one of Evie on the clifftop, a fact I'd ignored, or rather buried because it didn't fit with my random troll theory, but I can't ignore it any longer, can I? Because not only does this person have a picture of Evie the night she died, they have my phone number.

Who is this? I type quickly, looking up at the door Richard will be coming through any minute.

The reply comes quickly.

The wife.

I run through all of the wedding guests in my head, discounting all of the men and single women, along with Evie's Great Aunt Beth, just because. The wedding party was small, something I'm now certain Evie planned. Her closest friends from home, Harriet and Jessica, had been there as bridesmaids of course, and although neither of them were married I can't discount the fact that the person sending me the texts might just be lying. We'd had a WhatsApp group for the bridesmaids and although I'd barely spoken to either of them, let alone exchanged numbers, my phone number would show on the group, so feasibly it could be one of them sending these messages, or both. But why?

And then it comes to me. There was one wife, not a guest at the wedding, of course, but if *he* was there then it stood to reason she might have been as well. His wife. *Camille.*

Had Camille stood and watched Evie throw herself into the sea? Had Evie known she was there? And if it was Camille, what did she want from me now?

I'm unsure, now, whether I should let her know I'm on to her, or whether to continue to play dumb. If I tell her I know who she is, it's possible she will just give up on me – which is what I want, don't I? Yet she obviously has a reason for this little game she's playing, and I want to know what it is. Has her husband come clean? Told her everything? In which case, why is she taunting me?

There is another possibility, one that is much worse. I've only ever been contacted by this 'Evelyn Bradley' when I've been on my own, never when I've been in a room with Richard. Even now he is taking longer to get our drinks than he needs to – they are on the kitchen counter no more than a minute away. And if 'Evelyn Bradley' is Richard? That means he knows about Camille, and possibly everything else and he's been playing me all along.

10

Evie

'Come along, Evie, your father's guests have arrived.'

Evie looked up from her book and scowled.

'Do I really have to go and meet them? Can't you tell him I'm sick? I do feel a little off-colour today.'

'You're too late. Your mother has played the sick card today so your father needs you. They have their son with them and you are to show him around the gardens while the men talk business.'

When Evie pulled a face and returned to her book, Yasmin walked over and plucked it from her hands. Groaning in amiable defeat the young girl jumped from her window seat and made to follow her nanny through the door. Yasmin turned on her.

'Where do you think you are going?'

Evie frowned. 'To show some boy around the gardens, like you just said.'

'Looking like that? *Mon Dieu!* Your father would fire me on the spot! No, you must brush your hair, Evelyn, and if you can force yourself, perhaps put on something pretty, a dress maybe?'

Evie raised her eyebrows. 'A pretty dress? I'm not seven any more, Yasmin.'

'No,' her nanny shook her head. 'And my, don't we know about it. Sometimes I know not if you are nine or nineteen! Fine, just change into something that is not stained with jam and come straight down to the veranda.'

When Evie arrived downstairs, Yasmin gave her a smile and an 'okay' sign as her father gave her an appraising once-over.

'Evie, *finally*.'

'Sorry, Papa,' she replied, standing on her tiptoes for a kiss. 'I wanted to make myself look nice.'

He smiled indulgently and turned to a tall man who stood and offered Evie a hand so stiffly it was as if it was painful. He gestured to the young boy standing next to him.

'Pleasure to meet you, Evelyn,' he said, barely looking at her. 'I hope you won't mind showing James your beautiful gardens?'

'Of course not,' Evie smiled pleasantly. She knew how she was expected to act around her father's associates – even the rude ones – and *she* had no problem with being pleasant and courteous. Papa worked so hard to give them the nice things they had and the least she could do was be a good daughter. She glanced over to James, who was standing on ceremony, and felt a stab of recognition.

'Pleased to meet you.' James held out a hand and Evie shook it. 'I'm James Preston—

'Addlington,' Evie finished. 'I remember. I'm Evie.'

She hadn't recognised him instantly, but now she had, the memory of her parents' party just eighteen months ago resurfaced almost fully formed. Oh, how long she had spent seething with fury about this boy and his rudeness! She smiled to herself at the memory.

'Do I know you?' James asked as the two of them broke away from their fathers and wandered towards the path that led to the swimming pool. Evie motioned for James to follow her underneath the magnificent stone archway and ducked as the leaves from the trees overhead scraped at her ponytail, feeling a small victory as they sprung back from her head and hit him in the face.

'We met ages ago. At a party here, in my house. I was in my pyjamas.'

Recognition dawned and his eyes widened in horror at the memory. He seemed to have aged at least five years in what had not even been two. His features were less rounded now, Evie remembered a boyish chubbiness to his face that no longer remained. He had grown taller too; at the time she had imagined him to be nine or ten but now he looked at least thirteen.

'You never told me your father was Dominic Rousseau,' he screwed up his nose trying to remember. 'You told me your mum worked in the kitchens!'

'Well she does, sometimes. If Yasmin is sick,' Evie shrugged. If pressed she wouldn't be able to remember a time she'd even seen Mama walk into the kitchens but that hardly seemed like the world's biggest lie. It was possible, if not improbable.

'You lied to me. And you called me a bastard.'

'Well, you deserved it.'

James Preston-Addlington looked shocked, as though he had never been spoken to that way in his life, much less by a little girl. Then he let out a laugh and Evie saw that his blue eyes sparkled. He shrugged. 'I probably did.'

Evie was a little surprised at this admission. It wasn't very often that a boy would admit he deserved to be called a cuss word, especially one as insulting as a bastard. They walked along the lush flower beds in silence for a while, coming to stop at the water feature that fed into the pond.

'What does your father do?' Evie asked, trying to arrange herself on the edge of the wet wall. She felt the water soaking through the seat of her jeans and jumped up self-consciously. James smirked.

'Same as yours. We are the second largest IT recruitment firm in the UK. Our parents were good friends years ago, apparently, but they haven't spoken properly since not long after I was born. My father wants to reignite their friendship so they can work together again. He says that together they could become the richest men in England. My father says that one day he wants me to take over the business.'

'He must not like you very much,' Evie remarked.

James frowned. 'Why would you say that?'

Evie shrugged and pulled a flower from the bush next to her, inspected it as she spoke. 'Because I can't think of anything more boring than taking on my father's business. And if that was the future I had to look forward to I don't think I'd be in any great hurry to grow up.'

'You are impertinent and rude,' James replied flatly. 'What do you want to be when you are older then? Let me guess, a model.'

For a brief second Evie felt a small thrill that this boy thought her pretty enough to be a model. The idea was quickly replaced by disdain.

'No, not a model.'

'An actress then? Or a socialite living off your father's boring money?'

'I don't want to be any of those things,' Evie set her shoulders defiantly. The problem was, she hadn't decided what she wanted to be. After all, there were so many occupations, so much she could do with her time. How could anyone just settle for one and expect to be happy the rest of their life? Papa's words, the night she first met James Preston-Addlington Jr, came back to her now. She hadn't even remembered them until this moment. *You must find a way to make people see the world from behind your eyes.*

'I'm going to be a photographer.'

'A photographer?' Evie was waiting for him to make a derogatory remark, already formulating a comeback in her head, when he smiled and said, 'That's cool.'

Shouts broke through the air from the house beyond. James and Evie looked at one another quizzically.

'Come on, let's go and see what's going on.' James grabbed Evie's hand and she felt her fingers tingle under the warmth of his touch. As he pulled her towards the house a figure emerged.

'James,' Mr Addlington barked. 'Get here now. We're leaving.'

James dropped Evie's hand and scuttled to his father's side, turning around to give her one last wave before running to keep up with the grown man stalking in the direction of the driveway. Evie looked up at the window, where her mother was watching them leave.

11

Rebecca

When Richard comes back out he's avoiding eye contact, but I can't tell if it's the I'm-pretending-I-haven't-been-crying avoidance or the I'm-messaging-you-pretending-to-be-my-dead-wife avoidance.

The wife. Richard's wife? Makes sense, seeing as the person sending the messages is using Evie's name. It's possible Camille is the one contacting me, although I can't imagine why she would. She's got what she wanted now, surely. Why taunt me like this? Is she bored already? Without Evie to play with perhaps she's moved on to a new target. Me.

'Here,' he says, but as he passes me the bottle my co-ordination betrays how shaken I am and it slips through my fingers, smashing on the concrete patio. Beer froths and spreads across the floor and I jump to my feet.

'Oh God, I'm so sorry,' I say, bending to pick up the broken glass.

'Leave it,' Richard waves a hand but I carry on retrieving large fragments of the bottle, stacking them up to one side. 'Becky, leave it, you're going to—'

But before he can say the word one of the pieces of glass slices into the flesh of my palm, just below my thumb. I gasp as blood appears instantly from the wound, and Richard jumps up cursing and disappears inside. He returns almost immediately with a tea-towel to find me sobbing on the floor, blood flowing down my wrist. He kneels down beside me and takes my hand in his as I gulp air into my lungs. I feel like I'm suffocating.

'Calm down,' he says, and he seems sober now, efficient and clear-headed, more like the Richard I used to know. I'm staring at the blood that seems to be everywhere now, on both my palms as I try to hold the gaping wound shut. Richard wraps it tightly in the tea-towel, the pressure stinging.

'Get it off,' I say, only my words seem far away, like I'm hearing them through cotton wool. 'Get it off me!'

'Ssshhh, calm down, Becks. Calm down.'

He's lifting me to my feet and guiding me to the kitchen to wash the blood off my hands but it's everywhere, thick and red and it won't go away. It won't go away. *Why won't it go away?*

And all the time I can hear my own voice, completely alien to me, screaming at him over and over.

Getitoffmegetitoffmegetitoffme.

12

Evie

Eleven-year-old Evie Rousseau adjusted the maroon blazer bearing the crest of her new school, looked at her mother and gave a nervous smile.

'Does it look okay?'

Her mother gave a small nod, her eyes shiny with held-back tears.

Evie tried for a more confident smile. 'Come on, Mama, I'll be fine. It's one of the best schools in the country. And remember what you told me? It's like one huge sleepover. I know tons of girls there already, I have Jess and Harriet, it's just going to be like prep school but bigger.'

'And with no boys,' her father's voice came from the doorway of the drawing room. It was a mark of how special an occasion today was that Dominic Rousseau had stayed home long enough to see his only daughter off to her first term at high school this morning. He was usually out of the house by 7.30am.

Evie laughed. 'And no boys. Thank goodness.'

'I'm not worried about you.' Her mother looked at Papa, who put an arm around his wife's shoulder. 'Can you believe how grown-up she looks?'

'She is a real young woman now,' Dominic agreed. Evie pulled a face.

'Eurgh. Can we go now please?'

'Of course. Phillip is bringing the car around. He bought a new hat just for today.'

'Papa, no!' Evie squealed. 'You promised no driver!'

'Oh Evelyn, he was so looking forward to driving you this morning. Right up to the gate.'

Evie was poised to continue her tirade when she saw her father wink at her mother.

'Very funny,' she folded her arms. 'If you're finished, can we go now, *please*?'

As predicted, high school had become an extension of prep school, and Evie and her friends had fallen into an easy routine. So far life without boys, who had been sent to a high school nearly a mile away, was so much easier. There were less distractions in class, and Evie found that the girls were more relaxed and amiable when not in the company of the least fair sex. Boarding was much better than being at home, in that vast lonely house with only Yasmin for company. Now there was never a quiet moment – Evie was never alone and she quickly became used to being surrounded by chattering voices, so much so that she dreaded going back to Wareham for the summer.

There had, thus far, been only one thorn in the side of young Evelyn Rousseau, one person who never failed to take the shine off her good mood, and her name was Camille Darlington.

Even at eleven years old, Camille Darlington was what Evie could only describe as a pretentious little bitch. The Darlingtons were old money, a fact that Camille enjoyed reminding Evie every chance she got. Until now Evie had never even known the difference, and when she'd asked her father he'd told her with a wry smile that it simply meant he had earned his money by building his company from the bottom up, rather than relying on a fortune he had inherited. Evie thought this was much more admirable, but the scorn in Camille's voice when she said the words 'new money' made it sound much less so.

And to make matters worse, Camille was charming, intelligent, and perfectly adorable to every adult they came across. The teachers loved her, the other students loved her. Worst of all, Jessica and Harriet loved her. It seemed that Evie was the only person Camille showed her true self to, and she couldn't for the life of her work out what she had done to deserve it.

'My mother said that your mother is an alcoholic and an emotional basket-case and your father is a philanderer,' she'd hissed at Evie once, when Evie had dared to score the same as her on an eleven-plus English test. 'He probably slept with Miss Brady to get you that score.'

Evie had felt the elation of being joint highest in the year seep away. Imagine what Camille was going to say when she found out Evie had scored higher than her in maths.

'God knows how you got yours then,' Evie had replied with a scowl. 'Because your father looks like he's been hit by a bus.' Her triumph at Camille's face was short-lived however, when the other girl burst into tears.

'What's wrong?' Miss Brady had scurried over, her face full of concern. Camille shook her head.

'Nothing,' Camille sniffed. 'I just don't know why we can't all be happy for each other. Not everything is a competition,' she aimed her last remark at Evie, and Miss Brady shot her a dark look.

'That's very true, Camille,' she said, putting an arm around the girl. 'Everyone's journey is their own, and if people don't have anything nice to say they should not say anything at all.'

And with that, Miss Brady led Camille away, leaving Evie shaking with fury.

13

Rebecca

The pub is practically empty when we arrive, which is good I think to myself – neither of us have been out in public much these last few weeks and I'd suggested somewhere quiet and a bit further from home on purpose, rather than our local where Richard is likely to be besieged by well-wishers. This place is more of a gastro-pub, better suited for families to eat in than the dark, sticky-floored Duke we practically called home in our uni days. It's open-plan and the colour scheme is mock Farrow & Ball, with a large log burner in the centre. Despite being on the outskirts of London it looks like a countryside bistro. As we approach the table for four, Chris notices us and gives Sarah a nudge.

'Richard, mate. Becky.' Chris nods at me, Sarah hugs Richard and gives me a tight smile. I smile back, although I know she doesn't like me, never has. Evie was always the one so easy to get along with, an anecdote for every occasion – I was always too quiet, people never knew whether I was silently judging them and it made them uncomfortable. The truth was, I was always content to sit back and listen to the stories being bandied around, just happy to be in the company of others. I never felt like I needed to offer them anything.

Now though, now that I face a life without Evie, I wish I'd tried more. I wish these people were my friends too, that I hadn't always been Evie's plus one.

They were Richard's friends first, Sarah and Chris, since they were about sixteen, although they weren't together then. Yet he looks like he doesn't want to be anywhere near them. Maybe it's their good fortune he can't stand – they are still standing there together, tonight they will go home and eat together, argue about what to watch on the television and then go to bed together, wake up in the morning and watch TV in bed with their children. Life for them hasn't altered, and Richard looks like it causes him pain to be around such normalcy, to be reminded that life goes on, whether Evie is in the world or not. And how can that be possible? How can the people in the pub around him still be talking about last night's *X Factor* or *The Great British Bake Off* when his world has received its punctuation mark? When a mass tragedy occurs, when multiple people die in one instant, the world grieves. Those people's lives are celebrated on a nation-wide scale, there are pictures of them on TV and in the news – their every good deed held up as a symbol of what the country had lost. Why did Evie warrant any less because she died alone?

I can't help wondering if it was a mistake to push him into this, this façade of putting on a brave face – he wouldn't even be here if I hadn't noticed him looking at the text from Chris inviting him to the pub and badgered him to accept. He agreed eventually, but only if I came with him, which gave me a small thrill, the thrill of being needed, wanted, especially after my breakdown a few days ago. I'm supposed to be the one looking after him, and yet it was Richard who bandaged the cut on my hand – which turned out to be nowhere near as bad as it looked – and called me a taxi to make sure I got home okay.

'I can't imagine how you must be feeling,' Sarah's soft voice cuts through my thoughts. As she reaches out to put a hand on Richard's shoulder I can see him try not to flinch. 'We all thought so much of Evie. I hope you haven't been feeling bad about the argument, I'm sure it had nothing to do with what happened.'

Richard opens his mouth to thank her automatically, until I see her words register and I have to stop myself groaning.

'What argument?'

I see Chris shoot Sarah a furious look and she winces.

'I shouldn't have. . .' Sarah drops her eyes to the table. *Too late now, princess.*

'No, seriously, what argument?' Richard looks between them both. 'Sarah? Chris?'

'It was nothing, I'm sure. If you've forgotten it already. . .'

But Richard isn't going to let it drop now, is he?

'Forgotten what? Fucksake you two, spit it out.'

'I'm sure it was—' I start to interject but Richard shoots me the kind of look that tells me to *shut it*. Silence heavy with expectation sits between us at the table until Chris can't stand it any longer.

'We saw you,' he says. 'On the way up to the cliffs at the wedding. We'd been having. . . a walk.'

Once upon a time he'd have said they'd gone for a shag. They were those kinds of friends once, where conversation was easy and unfiltered. I barely knew Chris and Sarah but the few times I'd met them Chris had been loud and overtly sexual, Sarah more uptight, rolling her eyes and pretending she wasn't loving it. Then Evie had thrown herself off a cliff and in just a few short weeks Richard had become the kind of friend you have to watch what you say around, someone fragile, ready to shatter if you say the wrong thing.

'We were coming back down and we saw the pair of you arguing on the verge. You don't have to feel bad, whatever

57

it was Evie wouldn't have. . . it wouldn't be the reason she. . . Shit, I wish I hadn't said anything now.' Sarah puts her hands over her face, genuinely miserable, so she doesn't catch Chris' furious *'didn't I warn you'* look.

'I wasn't on the cliff with Evie,' Richard says quietly. 'So you couldn't have seen us arguing. It must have been someone else.'

Sarah uncovers her face. 'Someone else in a wedding dress and veil? Was there another wedding that day? There must have been, unless. . .' She stops, realising the implication of what she was going to say. *Oh do shut up, idiot.*

'Unless Evie was arguing with someone else. What time was this?'

'Nearly an hour before the police arrived.'

'Did you mention it to the police? Why didn't you tell me?'

Chris looks uncomfortable. 'We honestly thought it *was* you, mate. It was obviously Evie and we weren't that close, we assumed she was with you. If you wanted the police to know you'd been arguing you'd have already told them, didn't make much sense to stir things up for you, make you a. . . make things difficult.'

They were protecting him, and he hasn't twigged yet. They hadn't wanted to give the police a motive, make him a suspect.

'Anyway, the police said she was alone when she. . .' Sarah can't finish the sentence. 'So it doesn't matter who it was, does it?' She looks desperately between Chris and Richard for a sign that she hasn't caused a massive issue. I hope to God she hasn't.

'What did he look like? Did you hear what they were saying? Could it have been her father?'

Chris shoots Sarah another furious look but Richard doesn't care and I know why. If Dominic Rousseau had seen his daughter a few minutes before she'd died then he'd lied to the police.

'I don't think so,' Chris replies. 'He's quite tall, isn't he? I don't know, mate, I'm sorry. If we'd realised it wasn't you we'd have looked better.'

'He was wearing a black wax jacket,' Sarah speaks suddenly and my heart pumps faster. *What is she going to say?* 'And grey suit trousers like yours. He might have been a bit taller than you but they were on a slope so he looked smaller, Evie was up higher. She was crying a bit and you – I mean he – was waving his arms around, gesturing at the cliff. I heard her say something, or I thought I did, I couldn't have been sure and anyway we didn't realise it was important—'

'What did she say, Sarah?'

'She said it didn't make any difference. Whatever it was he was saying to her didn't make any difference. I'm really sorry, Richard, that's all I remember. I wish I could tell you more. . .'

Richard sighs and sits back in his chair. 'It's fine, thanks for telling me now. You're probably right, whatever it was wouldn't have made Evie do something drastic – we all know she didn't do anything without some kind of reason. I just wish I knew what the reason was. If she'd left a note or something. . .'

'And she definitely didn't? There was no indication?'

Richard shakes his head and picks up his coat – my cue to do the same. We've been here less than quarter of an hour – I should have known better.

'I'm sorry, guys, I can't really. . . It's too soon for all this. I just need some space.'

Sarah nods sympathetically but Chris looks troubled.

'Look, mate,' he said. 'If there's anything we can do. Anything at all. You know you can talk to us.'

Richard attempts a smile but the result looks alien to his face and it comes across as more of a grimace.

'Don't worry, I'm not going to do anything stupid.'

Sarah shakes her head frantically. 'He didn't mean that. We know you wouldn't. . .'

'Thanks, I appreciate it.'

They both stand and embrace him, giving awkward nods to me. I can sense their relief that it's over. They can walk away now back to their homes, their lives, safe in the knowledge that they've done their duty as friends while he goes back to his empty home, his empty life, his Lidl substitute for his Waitrose wife trailing behind him. But the last fifteen minutes have changed things for Richard – I can see that and it worries the hell out of me. Now he has a purpose. He will want to find out who Evie had been arguing with – probably the last person who saw her alive – and find out why they haven't come forward. And if he does he'll find out why his life had been imploding without him ever even realising.

14

Evie

A long, lazy summer heavy with promise stretched ahead of the three of them; Evie, Harriet and Jessica. Their sixteenth year and everything was changing. In September they would join the lower sixth, their transition into womanhood marked by the replacing of maroon shirts with white – an important distinction that separated them from the youth of high school. They would begin studies for A levels and choose universities, but for now they stood teetering on the cusp of womanhood – ever increasingly aware of the extra inches they were growing and the emerging mounds under their T-shirts.

The beach was heaving with teenagers making the most of the warm weather, mums with pushchairs so laden with supplies that they looked like they were spending a week camping rather than a day of sunbathing, and old age pensioners still as wrapped up in their coats as if it were mid-November, sitting on benches eating sandwiches peeled out of tinfoil.

'Over there,' Harriet pointed to the far end of the beach, next to a cluster of rocks which jutted out into the sea. Evie could just make out shirtless figures climbing over the slick boulders.

'That's miles away,' Jessica moaned. 'And there's nowhere to sit.'

'Are you going to complain all day?' Harriet snapped. 'We can sit on the rocks, or on that bit of dry sand there.'

Before Jessica could start complaining again Harriet stalked off in the direction of the rocks, the soft sand making her departure less glamorous than Evie thought she intended. Giving a shrug, Evie gestured her head towards Harriet's retreating back and trailed after her friend.

Evie laid out her towel and kicked off her sandals, well aware of the eyes of the boys on the rocks following her every movement. As they had approached she could see there were five of them, they were maybe a couple of years older and not completely unfortunate-looking. One of them let out a wolf-whistle as the girls peeled off their tops to reveal a bikini top – Harriet – and swimming costumes – Jessica and Evie. Evie wasn't anywhere near as confident as her friend, and the thought of anyone seeing her in her bikini had made her cringe. Although now, looking at her friend, she wished she'd had the guts to put hers on; her black swimming costume with white stripes down the side made her look like a stupid school-girl in comparison to Harriet. As her friend stepped out of her shorts, Evie looked at her slender legs and athletic figure, then glanced down, noting the way her thighs met at the top – Harriet's had an inch-wide gap – and the swell of her own hips where her friend had none. She left her shorts on.

Pretending to ignore the boys on the rocks, the three girls stretched themselves over their towels. Evie closed her eyes, basking in the warmth of the sunlight on her face and chest.

After less than five minutes she was bored beyond belief. How did anyone lie still for hours without going braindead? Lying in one place and trying to look grown-up might be Harriet's thing but it definitely wasn't hers.

On the rocks above, the boys had grown bored of the three prone girls and Evie concentrated on trying to hear what they were arguing about.

'You first, gutless.'

'You must be shitting me. After you, Doris.'

'I wouldn't want to take the honour away from you, Peaches.'

She opened her eyes, squinting as the sun hit them. They were standing on the edge of the rocks, peering over the edge at the water below, goading one another to make the first jump. Evie smiled to herself. Boys. At what point in their lives did things stop being about bravado and ball-swinging? She thought of her father, his flashy parties where he spent thousands of pounds a time catering for people who were too drunk or high or self-important to even notice that the napkins were all folded at perfect forty-five-degree angles. Never, then.

She stood up, adjusting the straps of her swimming costume, and slipped off her shorts. She was restless, the need for something to happen was overwhelming, and Evie had never been the type of girl to lie in the sun and let the boys have all the fun. Neither Jessica nor Harriet even opened their eyes. Evie thought Jessica might have fallen asleep but there was no chance Harriet would risk snoring or drooling when there were males in the vicinity.

Planting her hand firmly on the lowest rock and wedging her foot into a crevice, she clambered her way to the top, realising halfway up that she was inappropriately dressed for a rock-climbing expedition. It was too late now though, and thankfully none of the boys even noticed until she was standing behind them.

'Move out of the way then, if you're not going to jump.'

At the sound of her voice all four of them swung around.

'What, you're jumping off?' one of the boys scoffed, looking her up and down. 'Don't be stupid. Go back to sunbathing with your friends.'

'Evie!' Harriet had opened her eyes to find her friend gone and was now standing on the sand, staring up at Evie, her hand shielding her eyes from the sun. 'What are you doing?'

'Going for a swim,' Evie shouted back, and stepped up to the edge of the rock. It was barely a six-foot drop – hardly a distance to worry about – but there was no way of telling how deep the water was below, or what it might be hiding. It was too late to back out now though – there was no other way down. Climbing downwards would be impossible, she'd have to walk the long way around back to the beach. She took a deep breath and threw herself off the rock edge.

Evie pulled her knees up to her chest to lessen her depth. She hit the water – which was warmer than she'd been expecting – and her head went under. She released her knees and kicked upwards. Breaking the surface, she let out a piercing scream and disappeared once again, under the water.

15

Rebecca

I dropped Richard off at home last night hoping he would go to bed and forget about the mystery man Evie had been arguing with on her wedding day, but I know he won't. Would I, if I hadn't already known who she was speaking to, and why? Lately I've been wondering how I'd be reacting to all this if I didn't know what I know. Probably not too differently to Richard: a mournful silent acceptance, then so quick to jump on anything that might answer the question that will hang over the rest of his life.

Richard answers the door this morning in his bathrobe. Just when I thought we were getting somewhere. Thanks a fucking bunch, Sarah.

'God,' I wrinkle up my nose. 'You do realise it's eleven am?'

Richard rubs sleep out of the corners of his eyes and looks as though he is struggling to focus. His sandy brown hair, ever so slightly too long, sticks out at odd angles around his head.

'Yeah,' his cheeks redden. 'I was up late last night, um, thinking.'

'You need a shower,' I tell him, sniffing the air as if to prove how ripe he is. 'Go and sort yourself out and I'll find you something to eat.'

He doesn't even register the irritation in my voice. How long is he going to mope around, content to let me mother him?

I'm just debating whether the farmhouse loaf is still edible when I hear the doorbell. I debate ignoring it but after the third ring whoever it is isn't going away. Perhaps it's the police – perhaps there is a body. Pushing down the ever-present image of Evie, bloated and rotting, I answer the door.

Martin Bradley is three years younger than Richard, and the saying 'chalk and cheese' could have been written about them. He's somewhere in the region of 5'6, slightly shorter than his brother, and stocky, with the look of a rugby player about him. In fact, when he shows up today he's wearing a dark green rugby top, the collar upturned at the back, and navy jeans with brown shoes. Despite not getting the height advantage, Martin stole the typical good looks – that's not to say Richard is unattractive, but where the older brother is (or should I say, was, because these days you can't tell) always smartly turned out, Martin has the air of falling out of bed looking like he wants to get you back in it. Not my thing, but he has never been short of a woman or two, and he has never married.

'Martin,' I say, and I can hear the weariness in my voice. We've only met three or four times, the wedding being one of them, but I always got the impression he could never quite work out where I fit into Evie and Richard's relationship. Or perhaps he could, and that was the point. 'Lovely to see you.'

'Where's Richard?' he says, without preamble, and steps forwards to come in. I can hardly deny him entry into his own brother's house so I step aside. I follow him into the front room where he throws himself onto the sofa and I perch on the chair, as far away as I can.

'He's in the shower,' I say, immediately clocking his furrowed brows. 'I haven't been here all night, if that's what you're thinking. I only just got here and he smelt like three-day-old chicken so I sent him up to get washed while I did him some lunch. Breakfast. Well, brunch, I suppose—'

'Did you know about this argument?' Martin cuts off my culinary ramblings and gets straight to the point as always.

'What argument?'

'The one Evie's supposed to have had with someone before she jumped off that cliff. Richard rang me last night asking if I'd argued with her on the cliffs. Might as well have asked if I'd bloody pushed her.'

'Oh, yeah, Sarah and Chris mentioned something yesterday and I think he's jumped on it as a way to try and understand, you know.'

Martin grimaced. 'Well he needs to stop it. He'll drive himself mad analysing every step she made, every conversation or argument she had. I mean, what does it matter? It's not going to bring her back, is it?'

Richard would say, 'Typical Martin, all action' – if something couldn't be changed, what was the point in worrying about it? I always got the impression they weren't particularly close and I can see why.

'Surely you can understand – he just wants to know why she would have done it. He's heartbroken that he might have missed something that could have stopped her.'

'Yeah,' Martin ruffles his hair. 'Except from what he was saying to me it sounded like he was questioning *if* she'd done it. Like there might have been someone else involved. But the police ruled that out, didn't they?'

Biting at the loose skin on my lip, I nod. 'They aren't treating it as suspicious. I'm not sure if he's told them about this row, though. I don't think it would change much.'

'He should be moving forward, grieving. Not acting like there's some sort of investigation. If he's not careful. . .'

'What?' I ask. 'If he's not careful, what?'

'Well, don't they always look at the husband first?' Martin's voice is full of exasperation. 'I mean, if they open an investigation, and find out she was arguing with someone – won't they look at Richard as the main suspect?'

It's true, and that's how I'll convince him not to go to the police. Even his own friends thought it was him on the verge. It won't look good.

'Yeah, maybe. Look, I don't think you have to worry. He's been doing really well. This is a temporary setback.' I don't mention the other day, when I found him drinking at one pm. He has been doing well, just a couple of bad days. 'He'll move on in his own time.'

'And you're going to help him with that, are you?'

And there it is. Asshole.

'I don't know what you're insinuating,' I snap. 'Richard and I are just friends. I was, I mean *I am*, Evie's best friend. I'm just trying to help. I don't see you here every other day making sure he doesn't starve.'

Martin sighs. 'You're right, I'm sorry. I just don't see how he's going to move forward when you're here, as a constant reminder of her. And now his obsession with some black jacket guy. . .'

'Look,' I stand up, move towards the kitchen. 'I get your concern, I do. But if I'm not here for him now, who will be? He's having a hard time coming to terms with the fact that his wife killed herself, on their wedding day of all bloody days. Cut him some slack.'

'And you think that's what happened, do you? I mean, Richie was rambling last night about someone pushing her off a cliff, or hitting her so she stumbled and fell. You knew Evie better than anyone – do you really think she'd try to kill herself?'

I don't think, I know she threw herself off that cliff, and my life would be a lot easier if I could just tell them all why, but that would defeat the point.

'Yes,' I tell him. 'Yes I do. After all, it's not the first time, is it?'

16

Rebecca

Martin tries to be subtle with Richard, doing his best impression of a caring human being, but he can't seem to keep it up for more than a few minutes. Listening to them argue, I marvel at how different they are: Martin attractive in all but personality, Richard just ever so slightly the wrong side of cool. If they hadn't been brothers they never would have been friends. Although I suppose opposites do attract; Evie and I were proof of that.

'Get over it?' Richard shouts from the other room. I can feel Martin's flinch through the wall. 'Oh fuck off, Martin.'

'I didn't mean get over *her*,' Martin backpedals furiously. 'I just meant you need to stop obsessing over the way it happened. She did it. No one knows why but no one forced her, or pushed her. She chose this, mate, you have to accept that.'

And he's right. Evie chose this like she chose everything else in our lives. Even without knowing it she was always in complete control, the first to suggest a new place to go, the best place to eat, the perfect style to suit my short stumpy frame.

If it sounds like I was a pushover, maybe I was at first. At first, I just wanted to be near her. I'd even stayed friends with Steve in the hope I'd see her again. Except I hadn't, not for three whole weeks. She hadn't called Steve, and after a couple of weeks he got tired of me asking casually if he'd heard from that girl, Evie. His pride had been damaged by the fact that I hadn't cared about him enough to go mad at him for cheating on me. I hadn't screamed and shouted or staked my claim, I'd stepped aside and hoped she liked him enough to come back. She hadn't and, pissed off by the fact that he'd been surrendered by one woman and ditched by another in one morning, he'd casually suggested I stopped hanging around.

I found myself wandering past the Art department hoping to bump into her accidentally, although if you'd seen me and asked what I was doing there I'd have sworn it was a shortcut to wherever I needed to be. It felt like a crush, only different: I didn't want to sleep with her, I just wanted her to smile at me again and ask me what I thought about things. I'd pre-formed an opinion on just about every current issue there was; I just wanted to see her look impressed.

I'd about given up hope that I'd ever cross paths with her again and stopped looking for her around every corner when she injected herself seamlessly into my life for a second time. I was sitting in a greasy spoon copying out notes on *Organisational Culture and Change* when someone sat down beside me. Looking up from my book, ready to suggest they choose one of the other free seats in the café, my polite rebuttal died on my lips when I found myself looking into familiar green eyes.

'Becky, right?'

'Right. Evie?'

She looked pleased but not surprised that I'd remembered her. Today she was wearing a baggy grey knit and light blue jeans so tight they looked like they'd been sprayed on. She looked impossibly beautiful in something so simple and I couldn't help but feel dowdy – despite the fact that I was wearing jeans and a jumper not totally unlike the outfit she had on herself. Her hair was still messy, but this wasn't an 'up all night screwing your boyfriend' messy, it was the kind of hairstyle that would have taken me hours to perfect and still would have looked like I had a bird's nest on my head. It was pushed off her face with a pair of oversized sunglasses that probably cost my year's tuition. On her lap was a colossal multi-coloured handbag that hung open, giving a clear view of the chaos inside. People in the café were staring at her in interest – maybe thinking they should recognise her from the TV or somewhere.

'Look, I've got these. Do you like them?' She pulled some A4-size glossy photographs from a brown leather portfolio and handed them to me. The black and white images all showed the same subject with varying light and camera filters. The person facing the camera looked intense, deep in thought, and beautiful. I knew for a fact she was none of these things in real life, because the person in the photos was me.

'Wow, these are great. Are these what you took at Steve's?'

She nodded. 'Do you really like them? I hoped I'd see you again to show them to you. I think you look beautiful in them.'

It was a surreal moment. The girl I'd found myself wandering around university buildings hoping to catch a glimpse of again was sitting here calling *me* beautiful. I've tried again and again to figure out what it was about Evelyn that had drawn me to her so strongly, and over the years so many people after me. Everywhere we went people gravitated towards her, like she was a magnet collecting iron filings from a tray, and it wasn't just her beauty. I'd never met someone who could see beauty in everything her eyes fell upon, and yet at times could seem so lost, and so sad on the spin of a coin.

We sat and talked in that café until our lungs felt sticky from breathing in the grease. That was when she convinced me to go with her to an art exhibition at the Copperfield Gallery followed by drinks with the artist which turned into a 'gathering' at a townhouse across the city. We spent the next few days tumbling from one place to another, integrating ourselves into groups of people we'd never see again and crashing on everything from four-poster beds in Victorian houses to an inflatable sofa in the kitchen of a flat that seemed to permanently smell of tuna fish.

On the third day, wearing the same clothes I'd worn when I first met Evie in the café, feeling grubby and exhausted, my captor pulled me around what seemed like every charity shop in London until neither of us resembled the people we had been that morning. We showered and changed in the local swimming baths after sneaking in when the cashier was having a fag break and ended up in front of a four-storey white house with ivy growing practically over the front door and trash bags piled up in the front garden.

'This is my friend Philippa's place. Well, she rents the ground floor. She's a hairdresser.'

'Why do we need a hairdresser?'

'To get rid of the nits we picked up at that last place.'

I must have worn my shock plainly because Evie broke into wild laughter.

'I'm kidding. I'm getting my hair cut – she'll do yours too if you want.'

The inside of the house was as dirty and unkempt as the outside. Piles of rubbish overflowed the bin and someone had put a cardboard box underneath so they didn't have to empty it. Half-full glasses with cigarette ends floating in dubious brown liquid littered every surface and the musty smell of body odour and smoke hung in the air, so palpable it stung my eyes. Philippa greeted us both with hugs and, despite the condition of the place, she was clean and well turned out, and smelt of oranges.

'What am I giving you?' she asked Evie, running a hand through her unruly locks.

'Take it off.'

'What, all of it?'

'All of it.' The look in her eyes was fierce and made it clear the decision was not up for discussion. Philippa grinned.

'Excellent!'

She was as good as her word. I couldn't watch as her beautiful blonde mane fell from her head and gathered unceremoniously in a pile at her feet. When she was finished, Philippa had stepped back proudly.

'Wow.'

Evie looked stunning. Her hair was cropped short, the highlights more pronounced now, giving her face an impish beauty. Already I missed her long messy hair framing her face, but I had to admit the effect was amazing.

I'd had two inches off mine – thoroughly disappointing the adventurous Philippa – and we'd been starting a luke-warm Pinot Grigio when Evie's phone had trilled impatiently.

'My dad,' she frowned and cut it off. 'He's been in Europe for four months and hasn't called once. Now he arrives in London and expects me to run to his side like a bloody puppy. Bastard.'

'When did he get back?' The constant phone calls all weekend were beginning to make a bit more sense.

'Friday.'

I'd put down my wine and my stomach had lurched. We'd eaten some French stick smeared in brie for breakfast but it had been pulled from the fridge of whoever's house we stayed in that night and I doubted it was entirely fresh. That, combined with the cheap wine and the air pollution, and I wasn't feeling my best. I got the sudden urge to leave, get away from the smelly, mouldy flat, so damp and dim that silverfish had begun their night-time dance at only four in the afternoon.

'Need to get home,' I'd mumbled. To her credit, Evie looked concerned.

'Jesus, Becky, come on, let's get you back.'

I'd felt all eyes on me as we mounted the steps to the tube. I figured I must look pretty green and awful for people's eyes to be on me for a change.

'I need to swing by mine for some stuff, then I'll come to yours and look after you.'

I remember trying to argue, I just wanted to get back and try to sleep off whatever had come over me, but I was also starting to realise that it was easier just to go along with whatever Evie decided.

'Is this where you live?' Evie's cheeks reddened as I gazed in unadulterated wonder at the apartment block the taxi stopped in front of. We were on Bankside, a far cry from the student accommodation I was crammed into. 'Jesus, what's the rent like on a place like this?'

'No idea,' she muttered, utter embarrassment clouding her beautiful features. 'My dad owns it. And speak of the devil. . .'

A sleek black Bentley sat outside accusingly.

'He's here.'

She sounded neither surprised nor upset. I trailed behind her into an open-plan studio apartment where a man was sitting on the dark grey sofa, his head buried in a book. I hoped I wasn't about to throw up on his carpet.

'About fucking time,' he got to his feet and threw the book on the sofa. Even in my delicate state it struck me that this man was beautiful. Where his daughter was lithe and angel blonde he was muscular and dark haired – they looked like yin and yang. The minute he saw her his eyes darkened and narrowed into furious slits.

'What the fuck have you done, Evelyn?'

'Daddy!' Evie threw herself at her father, arms open wide, but he grabbed them and held her back.

'Don't "Daddy" me. What have you done to yourself? And where have you been? You invite me to stay then disappear for days on end? What if I'd phoned the police? Or is that what you wanted? Is this because I went to Italy?'

'This is Rebecca,' Evie pulled away from her father and stepped to one side to introduce me. There was no way I wanted to be introduced to anyone looking like I did, but I needn't have worried, he paid me no attention anyway.

'Hello Rebecca. I'm sorry if my daughter has dragged you into her silly little revenge plan but I'd appreciate if you could give us some time alone please.'

'Of course,' I'd mumbled, and without looking at Evie I'd stumbled out of the apartment to the sound of Evie's father starting another rant about 'your fucking hair'.

17

Evie

Firm hands grabbed her under the arms and yanked her upwards. Evie broke the surface and took in a deep gulp of air before thrashing her arms furiously.

'Let me go!'

She pushed locks of wet blonde hair from her eyes and glared into the face of her captor. A jolt of recognition hit her – she had seen him before, but she couldn't for the life of her think where. He was strong, and very attractive. She shoved him hard in the chest and he released her.

'Oh, you're fucking welcome,' the boy gasped, struggling to tread water.

'For what?' Evie dipped her head under the water to fix her hair. She looked up at the rocks where the remaining four boys were peering over.

'You were drowning.'

'Was not.'

'You screamed!'

Evie grinned. 'I was messing around. Seeing how many of you would jump in after me. Thanks, by the way. If it were up to your mates I'd be dead.'

The boy scowled and Evie wished she'd let him hold onto her a little longer.

'You can't be serious. How stupid can you be?'

Evie grinned. 'Race you back.' She turned in the water and swam away, knowing he had no choice but to follow.

'Evie!' Jessica ran over with her towel as Evie rounded the rocks back to where her friends were waiting. Harriet looked over her shoulder at where her rescuer was running up behind her.

'Here,' Harriet held out her towel to him. 'Your friends decided to walk down,' she pointed to where the other four boys were making their way to the railed-off walkway.

Ignoring her, he grabbed Evie by the arm. 'I don't know what you were thinking but—'

'Agh!' she fell to the sand, clutching her ankle, and his face dropped.

'Sorry, are you okay?' he knelt down beside her.

'I think it's twisted,' Evie massaged her ankle and sucked in a breath. 'Ow.'

'Here,' he wound his arm around her back and lifted her to her feet. She leaned into his firm, wet body for support and suppressed a smile. Harriet looked furious. Evie wondered how long she could keep up the damsel in distress routine before he caught on.

'They've probably gone back to the tents,' he inclined his head to where his friends had disappeared. 'We're camping on the other side of the dunes. Are you from the campsite?'

Evie let out a snort of laughter before she could stop herself. The thought of her mum and dad pitching a tent and sleeping on the ground was hilarious. But of course he didn't mean with parents – he was about eighteen and would be camping with his friends. No matter how adult and worldly-wise she thought herself, Evie had never been on holiday without her parents before.

'No,' she replied. 'We live in Hopton, we, erm, we got a lift here.'

'Evie,' he said, and her name sounded different coming from his lips. 'Evie Rousseau?'

She gave a start.

'How did you know? Have we met?'

The feeling of recognition she had felt when she first saw him – where did she know him from?

'A couple of times, actually,' he grinned. 'The bastard, remember?'

A memory tried to break its way to the surface but she couldn't quite grasp it. He laughed.

'You were quite a bit younger then. And I was an arrogant child. You told me I was a bastard because I said a maid's daughter shouldn't be attending a fancy party.' His eyes dropped to the sand. 'You were probably right.'

'James,' she said, the memory of their earlier encounter coming into focus. 'Your father was friends with mine? James Preston-Addlington Jr.'

'It's just Addlington these days,' James looked bashful. 'The double barrel Jr thing just sounded pretentious. And our parents aren't friends any more. Dad wanted to go into business with Dominic, that's why we were at your house. But they couldn't make it work – because your father is an asshole, apparently. Just his opinion.'

Evie squared her jaw. 'Well it's an asshole opinion, if you ask me,' she snapped. 'If my dad didn't want to go into business with your dad he had a good reason.'

James shrugged. 'Probably,' he smiled good-naturedly. 'Does the daughter of a business mogul make a habit of jumping off rocks and pretending to drown?'

'I wouldn't say a habit,' Evie smiled. 'But someone had

to show you and your jellyfish friends how it's done. Does the son of an asshole make a habit of saving damsels in distress and then twisting their ankles?'

'Only the pretty ones.' He looked as though he was about to move towards her and her heart sped up. What was about to happen? Was he going to kiss her? Was this normal – to meet a boy for the first time on a beach and kiss him? She knew that other girls in her school did things like this, maybe that's the way teenagers were supposed to act. Would they kiss here? In such a public place?

She never got to find out. A shout came from the end of the beach and they both looked up – James' friends were waiting on the other side of the barrier, fully dressed now and with a car parked alongside them.

James straightened up. 'That's my cue. Hope your ankle feels better soon, Evelyn Rousseau.'

Evie wanted to ask for his number, or if she could see him again, but the threat of humiliation in front of her friends held her back.

'See you then,' she said, shooting for an air of nonchalance she didn't feel. *Ask me to come with you*, she pleaded silently. *Ask me, and I'll come.*

'Take care of yourself,' he started to move away and hesitated, turning back. He leant forward, put a finger under her chin and, lifting her face to his, he kissed her lips – not a long lingering kiss, or a passion-filled tongue-clashing kiss she'd heard her friends talk about, but a soft, three-second meeting of the lips.

'That's for allowing me to save you,' he smiled. 'Best part of my week.'

She watched him walk away, her tongue glued to the roof of her mouth. When he got to the waiting boys, who started shoving his shoulder and banging him on the back, he didn't glance back until he was getting into the passenger seat. Evie lifted a hand made of stone and attempted a smile, her legs feeling like they were under anaesthetic. She wasn't sure any part of her would work properly for days.

18

Rebecca

Martin has not long gone and I'm in the garden having a cigarette when the police arrive. It feels weird even lighting up without Evie at my side, hopping from one foot to the other because she was perpetually cold. I hadn't even owned a lighter – I'd cried in the corner shop when I had to buy one after realising I always relied on Evie having hers. I wonder if I'll give up now she's not here. It doesn't feel the same. Nothing feels the same.

What have we done?

I'm picturing other bits of my life without my best friend, trying my own life on to see how it fits. Work is fine, she never featured in that part of my life, but watching the third series of *Doctor Foster* on my own might break me. That's when I see them standing in the front room. Richard has that confused look he seems to have permanently etched on his face. My first thought is, *They've found her.*

I can barely get the door open fast enough. I'm just in time to hear Michelle say, 'I'm sorry, sir, it's not her.'

'What then?' Richard sighs, and I feel the adrenaline that surged through me at the sight of the uniforms drop. God only knows how he feels. 'Why have you come all this way?'

'We haven't found Evie, I'm sorry,' she carries a bag I hadn't even noticed into the living area of the apartment and lays it on the floor. 'But there is something we need to show you.'

I remember them, kind, sympathetic Michelle and intense Thomas. Richard and I exchange a glance and both sit down, Richard on the sofa next to Michelle, me on the floor next to where Thomas is standing. I wish he'd sit down, he's making me nervous and I feel like just shouting, *What's in the bag, Michelle?*

'I want to tell you how sorry I am about what you're going through, Richard,' Michelle says as she reaches into the bag at her feet. As she draws out the once white satin of Evie's wedding dress, now looking as though it has been dragged through a mud bath, I can feel the little bit of breakfast I managed this morning churning in my stomach.

'We found this,' she stops short of laying the entire skirt out on the floor. 'Or rather a coastguard found it. He thinks it's been dislodged from some rocks near where Evelyn. . .'

I don't hear what she says next, because I am hurling towards the bathroom, where I lean over the toilet and vomit until my insides are empty.

When I return to the room Richard barely notices I've been away, but Michelle gives me a sympathetic smile. She looks like she wants to ask if I'm okay but doesn't want to interrupt the rant Richard is on.

'. . .doesn't help us to find out why she went over that cliff or where she is now,' he is saying. I sit down on the floor. The bag is gone, which I'm grateful for. I picture Evie's body smashing against those rocks. *Where is she?*

Michelle bows her head. 'Richard, I promise we're doing everything we can.'

'Except you're not, really, are you? No offence, but it's

not really your job to find out why someone commits suicide, is it? Once you have her body you're done. It's me who's left to wonder who she was fighting with on those cliffs, me to—'

'Fighting with?' Thomas interrupts. His voice is deep and sharp; he's definitely not had the family liaison training for a few years. 'What do you mean, fighting with? Green?'

Michelle shakes her head. 'I wasn't aware.'

'No, I haven't had a chance to tell you yet,' Richard lies. He's had plenty of time to tell the police, but I know why he hasn't. 'I met with some friends who had been at the wedding. They said Evie had been arguing with someone not long before she disappeared – just before actually.'

'We spoke with all the wedding guests,' Thomas frowns. 'No one told us this.'

Richard looks embarrassed. 'They didn't see the guy she was arguing with properly. They thought it was me. They didn't want to get me into any trouble.'

Michelle and Thomas exchange a look, and it's not a 'oh, isn't that interesting' look, it's something much darker.

'But it wasn't you?' Thomas asks. 'You're sure?'

Richard makes a weird snorty sound that's not quite a laugh. 'Don't you think I'd remember if I'd been arguing with my wife moments before she jumped off a cliff?'

'So you're certain she jumped? Do you have any reason to believe your wife would do that?'

'It was you who said she couldn't have been pushed,' Richard counters, getting flustered. I can see why, talking to the police is like talking to a child. You get yourself all tied up with their ridiculous logic, they tell you she was seen jumping then sound accusatory when you say she jumped. Not to mention that Thomas is scary intense; even his innocent questions sound like accusations. I liked him better when he wasn't speaking. 'You said there were witnesses. . .'

'Yes,' Thomas replies, but his eyes are fixed on Richard and it doesn't seem like an answer designed to placate. 'The witnesses.'

For the first time since Evie disappeared it crosses my mind that Richard might be a suspect. We'd been told that the police weren't considering a verdict other than suicide – two people across the cliffs had seen her jump into the water and not seen anyone else present. Now, looking at Thomas and the way his eyes have never left Richard's face – even when I ran off to throw up – I'm wondering if that's still their stance.

Don't they say the husband is always the first suspect when someone goes missing? And how does it look that I am always around – like Richard has moved his mistress in at the first opportunity?

'Richard,' Michelle says, and she gives Thomas a look that says, *Stand down.* 'Our enquiries are ongoing into what happened to Evie, and they will be so until an inquest makes a ruling. It is still very soon. For now, all we can do is follow the leads we have. If you could give me the contact details for your friends who saw your wife on the clifftops, that would be a great help.'

'They told me everything you need to know. I can give you all the details.'

'All the same, we'd need to speak to them directly.'

He lets it drop, thank God, and writes down a number, passes it to Good Cop. Bad Cop is still watching him as though he might break down and confess at any moment.

'These witnesses. . .' Richard begins, and I accidentally let out a groan. Shit. I screw up my face in an apology. But where is he going with this?

'Yes,' Michelle says, and I know she's thinking the same as me.

'Well, you've questioned them properly, have you? No,

listen, don't look like that, Rebecca. If you think about it, they are the only people who are saying Evie jumped off that cliff. Are you thinking they were wrong? Or could someone have paid them to say that? How do you know it wasn't them who pushed her, then called it in as witnesses? How good is their eyesight? You're spending all this time searching the sea and she might have been kidnapped by some lunatic.'

'We have no reason to believe the people who saw Evie on the clifftop were lying,' Michelle replies. Thomas looks as though he wants to say something but he doesn't and I wish I could get inside his head for a minute. He isn't as certain about the witness testimony, I can tell that much. And he latched pretty quickly onto what Richard said about a fight before she disappeared. Thomas thinks there's more to this case than a suicide, I'd bet money on it. The problem is, I'm almost certain he suspects Richard. Shit.

19

Evie

The day had been long, hot and humid. Everyone at the house was avoiding one another, for they were all in the foulest of moods, and Evie was the worst. She felt like doing nothing, yet when she did exactly that, lounging around on the lawn, she was overheated and bored in minutes.

This summer was dragging more than ever, and it was only the third week of the holidays. She thought back to the time two weeks ago – as she had every day since – to the day on the beach, and her heart quickened. She'd been desperate to go back, but Harriet had been in such a sulk over Evie's encounter with James Addlington that she had declared the beach 'one of the most boring places ever' and there was no way Evie was going back alone.

Now all her friends had gone away, travelling to exotic locations, it seemed, as a collective. Despite her family's money, Evie barely left England. She would look at travel magazines with a feeling of intense longing for the white beaches of Thailand and the landscapes of Botswana, and her stomach would ache with a yearning to get away from that small-town mentality where everyone knew who they were and she would never be anything more – or less – than the daughter of Dominic Rousseau. And she wanted to be less, much less. She wanted to be no one, to be anonymous, to be unseen and free to act out and make mistakes as normal teenagers were wont to do. At sixteen she often felt like a prisoner in her own life and she hated it. If ever she left Wareham she would make sure she went somewhere no one knew her face, or even her father's name. For the Rousseau name was a well-known one in their own county – how could it not be with the cars they drove and the house they lived in, the parties they threw? But they were not celebrities and their fame did not extend beyond the limits of England, perhaps not even beyond Dorset.

All *sans rapport* really, as her mother point blank refused to travel further than the county border, feigning one of her heads at the thought of getting on a plane. They had managed to convince her to holiday in Scotland once, but the journey left her in such a depression that the trip was cut short to get home to Dr Anderson. When Evie had questioned this with her father, screaming at him that it was bullshit – they had flown here from France, hadn't they? – he had threatened to ground her for the rest of the summer if she ever disrespected her mother or her illness again. Which was why, by the third week of the summer, Evie was alone in her garden, trying to keep from dying of sweat-related illnesses and reliving every moment of what was little more than a three-second kiss.

The swimming pool stretched out invitingly. Sunlight glistened off the still surface of the vivid blue water, just calling out for someone to jump in and break the surface, like freshly fallen snow that yearns to be stepped in. Evie looked up at the house; it would take her at least fifteen hot, sweaty minutes to go up to her room, find a bikini, change and get back down to the pool. In all honesty it was possible she might have passed out from heat exhaustion by then, or perhaps melted. There was no one around and this was *her* pool. There would be no harm in going in in her underwear. There wasn't any difference between her bra and pants and her bikini anyway.

She peeled off her shirt, grimacing a little at how ripe it smelt. It felt so good to be free of the confines of the material clinging to her body under the dampness of her skin. She gave another quick glance around to check there was no one watching before unbuttoning her denim shorts and wriggling them to the ground over hips that were now beginning to resemble a young woman's rather than a twelve-year-old boy's. Now there was no one here to impress, and Evie dived into the pool with her typical lazy grace. She had been swimming since she was tiny and loved the water, doing ten laps of the vast pool in ten minutes easily. She loved the resistance against her arms, the way the blood pumped in her veins as she cut through the water. Reaching the end of the pool, she turned expertly to begin again.

After half an hour of laps, however, she grew tired of the monotony of endless straight-line swimming and pulled herself out with ease. Water glistened down her lithe, tanned limbs and she realised with a groan that there was no towel here for her to dry herself on. Her underwear, once white, was now almost completely transparent and clung to her skin most obscenely in a way that she was certain her swimsuit did not do – even so she resolved to check before she wore it to jump from rocks again. She would not run to the house for a towel – if her mother saw her like this she would likely pitch a fit and thank goodness Papa was at work. No, she would simply lie here by the pool until she was dry enough to put her clothes back on and go in search of something else to relieve the boredom. Maybe she would get the bus into town and wander around the shops – you never knew who might be around.

She had barely closed her eyes on the warm grass by the side of the pool when she heard her father's voice booming through the air.

'What the hell do you think you're doing?'

Evie sat up quickly, thinking his angry words had been directed at her. Instead, her eyes landed on the target of his fury, a young man standing at the entrance of the courtyard. His dark hair and wide blue eyes were unmistakable; James Addlington.

Evie scrambled to her feet and grabbed at her white linen shirt, pulling it to her chest to cover her bare skin. James looked as though he had been hit with a thousand volts as Papa strode towards him and grabbed him roughly by the arm.

'Take your eyes off my daughter!'

'Papa, no!' Evie pulled on her shirt and shorts, almost tripping over her feet to get around the swimming pool to where the two men stood. James was red-faced now and Evie felt the heat burning in her own cheeks as she remembered the softness of his lips against hers. Papa continued to shout into his face.

'I want you off my property this instant!'

'Sir, I was just, I didn't know she was. . .' James tried to avoid looking at Evie as she stormed over to her father's side and pulled at his arm.

'Papa! Stop! You're hurting him!'

Her father turned his dark angry eyes to his only daughter. 'Evelyn Grace Rousseau, you will get back to the house this instant and go to your room. I will deal with you later.'

Angry, humiliated tears sprang to Evie's eyes but she didn't dare argue. Her shirt still hanging open, she clasped it together over her chest, and turned to run across the garden, into the house and up to her room without looking back.

20

Rebecca

Richard was more anxious than ever when the police left, so I made my excuses and left him to it, coming home to my single-bedroom rented apartment – all I could afford in Kensington without the financial backing of a rich father. It's homely enough, not as small as some I'd been to look at when we'd all finished our final year at university and Evie and Richard had announced they were moving to Kensington to be close to Richard's new offices.

At the time it hadn't felt like I was following them, more like we were all embarking on a new chapter together. The online PA service I'd been working for was flexible in its very nature and there had seemed little sense in staying put when everyone I knew was flying the nest, so to speak.

I'm curled up on my second-hand navy-blue sofa, my body melding comfortably into the worn cushions where I've been for the last hour, staring at the Facebook messages I received last week and ignoring the spreadsheet I'd opened with the full intention of catching up on the mountain of work that's been building up in my inbox. Since I blocked the Evelyn Bradley profile I can't see the picture any more

– thank goodness. There is just a blank face where it should be, but I can still access the messages.

YOU SHOULD HAVE SAVED ME.

Other than confronting Richard, I can't see how I can find out if he's behind the Facebook profile and the text messages, and sitting here now in the safety of my own front room, the idea of him creating a profile for his dead wife and using it to try and freak me out seems a bit ridiculous. If it hadn't been for the text messages I'd still be convincing myself it was a particularly macabre troll. Part of me still feels like it could be the wife – Camille – only I can't figure out what she'd want from me. Other than asking them there doesn't seem any real way of finding out who they are or what they want.

Unless. . .

I pull out my phone and scroll through to the number that Evie gave me for emergencies – someone I should only ever phone if things went drastically wrong. But they haven't gone wrong – not really – and I shouldn't be using it. Still, even as I tell myself it is a bad idea, I find my thumb hitting 'call'.

For a horrible moment I think it might tell me the number is out of service, and all of the implications of that hit me like a truck. Then it rings, once, twice, three times, and a voice answers.

'Hello?' the man says. I hang up.

21

Rebecca

Richard is up and about when I get there, and he answers the door looking more alive and upbeat than I've seen him look in weeks.

'Hello,' I say. 'What's got into you? It's barely midday and you're dressed.'

He looks embarrassed. 'Yeah,' he runs a hand through his unfashionable light brown curls – a little shorter than when I first met him but no less outdated. 'I thought you'd probably had enough of turning up and having to cattle prod me into clothes. And when the postman expresses surprise at you wearing trousers you know it's probably gone too far.'

He goes through into the living room and I follow, where I'm greeted with a table full of paper, coloured pens and scribbled notes. I try not to sigh, my joy at seeing him up and dressed dissipating.

'What's this?' I gesture at the mess all around.

'Oh, I was just making a list of everyone who came to the wedding,' he says. 'Thought it might help.'

'Might help what?'

He looks at me as though it should be obvious. 'Help find

out who Evie was arguing with. Look, I've written down every man who was invited.'

'And what they were wearing, their hair colour, their build – do you have mug shots of everyone so you can do Chris an identity parade?'

His eyes widen and I know he's considering the possibility.

'Richard, I'm joking. Don't you think this is all a bit over the top? Do you really think finding this guy will bring Evie back? It could have been a waiter who spilt wine on her dress for all we know.'

He points a finger at me. 'I hadn't even thought of the staff! This is why I need you around, Becky, you're an angel.'

It takes everything I have not to tell him who the man on the cliff was. Maybe I should, maybe it would help him move on if he knew the truth. But the time for telling the truth was four weeks ago, now is too late. Because if he finds out I knew all along he'll never forgive me. I have to stay strong, stick to the plan.

'Richard, you know this argument doesn't change anything.'

He half looks up from his notes, barely listening. 'What?'

'Well,' I hesitate before saying the words. 'Evie, whyever she did what she did, she's still gone.'

He looks up properly this time, and I see pain shining in his eyes.

'Remember when your tutor told you that you wouldn't pass your exam, because you'd missed too many classes?'

It's so off topic that I have to repeat his words in my mind.

'Of course I do. What's that got to do with any of this?'

'Evie felt terrible,' he says. 'She felt responsible.'

It was kind of her fault, but I don't say that. She *had* felt awful. I'd never failed at anything in my life and there I was, first year of university and told I might not pass three of my ten modules. I'd been stunned. I'd obviously been aware that

I'd missed a class or two since meeting Evie – they were nine am tutorials so I sure as hell wasn't the only one not to make it. Evie had practically been in tears when I'd recounted the conversation, too shocked and numb at the idea of flunking my first year to produce much emotion myself.

'She made up for it,' I smile as I remember what she'd done. She'd sent me into town for supplies, and when I came back to her flat she'd set up a complete revision area in her living room, my notes tacked to pure white walls, mnemonics scrawled across the back of rolls of wallpaper, a list of the syllabus highlighted with all the classes I'd missed. While I protested that it was too late, that I'd never catch up in time, she'd brewed me pots of coffee and made sandwiches like she was feeding the army. An hour later a private tutor had arrived. All the time Evie was taking photographs, my identity hidden, for a project on stress in the student population. We'd both passed our first year with points to spare.

'She didn't give up,' Richard reminds me. 'And she didn't let you give up. The least I can do is not give up on her. Not until I find out that the person she was arguing with had nothing to do with her death.'

Feeling like shit, I agree to help him call wedding guests, all the time knowing that none of them had said so much as a sharp word to Evie the entire day. I take the task of calling the hotel, mainly so I can pretend to make the call and speak to the catering manager and wedding planner who both fictionally agree to speak to the staff. After an hour of hearing the same condolences over and over, and assuring people there really wasn't anything to be concerned about, and no, there was no news about Evie, I offer to go and make us something to drink. Richard nods and makes a sweeping gesture, phone stuck to his ear, so I take the chance to escape. From the kitchen I hear him go silent and wonder if he's as fed up with speaking to people as I am.

Carrying the steaming mugs into the dining room where Richard has set up his makeshift call centre, I'm surprised to see he's not furiously making notes any more, or drawing arrows from one person to another, or sighing as he strikes through another name on the list. He's staring, in silence, at a phone on the table. My heart thuds as I realise it's my phone. Shit.

'What's this?' he asks, pointing down to where my internet browser is open to a page on Facebook.

'What are you doing with my phone?'

'I was making a call but they weren't answering. I picked up your phone to Google something and this was open on your browser. What is it? Some kind of joke?'

I lean forward and look. There's no point getting annoyed at him for using my phone, or at myself for being too lazy to have a lock code on it. He's seen it now and any wrong-doing on his part is eclipsed by his wife's name on the list of people I've blocked.

'It's my block list. I was being trolled. I didn't want to upset you.'

'When did you get it?'

I know what he's thinking, the same thing I thought straight away, what our brains are conditioned to believe – that the simplest explanation is true. This profile says Evelyn Bradley – therefore it is Evelyn's profile, therefore Evie is alive.

'A few days ago – look, it's obviously not her but. . .'

'What makes you think it's not? It might be her. Why did you block them?'

I sigh, but not unkindly. 'Richard, don't you think that if Evie had survived the fall, she'd have gone to hospital, or a police station? She wouldn't have set up a new Facebook profile and just contacted me.'

'Maybe she's lost her memory,' he says, then frowns as it

dawns on him how stupid that suggestion is. 'I don't know then – who is it?'

I shrug. 'No idea. They sent me some weird messages about me looking like I'd seen a ghost and I blocked them. I, um, I take it they haven't contacted you?'

I don't mention that for a while I thought it *was* him. Given his reaction that seems ridiculous now – Richard has never been the world's greatest liar. Unless he is literally the world's greatest liar, and so good that he's never been caught.

'I deleted the app from my phone,' he says, crossing the room to his computer. 'Notifications were doing my head in. I haven't checked it since.'

He boots up the computer and logs into Facebook. There are dozens of notifications, but no new friend requests. He looks almost disappointed. I pick my phone up off the table – if he hasn't seen the texts I'm not going to show them to him. In fact, I'm going to delete them the minute I get the chance.

'I've found it though,' Richard says, clicking around on the screen. 'Here, I can see the profile. God – is that her?'

You couldn't see the picture properly on my phone, but Richard has it on the screen now, a full-screen image of Evie on the clifftop. Only. . .

'No,' he says. 'It's just a woman in a wedding dress. See? That's not her. And it's been Photoshopped onto those cliffs – you can see the outlines. Bloody hell, some people really are sick.'

In the absence of any other photographs he clicks on 'friends'. She only has one, and it's one that wasn't there the last time I looked.

Camille Addlington.

'Yes,' I mutter. 'Some people really are.'

22

Evie

Evie preferred the clifftop when the weather was bad, when the wind sent furious water hammering against the rocks below. On days like that she would lean into the wind, certain she could feel the salty spray from the angry tide in her face – although she knew she was too high up for the wind to carry the mist this far.

Today though, the water was serene, undulating gently, dissipating against the rock rather than colliding. Today the sea seemed as solemn and sober as Evie herself. As she sat on the grass, her knees pulled up to her chest, her mind slowed down like a clock at the end of its wind. She closed her eyes and let every single thought drop away – which was not as easy as one might think – until she heard someone shout her name.

For someone so athletically inclined, James Addlington looked as though he had hiked two miles uphill. His face was blotchy and his breathing heavy.

'What do you want?' Evie asked, as he practically collapsed on the grass next to her. He lay on his back, rubbing his face. Her heart pumped faster just at the sight of him, and all thoughts of the empty bottles she'd found under the sink in her mother's bathroom evaporated.

She hadn't seen James Addlington Jr for months, not since the day her father had dragged him from their garden and threatened him with loss of limb or life should he return. He had been so furious, which in turn had angered Evie. How dare he be so protective of her! She was practically a woman. And her mother had been strangely silent, but something in the way she looked at her daughter made Evie think that she knew – she knew that what Dominic was unwittingly doing was making James forbidden, and therefore all the more attractive. Not only that but she knew the strength of a sixteen-year-old girl's emotions – in fact, Evie thought there was a lot her father the businessman could learn from his wife, if he ever solicited her opinion. Still, Evie had come to terms with the fact that if her father had anything to do with it – and he probably did – she would probably never see James again, or at least not up close. She'd gone back to school and listened to all the other girls talking about the boys they had met over the summer, all the time thinking about what might have happened if her father hadn't come home early the day of her swim.

And here he was, in her favourite place in the world, by the sea. She could hardly get up and run away, so she had no choice but to find out what he had come here to say. Although if he made any kind of wisecrack about her swimming in her pants she would indeed run away, and he hardly looked in a fit state to follow her.

'Your housekeeper told me she thought you were here,' he replied, pushing himself to his elbows. 'It's quite a trek from your house.'

Evie jerked her head towards the pushbike lying on the grass. 'Not if you take the road.'

James looked as though he might cry. Evie laughed.

'Don't tell me you walked up?'

He groaned and moved to sit next to her. Evie felt her face redden.

'Bit of a risk, going to my house. If my dad saw you he'd rip your face off. Although your father would probably be able to afford a new one. A better one,' she added, with a sideways glance. James laughed.

'You really are a charmer, Evie Rousseau, anyone ever told you that?'

'As a matter of fact, they do,' Evie raised her eyebrows. 'We have three whole members of staff dedicated to praising our every movement.'

He looked for a second as though he might believe her, then grinned.

'That sounds exactly like something both of our parents would do.'

'And yet they still don't get along. Why did you go to my house, anyway?'

'I wanted to see you.'

Evie swallowed. 'Why?'

'Because I like you. If I'm honest I think I've been a little bit in love with you ever since I was ten. No one had ever called me a bastard before.'

'To your face,' Evie joked. 'But I am sorry about that. I was a precocious child.'

'You were probably right,' he moved closer and Evie could smell Joop, the aftershave every teenage boy seemed to bathe in these days. He was going to kiss her, and this time there was no one to interrupt them. She lifted her face and closed her eyes.

Evie knew that the other girls in school assumed she'd kissed loads of boys, and she hadn't been without offers. It seemed like at this age boys expected to just walk up to you in the town and walk away with a phone number and a snog – they were obsessed with it – but Evie was glad she'd waited. It wasn't like in books or films; there was no background music for a start, no fireworks and her heart didn't 'explode with joy'. She was too nervous to really enjoy it at the time, it was only when she looked back later, replaying every second over and over, that she knew that no night as long as she lived would beat it.

They had stayed there on the rocks until darkness had crept in around them, and Evie began to shiver with the chill.

Back at home Evie felt sure her parents would hit the roof. How could they not know? Every inch of her felt bruised and raw from his strong fingers, there was nowhere he hadn't touched her and it had been glorious, but her body was unused to that kind of attention. They had stopped short of full sex – not that Evie thought she could have brought herself to say no if he'd asked her, but he seemed to understand it was too soon.

She needn't have worried. Neither of her parents would have noticed if James had bent her over the dining room table. Papa was in his office, his voice firm and uncompromising and her mother was asleep on the sofa. Evie closed the door as quietly as she could, fixed herself a bowl of Weetabix and retreated to her bedroom to relive the last three hours over and over until she fell asleep and dreamed of them too.

23

Rebecca

I can't get Evie's profile, or Camille, out of my mind as I go into town a short walk from my flat to have a wander around and escape from the confines of its ever-shrinking walls. Fair is foul, and foul is fair. Is she trying to make out that she isn't the villain in all this? That Evie was both fair and foul, that a darkness lived inside my best friend? Because that much I already knew.

The day is miserable, that glum drizzle which constantly threatens to transform into a full-blown storm, the clouds above thick with menace. My duck-handled umbrella puts up the obligatory fight before springing open and I button my jacket up around my neck.

The rain has driven people off the streets, save for the *Big Issue* sellers who work longer and in worse conditions than anyone I know and are still looked straight through, as if they are invisible. I fish into my purse to retrieve a two-pound coin and the man I hand it to tells me that God loves me. It makes me think of Evie, and how she would scoff at the idea that anyone could still believe in God when there was so much suffering and injustice in the world. *If there is a God*, she would say, *He gave up on us a long time ago. Either that or He has a pretty sick sense of humour.*

I'm still picturing her wry smile as she said this to the Jehovah's Witness who asked if they could talk to her about the 'true word of God'. *If He fancies a chat*, she said, *He can slide into my DMs.*

'You do realise, he's probably going back to his six-bed mansion,' a voice to my left says. As I turn I see the frowning face of a man in a navy jacket, scarf pulled up around his face. His eyes look familiar, although I have no idea where from. Then I realise, Detective Thomas.

'That's pretty cynical.'

'It's kind of my job to be cynical,' he says.

'You're a long way from home, detective,' I say, my pulse quickening. Does everyone immediately feel guilty when faced with a police officer? Or just those with something to hide? 'Is this a business trip, or a coincidence?'

'Business, I'm afraid.' As he says this I have a ridiculous image of him pulling out a pair of handcuffs and snapping them over my wrists. Of course, he does no such thing. Instead he clears his throat as if he is about to ask me on a date and says, 'Do you mind if I ask you a few things? I could use your help, as one of the people who knew Evie best.'

The only person who knew her at all, I think, but instead I say, 'Know.'

He looks taken aback. 'I'd have thought you'd want to help, given—'

'No,' I correct hurriedly. 'I wasn't saying *no* I won't help, I was saying I *know* Evie the best. You said *knew* but we can't really, I mean it's hard to think of her in the past tense. Not when. . .' I let my words trail off. Detective Thomas doesn't even look embarrassed.

'Shall we go somewhere drier?' I shove down the impulse to say, *Your place or mine*, in case he takes me to the local police station. Instead I nod at a coffee shop already packed with mothers wielding prams and students sharing one hot chocolate between four of them. Hopefully it will be torturous enough for him to keep it short.

Inside, my wet umbrella dripping onto the wooden floor earns us a few glares, as does Thomas boldly moving a push-chair out of the way to nab a table for two in the corner. As he brings over drinks I remind myself to keep my verbal diarrhoea in check.

'Is there any news?' I ask him as he sits down opposite me. I'm reminded now of the first time I saw him, of how I'd thought he belonged in a TV drama about police rather than on the actual force. He is everything you'd picture a police officer to be – dark hair, brooding eyes – although I've never met a real one who looks like him. His attractiveness is unsettling. It's not like Evie's beauty, which drew you in and made you never want to look away. His sets him apart and makes you want to look anywhere other than his intense gaze.

'Not exactly,' he says, but doesn't elaborate. As silence descends on the table I feel an urge to fill it – all part of the job, I suppose.

'So, what did you want to ask me?' I take a sip of the burning coffee to stop me saying more, confessing everything I know.

'I got the impression there was more you wanted to say in the hotel room that night, and at the house the other day, just not in front of Mr Bradley.'

It's not a question, just a prompt, so I shake my head. I must stay aware of these little tactics, these games they no doubt teach police officers in Interview 101.

'Not anything I can think of,' I say, my tone light. 'It was a horrible night, I just couldn't believe what people were telling me Evie had done.'

'But you believe it now?'

'Yes,' I say. Was that too quick? Am I supposed to hesitate, to question the official line that Evie jumped off those cliffs of her own free will? 'I have to, I suppose. She was seen, wasn't she?'

Thomas doesn't answer, another indication that he is in charge of the conversation.

'Have you had any more thoughts about why Evie might have wanted to kill herself?'

I wonder for a second if I should make something up – if the lack of motive is the only thing keeping him on his quest for answers. After all, people kill themselves every day, don't they? Surely it isn't the norm for a police officer to drive hours out of his way to question friends and family weeks later?

'Her mother had just passed away.' This much, at least, is true. Of course he already knows that. 'And her father, well, he didn't make it in time for the ceremony so I suppose she would have been sad about that.'

'Was it unusual for her father to let her down?'

I nod, warming to this subject. After all, this is the truth, there are no mines to navigate here.

'Dominic is a very busy man. I got the impression he worked a lot, that sometimes he put his work ahead of his family, Evie included. She looked – looks – up to him.' If he notices my slip in tense his expression doesn't change. 'In fact, I'd say she idolises him.'

'It seems a stretch to think she would kill herself because he was late to her wedding, don't you think?'

Yes, I do think. Evie was used to Dominic's overbearing presence and perpetual absence.

'I suppose. I just can't think of anything else.'

'What about the affair she was having?'

I put down my coffee cup so heavily that scalding liquid sloshes over the side. My face burns. *Keep it together, Rebecca. Keep it cool.*

'Affair?' I say, aware of how stupid my repetition sounds. 'What are you talking about?'

'You mean you didn't know that your best friend was seeing someone else?'

'She wasn't,' I argue. 'She would have told me. What evidence do you have?'

'Because she told you everything, did she?' He ignores my demand for information, his intense eyes watching my every reaction.

'Yes, she did,' I say, knowing this to be a lie. There were so many things Evie never told me, things I had to discover for myself.

'But not that she was going to jump off that cliff.'

It doesn't sound like a question but I answer it anyway, because that's what you do when a police officer throws a curve-ball at you. They knock you off guard just to see what happens. I'm being played, like this is a production but I'm the only one who doesn't know the lines.

'Obviously not. I'd have never let her do it – that's why she wouldn't have told me. I'd have helped her, talked to her, convinced her not to do it.'

'How well do you know Mr Bradley?'

His sudden change of tack blindsides me again. This isn't as easy as I thought it would be. What does he know? What isn't he saying to me?

'What's that supposed to mean?' I buy myself time. Calm down, Rebecca. He knows nothing. If he did you wouldn't be sitting here drinking coffee. 'He was marrying my best friend – we've known each other since university.'

'Did he know about his wife's affair?'

I take a deep breath. 'If Evie was having an affair – and you still haven't told me what proof you have that she was – then I very much doubt Richard would have married her, knowing all about it.'

'Evie was a very wealthy woman,' Thomas says, taking a sip of his drink to give the words full effect. The implication hangs in the air between us. Married, Richard inherits everything.

'I don't see what relevance that has,' I lie.

Thomas leans forwards. 'If Richard found out about his wife's affair, what do you think he'd do?'

'Not throw her off a cliff if that's what you're thinking.' The words tumble out before I can think and the detective sits back looking satisfied. I can feel the anger at myself and at him rear up in my chest. By saying it out loud I've been the one to put that possibility on the table.

Thomas shrugs. 'He was seen arguing with her just before she fell.'

'That wasn't him. Besides, your witnesses. . .'

'It was dark,' Thomas argues. 'They were far away. People get these things wrong all the time.'

'Do you have proof Evie was seeing someone else?'

'It's my job to ask these questions, Rebecca. A man finds out his wife was having an affair on their wedding day, then she ends up at the bottom of the cliffs. It's my job to question people's stories. So I leave you with the question. How well do you know Richard Bradley?'

'Well,' I reply firmly. 'Well enough to know that whatever you think of him is wrong.'

I never imagined, and neither did Evie, that Richard would be under suspicion. A whole wedding full of people, someone must be able to alibi him for the moment Evie jumped. But unless someone is willing to say for certain that they were with Richard the exact moment his wife went over the cliff he will remain a suspect.

'Besides,' I say, hoping I won't come to regret the lie. 'At the time those people saw Evie jump off the cliff, Richard was with me.'

24

Evie

Evie stretched her legs out carefully to avoid cramp and opened her eyes. James Addlington Jr lay with his smooth tanned back to her, breathing steadily.

So it hadn't been a dream. Last night, their first full night together had really happened, and it had been everything she could have wished for.

Ever since that night on the cliffs Evie and James had been an item. As their fathers still couldn't stand one another it had been best they kept their relationship to themselves, although it seemed to Evie like everyone could see it all over her face, that infatuation shone from her every pore. And now they had made the ultimate commitment.

James had insisted they wait until she was ready, and eventually, after nearly six months of dating, Evie had had to take matters into her own hands. She would be seventeen in a few weeks, it was about time everyone in her life stopped treating her like a child. She felt like a woman already, booking the hotel, finding something to wear and arriving early to sprinkle the bed with rose petals. He'd laughed at that, but in a teasing way. And she'd led him to the bed, acting far more confident than she felt, her legs feeling numb, her heart racing, and begun to kiss him, knowing that this was it – this was really it – and hoping to hell she didn't screw anything up, or make a complete fool of herself. And yet James had been calm, confident, and so loving. There had been nothing that wasn't absolutely perfect – if she ever told Harriet about last night her friend would put her fingers down her throat and pretend to puke but Evie didn't even care.

She looked over to the table, where the box still sat. Afterwards – he said she hadn't given him the chance before – he had opened his suitcase and pulled out a box.

'For you,' he'd said, handing it to her. As she opened the lid she gasped at what lay inside. Lifting out the camera, she put it to her eye and clicked. The camera whirred and the photograph instantly began to emerge from the bottom.

'So the world can see through your eyes,' James told her.

He would probably never know what he'd done for her – what he had done for her just by listening to what she said and taking her seriously. And neither did she. Because what James Addlington had done was to steal her heart – and sign her death certificate.

25

Rebecca

I don't know what made me lie about Richard being with me when Evie jumped off that cliff – I only know that I didn't want him to be blamed for what happened. I'm confident that no one will dispute my story anyway – at the time no one knew they would have to remember where they were at exact points of the evening, and who looks at the time at a wedding anyway?

The bigger question is what does Detective Thomas know about Evie, and her life before the wedding day? Was he just testing me when he told me she was having an affair, to see how I'd react? And if it was a test, did I pass?

And now I've got to decide whether or not to tell Richard, all the while second-guessing what Thomas expects me to do, what will make me look guilty, what will make *Richard* look guilty. The words *If Richard found out about his wife's affair, what do you think he'd do?* run through my mind over and over until all I can picture is a grief-torn and broken Richard standing in front of a jury of twelve people insisting that he didn't murder his wife. Would I have to tell them the truth then? Or would I keep Evie's secrets even as they dragged him away in handcuffs and sentenced him for her murder? How far am I willing to go to protect a woman who betrayed us both?

26

Evie

Three minutes had never felt so long. Alone in her sterile white en-suite, Evie sat on the closed toilet lid with her knees pulled up to her chest, watching the time as it dragged itself towards that third minute, the minute that could change her whole future.

Dread wrapped itself around her insides, snaking through her ribcage and clutching at her heart, lungs. Maybe she would die now of fear, and never have to deal with the consequences of her actions.

A small bleep indicated that her time was up. The walls of the bathroom seemed closer together, claustrophobic and suffocating. Evie put her face in her hands. What the hell had she done?

Slowly she stood on legs that didn't even feel like hers. When this was over it would either be the end of life as she knew it, or a silly overreaction. This was a moment of extremes – there was no in between.

Picking up the small white stick, she turned it over. It only took a second to see, two bright pink lines marking out her fate. Strangely, she didn't fall to the floor, faint or be sick. Evie simply slipped the stick into her handbag, a light feeling of finality seeping over her. The waiting was worse than the knowing. That was that, then. She was going to be a mother.

27

Rebecca

I've already decided I'm not going to tell Richard about Evie's affair when I go to visit him the next day. I'd contemplated not telling him about Thomas turning up here at all but he's going to find out eventually, that bastard has a stone in his shoe about something and he isn't going anywhere until he dislodges it. Even if that means dislodging our lives at the same time.

Plus, of course, I have to make him aware that I'm his alibi as quickly as possible – before Thomas goes to question him and he gives me away completely. Truth is, I'm not exactly sure where Richard was at the moment Evie went over those cliffs – I was too busy watching for the man she was arguing with to reappear, waiting to see if he had been successful in dragging Evie back off the edge. For all I know Richard could have been swinging from the chandeliers with both of Evie's bridesmaids – the thought makes me chuckle.

I bang on his front door, noting that the house is in darkness. It's a long while before he appears, fingers clutching at the doorjamb. All the blood has seeped from his face, leaving it a deathly grey. His pallor makes his deep brown eyes, underlined with heavy grey circles, stand out.

'What is it?' I ask immediately. 'Have they found her?'

'What?' He looks distracted, thrown by the question. He's leaning against the doorframe as though it's the only way he can stay upright. I think he might be sick.

'Have they found her, Richard? Have they found Evie?'

'No,' Richard shakes his head. 'Nothing like that.'

'Then what's happened? You look like you've seen a ghost.'

For a moment I think that maybe he has. Maybe he's seen Evie's ghost the way I've felt it – at times the air so thick with her that I can feel her fingers around my neck, choking the life from me.

'She wasn't sick.'

I have no clue what he's talking about. Who wasn't sick? Evie? And then it dawns on me. He'd asked his solicitor to get hold of Evie's medical records to try and fathom her actions. If she had been dying it would all make sense, an unselfish act by someone who didn't want to make her friends and family suffer. But she wasn't sick. I already knew that. I just didn't think Richard would be allowed access to those records until she was officially registered as dead – seven years from now. Shit.

'Well that's good, isn't it?' I hope he can't hear the falter in my voice. Because I know what's coming. 'That she wasn't coping with some terminal illness on her own? I'd feel terrible if she felt she couldn't tell me that—'

'Because she told you everything, right?' Richard snaps. I recoil at the malice in his voice. *He knows.*

'Obviously not everything, otherwise I'd know why. . . but I thought she did, until now. . .'

'No, she didn't tell you everything. She didn't tell either of us everything. She was pregnant.' His face crumples. 'She was pregnant, Rebecca, and she never even told me.'

28

Evie

'Oh dear God, Evie.' Her mother stumbled to her feet and pushed past her into her bedroom's en-suite where Evie could hear her retching into the toilet. When she reappeared she leaned against the doorway for support, her face as pale grey as the wall. She lifted a towel to her face and Evie heard her mumble through it, 'This is all my fault.'

Given the seriousness of the situation, Evie fought back her instinct to laugh bitterly. Leave it to her mother to find a way to make everything about her. As much as she loved Monique, she didn't feel up to consoling or reassuring her that her teenage daughter getting knocked up wasn't her fault. Just once, she'd hoped for some comfort of her own, for her mum to hold her and tell her it would all be okay.

Now Monique stalked the floor on unsteady feet, her hands working furiously at whatever she could get them on, picking at her nails, fingers raking through her hair. If she was having another episode Evie would have to call the doctor, again.

'Have you told anyone else?'

Evie shook her head. She had wanted to tell Harriet, but her best friend had never been the type to keep secrets, and unless Evie wanted the news all over town before the end of the day she was best to keep quiet.

'Okay,' her mother nodded, pleased with her answer. She looked at Evie again and her eyes brimmed with tears. 'I know what we're going to have to do.'

Evie felt a wash of relief at the word 'we'. She wasn't alone any more. For once in her life her mother was going to be on her side, she was going to be there for her, support her.

'We need to deal with this before your father finds out. He can never know, Evie, do you understand?'

Evie shook her head, confused. How would he not know? Even her father, as busy as he always was with work, would notice something like a baby popping up around the household.

'We're going to have to tell him eventually,' her voice was small.

'No,' her mother shook her head. 'Here's what we're going to do. I know a doctor in Pembrokeshire who can help us. He will be very discreet, not like Patterson, who would have called your father by the end of our session. This man, he's helped me before. He's kind, and he will be able to get us the referral you need. You don't have to worry, baby, I will be with you the whole time.'

Evie was no longer confused, she knew exactly what her mother was talking about. At the word 'referral' her heart had begun to pump faster in her chest, her throat closing in around her words. She knew now how her father would never find out, and why they were going to Pembrokeshire. Her mother wanted her to abort her baby.

'I'm not getting rid of it.'

If it were possible for her mother's already pale face to turn any whiter, Evie was sure it did. She froze, and gripped one hand with the other, her nails scratching at the inside of her palm.

'What do you mean, you're not getting rid of it? Surely you don't think you can have this baby?'

'I'm not saying it will be easy,' Evie said. 'I know how hard it is, Mama. But I can't just kill my baby.'

Her mother moved towards her, wrapping her arms around her daughter's shoulders in what Evie assumed was supposed to be a comforting gesture. But Monique's arms were spindly, bony and cold, and the gesture just felt stilted. There was none of the warmth Evie so desperately craved. She could feel her mother shaking and wondered who was comforting who.

'You don't understand, Evelyn, you're so young, you wouldn't understand. But your father would never allow it. And it can't be allowed. . . If it were any other boy perhaps, but not this one. . .'

'This is pathetic!' Evie screamed, pulling away from her mother who flinched at the sound. *Ladies don't shout, remember, Evelyn? And they certainly don't get pregnant – especially by boys their daddies don't like very much.* 'Your stupid feud with these people – you would force me to kill your grandchild because you don't like its grandfather? For God's sake, it's all a bunch of playground crap! Dad will just have to get over it, and the pair of them will have to act like adults and accept that James and I are together and there's nothing you two can do about it.'

Her mother's hand connected against Evie's face with a sickening snap. Evie stepped back in shock, her cheek burning hot. In seventeen years her mother had never raised a hand to her. Even Monique's eyes were wide with shock and fear.

'I'm so sorry. Sweetheart, please.' Her mother stepped forwards but Evie recoiled in shock, avoiding the hands grasping towards her. 'I'm sorry, I. . .'

'Don't touch me!' Evie turned her face away, blinking

furiously to stop the tears from falling. 'I'm keeping this baby, Mama.'

'Fine.' The apologies had dried up as quickly as they had begun. 'If you're determined to go ahead with having this. . . *it,* I think we should see what your father says about the whole thing. Yes,' she muttered, almost to herself. 'Let Dominic deal with it.'

29

Richard

Pregnant.

Richard pictured Evie as he'd last seen her, long white dress swooshing around her dirty bare feet, her hair falling from the pins that had held it tightly in place for the ceremony. Her green eyes sparkling with happiness, a glass of water in her hand.

Water. He'd thought she was pacing herself, assumed she'd been drinking champagne in between the glasses of Pellegrino, but now he thought about it he couldn't actually remember her drinking at all for a while. She hadn't made it obvious but hindsight, they say, is twenty-twenty. Not to mention that, despite how nervous she'd been about the wedding day, he hadn't seen her slip off for a cigarette lately either. Evie didn't smoke in front of him – he hated the smell – but when he wasn't around he knew she would sneak off to light one up, a mischievous twinkle in her eye when she returned. He'd lost count of the amount of times he'd been working all evening and come home to the faintest smell of weed under the air freshener. It made him smile, to think of his carefree, bohemian wife who had never been controlled by anyone in the years he'd known her – probably in her

119

life – spraying the patio with air freshener and scrubbing her teeth before he came home. She didn't have to, Richard would have let her get away with murder, but that glint in her eye as she covered up her 'crime'. . . He had enjoyed acting like he didn't know, letting her have her moment of defiance.

Something about all this felt so wrong. A baby? Why hadn't Evie told him she was pregnant? How could she be so selfish as to kill herself while she was carrying his child? She hadn't just deprived him of a wife now, she had deprived him of a whole family. And why had she stopped drinking and smoking if she'd known she was about to kill herself, and her child? But the biggest one – the one he didn't have room for in his head it was so huge and yet it continued to slip in at the edges anyway. *Was the child his?*

No, he wouldn't entertain that. Instead he fixed on all of the reasons that this new information changed what he already knew. None of it made sense. Why would you take such care of something you knew you were about to kill? And why bother with doctor's appointments at all? Unless it was a spur-of-the-moment thing – Evie was all about the last-minute decisions. Until now he'd pictured this as a planned event, a meticulously contrived betrayal, but her pregnancy put an entirely new spin on things. She wouldn't plan to kill her baby, he was sure of it. Evie was a wonderful, gentle, loving woman and would have been an amazing mother. He wouldn't say out loud what this meant to him, he didn't want to hear Rebecca tell him he was being stupid, overreacting, that he was emotional or in shock.

Because now, more than ever, he believed that his wife had been murdered.

30

Evie

Evie lay on her bed, watching a small spider crawl across the ceiling, stop halfway and make its way back. How easy it must be, to spend your days weaving webs and laying eggs, she thought. No one to scream at you that you were ruining your life, the way her father had done, no one to put you under house arrest. House arrest. It sounded archaic, a historic way of dealing with naughty children, and yet that was the exact situation seventeen-year-old Evie Rousseau found herself in now. Confined to her bedroom while the adults decided what to do with her.

Telling him had been worse than she'd imagined.

'How could you be so stupid?' he'd yelled, every word worse than a slap to the face. Her father had never raised a hand to her in her life but at that moment she swore he was close. 'Do you have any idea what you've done? No, of course you don't. I warned him I would kill him if he ever went near you—'

'Dominic,' her mother said softly as Evie began to sob.

'And you!' he rounded on her mother now, his face growing redder by the second. 'This is all your fault! Can you see what you've done? Do you understand?'

'Of course I see,' her mother whispered, but she shrank backwards and Evie knew her support was wavering.

Once his yelling and hand-waving, complete with a diatribe of expletives in his native tongue, had subsided she had been sent away in tears so that he could talk to her mother in private, her phone confiscated, all contact with the outside world forbidden. She was lucky she wasn't shackled to the wall in the cellar, although she may as well have been. However comfortable her bedroom, she was no less a prisoner.

Evie's hand slid to her belly. It was too soon to feel the life growing inside her move – her baby was less than ten weeks in the womb – but still she felt its presence as keenly as though it was in her arms. She'd never expected to feel this way. She'd ignored her first missed period and put it down to confusion over dates, but when it still hadn't come a month later she'd known in her heart, and she'd been petrified. She didn't want a baby, she would get rid of it, she decided immediately. It wasn't until she'd seen those two pink lines that the reality of her situation had hit her, and she'd known that she could never kill something that was a part of her – and a part of James.

James. Not being able to contact him was the worst part. During the weeks following that day in the hotel they had barely been out of contact – snatched moments in the village at weekends, text messages late into the night. Now, not being able to have him comfort her, share her anxiety and excitement about their child – it was all she could do not to climb out of the window and walk the five miles to his home.

After what seemed like hours of waiting to hear her fate, and the fate of her baby, there was a knock at the door. Evie expected it to be Yasmin, calling her downstairs like a prisoner to face the jury, but it was her mother's face she saw, raw and puffy from her tears.

'I brought you some stew,' she said, carrying the tray in and placing the steaming bowl on the dresser, next to a plate of crusty bread. 'You need to eat.'

'Where's Papa?' Evie demanded. 'What did he say?'

'Your father has gone to the Addlingtons, to speak with James and his parents.'

Evie froze. 'Noooo,' she moaned. 'I should be the one to tell him. What is Papa thinking?' How humiliating. Even now, now she was to be a mother, she was still being treated like a child. 'He should have at least taken me with him.'

'No,' her mother shook her head. 'He doesn't want you to have the stress of confrontation,' she lowered her voice to a hushed whisper, although God knows why because there was no one in earshot that couldn't have already heard the screaming that had taken place earlier. 'He has gone to demand that James marries you before the baby is born.'

Evie groaned as though she was in physical pain. 'No! Mama – do you have any idea how humiliating that will be? And not to mention that neither James nor I want to get married yet! This isn't the Victorian era – plenty of people have babies without getting married. And let's say for a moment James says yes – how will it look, me rolling down the aisle the size of a house? You think people won't know it's a shotgun wedding? It will be the talk of the town anyway.'

'Do you think we don't know that? Do you think any of us have the first idea how to deal with this? Evie, your father is just trying to do his best by his little girl – and yes, his approach may be a little hot-headed and over the top but believe me when I say he loves you and he's only trying to do the right thing by you. He's so, so frightened.'

Of course she had thought about marrying James in the future, didn't all seventeen-year-olds in their first throes of love? But it had been on their own terms, with James making a grand gesture of a proposal, down on one knee, perhaps on the Eiffel Tower – Papa would like that touch. Never in her dreams had it been some forced, arranged affair, James bullied into marriage by her father. She pictured Dominic holding him by the ear and dragging him down the aisle while she stood back, her circus tent of a wedding dress billowing behind her. Evie took a few deep breaths to steady her nerves. Okay – this wasn't the end of the world. As long as James just agreed to the wedding for now – they had plenty of time to convince their parents to wait a while, until after the baby was born and they'd had time to adjust to being a family. This was all about damage control – and hopefully James would see that too.

She wondered how he would react to the news of the baby, wishing she was there to see his face when her father told him that there was a little piece of him growing inside her. Would they have a boy, or a girl? What would it look like? Would it have James' dark shock of hair, or her fair golden halo? Whose eyes would it get? More than anything she wished she could see his reaction, have him take her in his arms and tell her that it would be okay – that yes, they may be young but they would face this together.

She glanced at the clock. How long had he been gone? Would he bring James back here, to welcome him into the family properly? The waiting was too much to bear.

31

Evie

When the front door slammed closed Evie jumped from her bed and practically threw herself down the stairs. Her father was waiting at the bottom, his face solemn.

'Did you see him? What did he say? Was he excited? Scared? What did he say about the wedding?'

'Evie, come,' her father guided her into the small sitting room – the one they kept for themselves – and gestured for her to sit, and her mother followed them in and joined her, one arm wrapped protectively around her shoulder as though she were six again.

'Did you see him? What did he say? Just tell me!'

Her father sighed. 'Yes, I saw him, Evelyn. And I'm sorry that I did. As I expected, that boy is every inch his father's son. He flat out denied that the baby could be his – as far as he was concerned you were sleeping with a host of different boys. I take it this isn't true?'

His voice sharpened on the last sentence and Evie shook her head, tears swimming in front of her eyes.

'I didn't think so,' Dominic's voice softened again. 'And I told him as much. James Sr said that should you wish to proceed with the pregnancy there is to be a DNA test after birth. If the baby proves to be James' child they will support him or her financially – but outwardly they will not accept any child born out of wedlock into their family. I believe his words were "I will not let my son's future be marred by a quick fumble."'

The tears spilled down Evie's cheeks now, and she pressed her head into her mother's shoulder – her cheek uncomfortably wedged against a sharp collarbone.

'I'm sorry, *ma princesse*,' her father stroked her arm. 'I can see how much the boy meant to you. But teenage boys – they are all the same. And having a child, it is something to be celebrated, brought into a loving home after much consideration. Not as an accident, always to be resented.'

Evie gave a sniff and looked up in time to catch her mother throwing her father the strangest of looks. Before she could question it, however, her father passed her her mobile phone.

'Here,' he said. 'Take this, in case he tries to apologise. I really am sorry, my sweetheart. Why don't you go and lie down. Your mother will phone the school to tell them you won't be back this week. You have a lot to think about, and you need some rest and time alone. When you need us, we will be here.'

Evie nodded, still unable to believe what her father had told her was true. Was James just putting on an act for his father's sake? From what he had told her, James Addlington Sr could be a cruel man, harsh in his opinions and quick to use force. Perhaps he would call her now, tell her how sorry he was and that they could work things out.

Composing her third message to him and still unable to find the words, Evie jumped as her phone vibrated in her hand. One new message – James.

How could you be so stupid? Did you do this on purpose? Did you really think I would marry you if you got pregnant? You are not the person I thought you were.

Each word was like a knife to her chest. He sounded so angry! She tried calling him but the phone rang and rang, so instead she typed back:

It was an accident. Please don't be mad. We can make this work. I love you.

It felt like an eternity before her phone buzzed again.

U must be as stupid as U are easy. Don't call me anymore.

Evie hurled her phone across the room with a sob and fell crying onto her bed. James was right – she was stupid and easy. And now everyone would know. She would be a laughing stock – the single mum, the girl who had tried to trap an Addlington into marrying her. She pictured Camille's face at school, as Evie tried to cram her ever-expanding stomach under her stretching uniform. Thank God it wasn't too late to put an end to this nightmare. She knew what she had to do.

32

Rebecca

When Richard told me about the baby I tried my best to look shocked, then looked away. I couldn't bring myself to discuss the whys and hows with him, not knowing what I do. I'm finding it harder and harder to keep up this façade. Why had we not thought about the fact that I would be the one left here to pick up the pieces? Had we been so naïve to think that Richard would just blindly accept Evie's suicide, question nothing? We'd talked about where she would go, how she would live, she'd squirrelled money away and hidden her passport in her suitcase, yet we'd never talked about what *I* would say or do when the time came. It was always just assumed that I would act surprised and devastated, and everyone would slowly move on. Which is why I'm reacting to the news of my best friend's pregnancy with shock and confusion – just like the first time I found out.

My sister's thirtieth meal has been planned practically since her twenty-ninth birthday, and although she's texted me to assure me that she won't be upset if I don't feel up to going, I know that I'm expected to be there and put on a brave face. The whole family will be there, all wanting to ask if there has been any news, or how I'm coping, but no one wanting to be the first to dig for the gossip.

The first person I bump into in the car park is Sam, my older brother, and I'm hellish glad to see him. Although he was a horrible shit to me when we were younger we've grown up into a comfortable sibling relationship – he's easygoing with no airs and graces. Unlike my older sister who has acted as though she's too good for us ever since she married up, an awful prig of a man who reminds me a lot of Richard's brother. Two of Sam's boys, Alfie and Edward – Teddy – have already run off into the restaurant, leaving him holding two-year-old Harry who is fast asleep on his shoulder.

'Bex,' Sam offloads Harry onto his wife Jemma and pulls me into a bear hug. 'I'm so sorry, mate,' he mumbles into my hair. 'I can't imagine how you must feel.'

We break away and Jemma passes Harry back so she can give me an equally tight hug. She smells of baby wipes and bananas.

'How are you?' she asks, holding me at arm's length and searching my face.

'Shit,' I reply, shrugging my shoulders. 'And not in the mood for this.'

Jemma pulls a face as if she knows exactly what I mean. I like to think that if we'd lived a bit closer to one another Jemma and I would have been more like sisters than me and Lucy have been these last few years. Although I'm closer in age to Lucy, and she's put having children on hold to 'concentrate on her career' (she's a florist), Jemma is like the female form of Sam and I just feel more comfortable around her than I ever have in Lucy's immaculate house with its Farrow & Ball walls and spotless kitchen.

'Stay for an hour or so then fake a migraine,' she grins. 'Once Harry wakes up she'll be so busy tutting at him crawling under the tables and the boys playing swords with the bread-sticks that she won't even notice you leave.'

'Give him to me,' I say, holding out my arms and the baby doesn't even stir as Sam hands him over. His weight against my chest feels comforting and I didn't realise how much I've missed him until this moment. 'I'm so sorry I haven't been in touch more, Jem. He's growing up so fast.'

Jemma's smile is sympathetic. 'You've had a lot going on. You know if it gets too much down there you can always come and stay with us for a bit? It's a bit mental but you don't really have time to be sad.'

'Thanks,' I take a deep breath as we go into the restaurant, just the kind of fancy-looking place that I'd expect my sister to choose with no regard to whether it's appropriate for the children, or my parents who likely don't spend this kind of money on their mortgage.

'Becky!'

The minute I step into the private room reserved for our party, Lucy throws herself towards me in a completely uncharacteristic display of affection. She gives me a quick squeeze then plasters a look of concern onto her 'sponsored by Benefit' face.

'How are you?'

I give her a tight smile. 'I'm okay, thanks Luce. Happy birthday.'

She looks momentarily disappointed but recovers quickly. 'Thank you! Big three oh – how scary! Come on, sit down, I've put you by me,' she lowers her voice. 'You know what some of them are like, they will just be after a bit of gossip.'

I look at Jemma and I know she's overheard because she's bowed her head and is biting her lip to stop her laughing out loud.

'Thanks,' I say and take my place.

Sam and Jemma are stuck down the end with the boys

– which shows how little Lucy knows because now they are constantly running backwards and forwards to their nana and grandad. Mum and Dad are opposite me; Mum shoots me concerned looks and mouths 'Are you okay?' every five minutes or so, while Dad has spent the last ten minutes frowning at the menu and avoiding eye contact.

Lucy beams over at the doorway.

'She's here!'

As I look up to see who has come in, expecting perhaps Kate Middleton, given the delight on my sister's face, fake aunty Barbara – Mum's best friend from when they were kids – leans across the table and lays a hand on mine.

'We were so sorry to hear about Evie, love.'

As she says my best friend's name the figure emerges from the doorway and my breath catches in my throat.

She is wearing a long white dress saturated with water and clinging to her figure. Her veil trails limply behind her, hanging by one pin from tendrils of wet hair plastered to her face. Blood flows from both of her eyes, cutting bright red lines down her pallid grey cheeks. In her arms she holds a tiny baby, presenting her to the room like a trophy. They are both crying: Evie silent blood red tears, the baby high-pitched wails, razor-sharp like a piglet sent to slaughter.

I don't even remember getting up but I'm on my feet. Everyone is looking at her, Evie, as if she is a prize, a special birthday gift just for me.

'Evie,' I say, her name catching in my throat and coming out as a croak. 'Evie?'

She turns towards me but there is no emotion in her face, nothing but those silent tears of blood that pool at her feet. She looks down at the baby in her arms. The room begins to swim.

I feel a hand on my arm, hear someone speak but I can't make out the words. Why is she just standing there? What does she want? The people at the table are looking at her but no one reacts. I look frantically at my sister, my mother, they are smiling as though they expected to see her there, as if it is all one big, wonderful joke, a joke that only I don't understand. How can this be? *How can this be?*

'Evie!' I shout, and the buzz of excitement stops – all the sound in the room stops except the cries of the baby in Evie's arms and I can feel everyone looking at me as I take a step forward and stumble. Someone catches me and begins to talk in my ear, the voice soothing. Strong arms wrap around me but I can't look away from where my dead friend stands in the doorway.

'Becky, Becky, listen,' the words are urgent and at first I think they are coming from Evie but then I realise it's the person in my ear, my brother Sam, who is whispering my name over and over. I look at my mother, at Lucy, they look aghast, no longer happy in their surprise. My father is half out of his chair, everyone is staring at me. I look back at Evie but she is no longer there. In her place stands another woman, the same blonde hair but much shorter and fatter than my best friend. Her hair is dyed blonde, black roots at least an inch down her head. She too is staring at me. In her arms is a newborn baby.

'You came!' Lucy rushes over to the woman, scowling at me as she pushes past the other guests.

I turn into Sam's warm chest. 'I thought. . .' I mumble.

'Ssshhh,' he says, and leads me to the door, past the nervous-looking woman who doesn't even vaguely resemble Evie any more and out into the fresh air beyond.

33

Evie

It was done now, and all she felt was a scaring emptiness. Her mother had gone with her to the clinic. Papa had driven them – today there had been no driver – and waited outside in the car. The whole thing had taken less than fifteen minutes, although the doctor had insisted she stay in that stark cold room for observation for forty minutes, a lifetime of her mother wringing her hands and asking if she was 'okay'. There were too many answers she could have given, too many sarcastic comebacks that would have slipped from her lips without thinking before today, but Evie was too drained to even answer. She felt as though her energy, her soul, her very life, had been tethered to her like a balloon and the doctor had snipped the string. She heard the doctor and her mother speaking in hushed tones outside the door, talking about her, and she couldn't care less what they were saying. It was done, there was no undoing it now.

The tension sat between them all on the drive back home, making the air thick and uncomfortable. Evie curled up on the back seat, her seatbelt undone and her knees pulled up to her chest, making herself as tiny as possible. For once, her father didn't complain or tell her to buckle up – even though Evie wished he would, anything to bring some normality back.

This is normal now, she told herself. This secret, thick and bitter between them, this burden of what she – what they – had done. The doctor had been pleasant, nice even; he'd told her that thousands of young women made this choice every week, that it was her body and she should be in complete control of what happened to it. But she didn't feel in control. She felt as though her thoughts were spiralling in her mind, bashing into one another, so none of them had a chance to become coherent. She didn't know how she felt because none of those thoughts had room to translate into feelings of relief, pain or grief. She felt empty and full all at the same time and it was exhausting. But she knew there was something that would help, something that would take her out of her own head. And thanks to her mother's apathy for finding new hiding places, she knew where to find it.

34

Rebecca

I dreamt of Evie again last night. After lying awake for hours I had come to think that sleep had all but been murdered – that might be preferable to the dreams I had been having of flower beds filled with writhing snakes and falcons being plucked from the sky by owls. Instead I woke with fragments of a dream, as though it had been torn up into pieces and thrown in the air, and I could only catch one or two. On one piece we are standing in a square in London. It's raining and I know this isn't just a dream, it's a memory, of a time I had almost forgotten. We are soaked to the skin, the only two people watching as a group of street artists perform under a tarpaulin held up by two tall planks of wood. Evie wants to join in, she's tugging at my arm and laughing, asking me what's the worst that can happen. Another fragment now, and the dream switches to another memory, this one of the day before, the reason I had lain awake so long and fought sleep. The dream I feared would come.

I'm walking down a street in Kensington, on my way back to Richard's house and keeping my eye out for a shop that I know Evie used to love, when there she is.

Evie is standing in the darkened shop doorway watching

me. I can't explain how I feel when I see her, I should be confused, of course, but should I be this scared? My hands are trembling so much that my grip on my purse is weak and someone pushes past me, knocking it to the floor. Instinctively I swoop down to grab it and when I look up again Evie is disappearing into the throng of people crossing the main road.

'Evie!'

She doesn't look back, so I give chase. She's moving quickly and doesn't slow when I call her name again. Where is she going? Why doesn't she stop? I see her blonde head turn into a side street and I break into a run – first I will confront her, then together we will work out what happens next. We were always stronger together – I'd almost forgotten that. I've got no reason to be afraid, she's my best friend, and despite the dream that lingers in the back of my mind – *You could have saved me* – she wouldn't hurt me.

I sprint into the side alley – it's empty. It's not even a through road, it's a complete dead end, and there is no one in here, not the dripping, decaying Evie of my dream or the smiling, teasing Evie of my reality. No one.

Am I going insane? Maybe. Probably. Grief, confusion and guilt will do that to a person I suppose. Am I to blame for what Evie did? Are these visions my mind's way of telling me I'll never be free of her? No, I don't think one person can take responsibility for the actions of another – Evie's death is not my cross to bear. And if she has survived – which every day is looking less and less likely – she wouldn't be lurking in abandoned shop doorways or disappearing into thin air in alleyways. I wouldn't have to find her, she would find me.

Taking a few steps backwards – *why don't you want to turn your back on the alleyway, Rebecca? If she wasn't real, why are you afraid to turn around?* – I step back into the bustling street, take one final look at the empty alleyway, and run home, not wanting to be anywhere near Richard or the house where Evie no longer lives.

I wake drenched in sweat and with my own screams still ringing in my ears. Am I losing my mind? When will this all end?

35

Evie

Time, it turned out, wasn't exactly the healer everyone claimed it to be. Evie returned to school, thanked her friends for their concern and flowers – she was feeling much better now, thank you, and yes, it was quite the flu and hadn't it been going around? – and no one was any the wiser. Despite how different, how raw and bruised and tarnished she felt inside, not one person saw that reflected in her face or in her smile. And because of that, because no one knew to pity her or show concern, and no one – least of all her closest friends – could understand her abrupt change in attitude, why she seemed to care so little for her school work or her sudden rudeness towards the teaching staff.

She was sitting on her desk, double-checking her homework against that of one of the other girls and rubbing her temples to make the pounding in her forehead subside, when Camille's voice commanded her attention, along with that of everyone else in the immediate vicinity.

'I heard you and James broke up.'

Evie cringed. She'd thought she'd got away without their relationship being public knowledge – and by extension their break-up a secret – but one look at Camille's smug face told

138

her otherwise. She attempted a 'fuck you' expression, unsure if her face was capable of anything but hungover today.

'Ears that size I'd be surprised if there was much you didn't hear.'

Camille gave a pinched smile. 'There's no need for that. I just came to say thank you.'

'Thank you?'

'Yes,' Camille was practically purring and Evie would have kicked her in the face, if she thought she could lift her foot. 'For a wonderful weekend. James had a *lot* of fun getting over you.'

Before Evie had a chance to respond, and as if she had timed it to the second, the bell rang and Camille was gone.

36

Rebecca

'Since you've been goooone,' I wail along with the radio, tossing dirty pants and socks into an oversized IKEA bag. Jeans that are at least a size too big go into a bin bag, along with drab black hoodies and baggy T-shirts. I've been through my entire wardrobe throwing out everything that doesn't fit, either my body or my mind – now I'm tackling my growing washing pile. Anything to try and avoid thinking about what happened at Lucy's meal, or the dreams that have plagued me ever since.

I haven't been to see Richard in days, ever since he found out about Evie's pregnancy. It's the coward's way out – he probably needs me more than ever – but I don't know what to say, and I can't afford for what I know to show on my face. Damn Evie for putting me in this position. I've decided that time and space is what Richard needs at the moment. Martin might be right, though obviously I'd never tell him that – with me around so constantly Richard can't begin to move on. So I'm taking a break from looking after him and so far I've spent my days working, spring-cleaning my house, and clearing out my head. I feel like a caterpillar casting a chrysalis around—

My thoughts are interrupted by the doorbell – probably the postman with the dresses I ordered in my middle-of-the-night shopping spree. Except it's not the postman, it's Richard.

'Oh,' I say. 'Is everything okay?'

'You could attempt to look pleased to see me,' he mutters. 'At least I'm not waking you at an unholy hour and forcing you into the shower.'

'Do you mind?' I hissed, stepping aside and letting him walk past. 'If my neighbours hear you say something like that I'll be the talk of the complex.'

'Do you even know what your neighbours look like?'

'Yes,' I scowled. 'That one across the hall has brown hair and smells of citrus, and freaky downstairs has a nose ring. Actually.'

'Septum.'

'*Gesundheit.*'

'No,' Richard grins. 'It's a septum ring.'

I shake my head irritably.

'Do you have a point? What are you doing here? Is there news?'

'Nope,' Richard holds up his khakis and I almost see the old twinkle in his eyes. 'I came to see if you wanted to go for a picnic.'

'A picnic?' I don't try and hide my surprise. Is he drunk again? 'You made a picnic?'

'Well, I brought pre-mades and crisps,' he admits. 'It's a veritable buffet – you want in or not?'

'Sure,' I shrug. 'Why not? Where are we going?'

Richard smiles. 'It's a surprise.'

It takes me half an hour of rolling my eyes at Heart FM to realise I've been had.

'Richard?' I ask, still staring out of the window.

'Hmmmm?'

'When were you going to tell me we were going to Lulworth?'

I sense him stiffen.

'What makes you think that?' he asks in the worst fake-casual voice I've heard anyone use.

'Is this a kidnapping?' I demand. 'Because unless you are kidnapping me – and by the way, even if my family noticed, they can't afford the ransom – then you need to tell me why we are driving to Lulworth.'

'There's something I wanted to check, that's all. You don't have to make it sound so sinister.'

Oh yes, I think. *Nothing sinister about going for a picnic where your wife threw herself off a cliff.* But I stay silent.

We make some small talk on the journey but as we get nearer to the place we both last saw Evie alive an uncomfortable silence descends. When we get to the hotel I expect Richard to park up, but he carries on as far as the road will take us. When he finally stops I look at him expectantly and he takes a deep breath.

'I need you to go out there,' he says, motioning to the clifftop ahead. 'There's somewhere else I need to go.'

'You're coming back for me though, right?' I half joke.

'Yeah,' he says. 'I won't be long.'

37

Evie

James' betrayal had been like a knife through her back but, although sharp, it wasn't fatal. Sometimes it would hit her, if she were to accidentally wander past somewhere they had visited together, or see a couple who looked like them holding hands, her body leaning into his as they walked, so in love that they fed from each other's touch. A young mother out for a stroll with her baby wrapped to her chest. Yes, those things would hurt, but the pain wasn't as real, as raw as those moments when she could smell him in the air, with no idea of where the scent had come from – was he there? Had he come to apologise, explain? – or those times she would actually hear his laugh in a crowded café, the instant flush of anticipation followed by crushing disappointment when it turned out not to be him at all.

But she was young, and in her youth had a way of mini-mising the pain, wrapping it up tightly in a ball and burying it deep in the pit of her stomach while on the outside she became the life and soul of every party. She laughed a little louder, drank a little more, pushed boundaries and broke school rules.

Life in the upper sixth was more relaxed but Evie seemed

determined to prove that she was okay, and to do that she must be having a good time. Her schoolwork began to suffer – who could do algebra when there was so much pounding in their head? – and the school's calls to her parents became more frequent and more serious. When she got wind of her father's imminent arrival she convinced Jessica and Harriet to take the ferry to France for the weekend, turning off her phone to avoid an angry barrage of calls and messages. And ever present was the constant knowledge that the malignant tumour of grief which remained lodged somewhere inside her might flare up at any given moment, rendering her utterly heartbroken where seconds before she had been pain free.

She sensed that something was wrong the minute she arrived back in the boarding hall. The way people stopped to look at her, the sympathetic glances they shot her way. What had happened? Had there been an accident? She got her answer the minute she walked into her dormitory.

'Evelyn,' her father's voice was calm, but even so she could tell he was furious. Had he been here all weekend?

'Papa!' Evie threw herself at his chest, hugging him tightly. 'It's so good to see you! Why didn't you tell me you were coming?'

'Where have you been?' he asked, extracting himself from her grip and walking around her bed. 'I've been here all weekend, waiting for you.'

'But we had that trip to Paris, don't you remember?' She waited to see if the boldness of her lie had worked.

'No, I don't,' he replied evenly. His face was a mask, fixed and unreadable. 'And yet I must have known you were going, because I signed the release forms.'

Evie gave a feeble smile. 'Well, you are so busy. You're bound to forget things sometimes. But you're here now. Would you like me to show you around? Wait – you didn't sleep in here, did you?'

'I tried, but apparently it's against school policy to let men sleep in teenage girls' dormitories. I've been staying at the bed and breakfast in the village. And no, I think we are fine here. Tell me, Evelyn – what am I paying thousands of pounds for this place for?'

'So I can have the best education money can buy,' Evie responded in a monotone voice. She knew what was coming next – she'd heard this speech before.

'And do I enjoy wasting money?'

'No, sir.'

'So tell me why it is that I am receiving letter after letter from this very school to tell me that your behaviour is falling well below the standard expected of Haverton Academy students? And why it is that your grades have slipped from exceptional to *below average*?'

The last two words came out like they had a bad taste to them.

'Perhaps the work is too hard. Perhaps I'm not the daughter you thought I was. Maybe I'm just not the perfect princess you expected me to be. After all, it's not exactly the done thing to get knocked up at Haverton Academy either, is it? Not in the school handbook, breastfeeding and antenatal classes?'

Dominic's face flushed bright pink with fury. 'Evelyn Rousseau, you keep your voice down and change your tone. I did not raise my daughter to speak to me—'

'Raise your daughter?' Evelyn let out a bark of laughter. '*You* raised me, did you? Not Yasmin, and Phillip, and a whole cast of staff, while you spend evenings rotating between the office and some whore's bed and Mother drinks herself into an early grave because you've made her feel like that's all she's worthy of?'

'Your mother is ill, Evelyn, and I work all hours God sends so you can have your private education and the privilege of acting like such a spoilt ungrateful brat! You know nothing of adult life. You think that marriage is easy? You think that your mother is blameless? You have no idea!'

Evie couldn't think of a time she'd ever seen her father more furious. He looked like he wanted to burst into tears and slap her in the face all at once.

'Papa, I'm sorry—'

Dominic shook his head. 'Don't give me your apologies. You will get your things together and I will arrange for you to come back to finish your final exams in a few weeks. I want you where I can see you, before you get yourself expelled entirely.'

38

Rebecca

We haven't been back here since the day after the wedding and as I stand at the clifftop I have a vision of looking over and seeing her floating there, a white doll in the sea, surrounded by chiffon. Bile rises, burning my throat and pinpricks of light dance in front of my eyes. *If you faint you will fall*, a voice tells me. *Then you can be together again*. I push down the thought and blink a couple of times to clear my head.

On the cliff the air is still warm but the light is fading away to dusk. Richard hadn't picked me up until three, which I'd thought was late for an impromptu picnic, but I'm guessing now that he wants it to be the same as when Evie was up here – just half an hour to go. The silence is disquieting; there's no one out walking tonight and the hotel can barely be seen at the bottom of the slope. If I didn't know there were hundreds of people eating dinner at the bottom of the hill I could well believe that I was completely alone.

I sit on the grass and wait as the light fades more rapidly, cursing Richard and whatever stupid plan has led him out here. How long does he want me to wait? He said he wouldn't just leave me here, he'll get here, but now I'm starting to doubt that he's ever coming back. I pull out my phone to call him and it vibrates in my hand with a text message.

Go to the edge.

I oblige, hoping he's not going to want me to jump off just to see if I survive. I nearly smile at my own joke until I realise how inappropriate it is. I am contemplating peering over the edge to see exactly how far down it is when I hear the voice.

'Careful, it's not safe, you know.' The voice is familiar, the deep intensity. I resist the urge to groan as I turn to see Thomas looking out over the sea.

'Did you follow us here?'

His appearance is too convenient to be a coincidence. Did Richard tell him we were coming? Is he following us? That day in the coffee shop he'd admitted to coming to Kensington to ask me some questions, but how had he known where to find me? And now here he is again, closer to his hometown this time, but unless he can see these cliffs from his house it would be impossible for him to know we were here.

He avoids my gaze and exercises his right to remain silent. *Fine, have it your way. This time you're getting nothing from me.*

'I'm not planning to jump, if that's what you think.'

'No, you're too clever for that,' he replies. 'Your friend, he's the one you need to look out for.'

'Richard? He's upset but I can't see him. . .' I stop, think about what I'm saying. I don't actually know if he's upset enough to do something stupid. Is he planning to join Evie down there? Am I his witness?

'Did you tell him about what I told you at the coffee shop?'

He means about the affair. Should I have told Richard? Is that what an innocent person would do?

'No,' I reply. 'He'd want to know what proof you had, and you wouldn't tell me, remember? I'm not just going to drop that bomb on him without anything to back it up.' I pause. 'Are you going to tell him?'

148

Thomas looks out across the navy sea. 'I was waiting to see if he told me.'

'He doesn't know!' I practically shout. 'I'm telling you, he's not who you think he is. He's not some master criminal, he's a grieving husband. If he knew about Evie and James he wouldn't be keeping it from you.'

Thomas looks triumphant and I can't for the life of me think why until. . . oh shit. He hadn't mentioned any names.

'So you did know.'

'Not until you told me at the café,' I try not to sound like I'm backpedalling furiously. 'But of course I thought about it afterwards. He's the only person I've heard her mention recently. So I assumed. . .' I close my mouth tightly but the damage has been done.

'Visibility is bad between there and here,' he changes the subject again, points across the cliffs to where I can just about make out a figure on the other side. 'Ask your friend. That's where he is now, checking how much the witnesses could see. Maybe he's checking whether he could be identified from that distance.'

'He wasn't up here. I told you, he was with me.'

'Perhaps,' Thomas says. 'Or maybe you're both lying. When he gets back here can you tell him we'd like to see Evie's passport, please?'

The accusation of being a liar and yet another change of subject throws me.

'What do you need her passport for?'

'Just a formality,' he gives me a curious look. 'Is there a problem with that?'

'No,' I lie. I'm getting quite adept at it now. 'I'll have him bring it in as soon as he can.'

When Richard arrives at the clifftop Thomas is gone, as completely as if he'd never been here. If I was the type of person to question my sanity I'd wonder now if I'd seen him at all or if I'd imagined the whole conversation. The warm air has chilled and as Richard walks over I realise I'm shaking, although how much is from the cold and how much is from the conversation I've just had with Thomas I'm not sure. Does Richard know that Evie was having an affair? If the police know, do I tell him? If he doesn't already know it will break his heart – can I bear to put him through any more pain?

Does he already know?

'Thanks for coming, sorry I took so long,' he says as he jogs over to me. 'I wanted to go over to the other side, see what they saw.'

'I know,' I say, watching his face. 'I saw you.'

'Could you tell it was me?'

'No. Could you see me?'

'Some of the time. Not very well though, although I suppose Evie was wearing a long white dress which would have made her more noticeable.'

'Yes, and she would have been closer to the edge. Thomas said—'

'Detective Thomas? The police officer?'

'Yes,' I clock the confusion on his face. 'Are you saying you didn't see him?'

'No,' Richard shakes his head. He's looking at the spot where I had been standing as I spoke to the police officer.

'He said they want to see her passport,' I tell him. 'Just a formality.'

I'm not sure he's heard me but after a few seconds he says, 'Yeah, right, I'm not sure where it is though. I'll find it.'

We stand in silence, me staring out to sea and Richard still looking at the grass beyond. Eventually he points.

'Look, the grass slopes that way. If you were blocking him

he would have been easy to miss – especially given how dark it was.'

'But if he could stay out of sight. . .'

Richard picks up on my train of thought immediately. '. . . Then so could the person Evie was arguing with.'

39

Evie

Evie shoved the money into the hands of the taxi driver, not bothering to count how much was there. The alcohol buzz was warm in her chest and her head swam as she climbed out of the car and looked up at the house blanketed in darkness before her. As the taxi pulled away she realised there was no going back now. She had come this far and she wasn't leaving without speaking to James.

It had been six weeks since her father had told him about the baby, five since there was no baby and a week since her father had arrived at school to drag her home, and she had been spiralling dangerously, her life in freefall ever since. She had to do something, she had to speak to someone, and the only person she wanted to be near was the only boy she had ever loved. It didn't matter that he hadn't loved her back, or that his callous words had been the reason for her drastic actions, she needed him.

The sleek, modern mansion was, of course, encased in a grand brick wall that ran around the entire property, large wrought-iron gates guarded by a small black box that decided who would be admitted entry. Evie had no key fob, so her only choice was to press the silver buzzer and wait.

After a few minutes there was no answer, so she pressed her finger against the button harder now, keeping it there, the angry buzzing somewhat satisfying. It sounded like she felt: determined and pissed off.

'Who is it?' a female voice sounded tired and apprehensive. Evie pulled out her phone and checked the time. Christ, it was after eleven. Where had those hours gone? She remembered digging out one of her mother's secret bottles – she wouldn't miss it and even if she did remember where she'd stashed it she'd assume she'd drunk it herself – but that was around eight thirty. Had it really been nearly three hours ago? It wasn't until she had been nearing the end of the bottle that she'd decided to call a taxi to the Addlington residence, so yes, it probably was quite late. Fuck it, she hadn't slept properly for weeks – let this woman lose a few minutes' rest.

'I'm here to speak to James,' Evie spoke into the box. 'My name is Evie, he'll know why I'm here.'

'James isn't here. Do you realise what time it is?' The voice wasn't dissimilar to her mother's, a cut-glass accent tinged with annoyance. Well screw her, Evie had more reason to be annoyed, didn't she?

'I'll wait here then,' she said, injecting as much defiance as possible. 'Unless you want to let me in?'

There was a pause. 'Evie who?'

'Evie Rousseau.'

She waited for the response, knowing the information wouldn't go down well. This woman didn't sound like a housekeeper – was she James' mother? Did she know about Evie? About the grandchild she had lost?

'Rousseau? What do you want? Did Dominic send you? What does he want?'

Obviously not. If she'd known then she would have been aware that her father would never have sent her here, would never have allowed her to come had he been at home when the taxi had arrived to collect her.

'I told you, I'm here to see James,' Evie's voice was thick from the drink and she was cold and impatient. 'It's nothing to do with my father. James and I,' she felt stupid all of a sudden – she had barely said this out loud to anyone, now she was declaring it to a box – 'James and I were together. And now we're not. And I want to hear him say he didn't want me.' She hesitated, unsure whether to add the words, but the alcohol lowered her inhibitions and loosened her tongue. 'Or his baby.'

She didn't hear the woman gasp – she'd obviously taken her finger off the intercom as the air was dead and silent. Without another word from the box, the gate buzzed and Evie pushed open the pedestrian entrance.

The front door of the Addlington residence was open when she reached it, and a silhouette of a woman was blocking the light from the hallway. James' mother stood in the doorway wearing a housecoat, her blonde hair piled in a messy bun on top of her head and her face devoid of make-up, but still Evie could see how beautiful she was, the same fresh-faced beauty of her only son.

That beautiful face creased into a frown as she watched Evie stumble up the pathway.

'You're drunk,' she stated, her frown changing to disgust mingled with confusion. 'I thought you said you were pregnant? Was that a lie?'

'I was,' Evie scowled. 'But your wonderful son refused to admit the baby was his. Told me I was easy and stupid. I. . .' Evie choked back a sob. 'I'm not pregnant now.'

Understanding dawned on Daphne Preston-Addlington's face. Yes – now she knew what her son had done, and what Evie had been forced to do to *her* grandchild. Evie hoped it hurt.

154

'I told you, James isn't here,' Daphne said, her chin jutting out in defiance. There wasn't a flicker of compassion in her face, no sympathy or apology. She cared as little about Evie and her baby as her son had. 'And he won't be back tonight. You should go home.'

'And I told you, I'll wait. Even if I have to wait all night.' Even as she said the words Evie debated the intelligence of the idea, but she'd said it now, spurred on by anger and alcohol. There was no way she could leave with her tail between her legs now. This was her only chance to speak to James and if she had to she *would* wait all night.

'Fine, have it your way.' Evie's mouth dropped open in shock as the woman swung the door shut in her face, leaving her standing on the doorstep in the freezing night.

She stood there for about twenty minutes, stepping from one foot to the other to keep warm, throwing the occasional look up to the only lit window in the house – presumably James Sr and Daphne's bedroom. No one looked out, the house stayed stubbornly silent and closed.

Finally, the crunch of tyres on gravel made her head whip around to the driveway where the gates were opening automatically. Evie couldn't make out the car, just the headlights moving towards her, but she knew it must be James. His mother must have called him and he'd come back from wherever he was to see her.

Evie's heart leapt. This was it, she was about to see that face again. Maybe he would take her in his arms and kiss her, tell her how sorry he was. How would she feel when that happened? It was too late for their baby – could she ever forgive him for that? But she knew she could; she was there, after all.

She smoothed down the front of her jacket, hoping her breath didn't smell too much of the whisky she had downed earlier and her make-up wasn't spread across her face. As the car pulled to a stop and the driver door opened she thought she might stop breathing. Then, as her father's profile came into view, she wished she had.

40

Richard

Richard tore through the upstairs of the house he'd once shared with the love of his life, pulling underwear from drawers, overturning mattresses. He had started in the bathroom, despite how unlikely Evie's passport was to be in there, the little bottles of lotions and potions like tiny knives to the heart. Finding nothing unusual he braced himself to move on to their bedroom – the room he'd barely been in since coming back to the house. He'd been sleeping in the spare room, his bed too much to bear alone.

If Evie's passport was still in the house – and it had no reason not to be – then it was either going to be in here somewhere or the study, another place so filled with her that it seemed impossible to approach. He couldn't believe he was even having to do this – until six weeks ago they had been a normal couple, engaged to be married, as in love as any two people he knew. Since that night he had been in freefall, being knocked from side to side by one detail or another, all mounting up to the conclusion that he'd had no idea what was going on in Evie's life. But he intended to find out.

Rebecca was downstairs again – she barely left him alone for five minutes these days. He knew she was only looking out for him but her presence could feel so oppressive, and so. . . unfair. Why Evie? Why not her shadow?

He was being unfair and he hated himself for it. If there was anything to be said about Rebecca it was how much she loved Evie. Her devotion to her best friend couldn't be questioned, even if it had seemed a little weird to him at times. And the way she had looked after him these last few weeks – he didn't know what he'd do if she gave up on him now.

Pushing open his bedroom door felt like an immense task every time he did it. Walking in felt like bumping into an ex-girlfriend on the street and feeling as though they belonged to another lifetime, another world you no longer lived in. He tried not to look at any of her clothes or jewellery but it was impossible. She was everywhere. The first time he'd been in here he'd broken down at the sight of a T-shirt discarded carelessly on the chair. He remembered telling her not to leave it there, she'd only have to come back to a messy room and tidy it anyway. The realisation she was never coming back to put the T-shirt away had been unbearable.

He pulled things from the top of the wardrobe: their electrical box full of wires and chargers to items they probably threw away a long time ago; some photography magazines; Evie's camera box. As he pushed it to one side he realised it was lighter than it should have been if Evie's camera was still in there. Not her professional top-of-the-range model that he'd bought her as a Christmas present; that still sat in its box, patiently waiting for her to come back and pick it up, put it to her eye and begin to click. She would smile to herself, as though with a camera in between her and the world everything took on a magical quality that she could only see through the viewfinder.

No, this empty box used to contain her first ever camera, an ancient model given to her when she was seventeen, although he doesn't recall if she ever said who by. And now it's missing, the box instead filled with small beige envelopes.

41

Evie

'What are you doing here?' Evie demanded as her father marched towards her in the darkness.

'I could ask you the same,' Dominic Rousseau replied. 'But looking at how you can barely stand up straight I'd say the answer lies at the bottom of a bottle.'

'I have every right to come here,' said Evie obstinately. 'I'm seventeen. It's ridiculous to just ban me from seeing someone, like it's 1952! I'm allowed friends, you can't just lock me in the house!'

Dominic raised an eyebrow. 'And do you really want your *friend* to see you in this state? Do you even realise how drunk you are, Evelyn? You should think yourself lucky James wasn't in and—'

'How do you know he isn't in? And how did you know where I was anyway?'

'Daphne called me, in the middle of a conference call to Japan, I might add. She was concerned about you.'

'Not concerned enough to let me in the house,' Evie retorted.

'Well, let's just say things between our families are. . . tenuous. I gather you told her about the. . .'

159

'The baby?' Evie saw her father flinch. 'Yes, as no one else had bothered. Don't worry, she didn't exactly look heart-broken when I told her it was dead.'

'That would require having a heart to break,' Dominic muttered. 'Come on, Evelyn, I know you're upset—'

'You know nothing!' Evie screamed. 'You know nothing about how I feel! I killed my baby – our baby – do you understand that? A living thing inside me that relied on me to keep it safe and bring it into the world and I killed it as easily as stepping on an ant. How do you think that makes me feel? I'll tell you – like a murderer. Well if I'm guilty of murder then he's,' she jabbed a finger towards the house, 'guilty of manslaughter. And so are you, and *Monique*, and *James bloody Addlington Senior*. All of us, we all are!'

Dominic moved towards Evie, his arms outstretched. 'Sweetheart, you had a difficult choice to make but you made the right decision. In time you will see that.'

'Get away from me!' Evie screamed, stumbling backwards. 'I want to see James!'

'If you stay here causing a scene Daphne will call the police,' Dominic said, his voice hardening. 'Now get in the car, or I will drive away and let her have you arrested.'

Evie looked up at the huge house. All of the lights were out now, as though the house and its occupants had turned their backs on her, trying to pretend she wasn't there. Was it true, was James out living his life, having fun while her heart lay broken on his front doorstep?

Her head hung in shame and misery, Evie got in her father's car and sobbed the entire way home.

When she woke the next morning she was grateful to find that her father had already left for work. She could barely remember getting out of the car and into bed, yet that's where she awoke, so someone must have put her there. Her head throbbed with pain and shame. Thank God James hadn't been home. Would his mother tell him she had been there? She hoped not.

Sneaking out of her bedroom and into the kitchen to search out painkillers and a bottle of water, Evie noticed a brochure lying on the kitchen table. Turning it over, hoping it was for some exotic holiday at long last, she saw it was a prospectus for a photography course at the University of London, complete with welcome pack bearing her name. So her father had decided what to do with her. He was sending her to London.

42

Rebecca

I hope you didn't think you'd got away with it.

'What is it?' My eyes go from his pale face to the paper in his hand. 'Richard?'

When I emerge from the downstairs toilet – yes, I rent a flat whose rooms I can count on one hand, yet Evie and Richard have a downstairs toilet – Richard is staring at a small bundle of envelopes on the kitchen worktop, an elastic band sitting discarded nearby. I recognise them instantly but try not to look too shocked until I see what they are, try to forget that I've seen the letters before in a different pair of shaking hands.

'These,' he jiggles it slightly, 'were in the box where Evie kept her first camera.'

'Well what are they?' I snap a little impatiently. When he doesn't answer I just take one from the counter and scan it, just like the first time, when Evie showed them to me. It's a printed sheet of A4 with just one line:

I hope you didn't think you'd got away with it.

'Is this Evie's?'

Richard frowns. 'Whose else could they be? It's not mine so unless the cat put them there I'd say they were hers.'

'What do the rest say?' I'm careful not to let my emotions show on my face, Richard is on a knife edge and one wrong word at the moment feels like it could tip him over. *Don't make a big deal of this. Be cool.*

'More of the same,' he says, opening the others in turn. 'Cryptic "I know what you did last summer" style things. And none of them actually mention what they know about.'

'Then it's probably nothing,' I assure him, wishing I had just told him weeks ago, so I didn't have to lie to him now. 'You hear about these things all the time, people sending these vague kind of things in the hopes that the person has done something wrong.'

'Do you?' He's going through the notes again, spreading them out on the worktop, five in total. Actually I've never heard of that happening but I'll say anything at this moment to put his mind at rest. 'I've never heard of that. And why would she keep them?'

'Maybe she was going to show them to you and forgot?' It sounds weak even to me. If Evie wanted to show Richard the notes she would have done so when she got them – blackmail isn't the type of thing you forget about. And she'd shown someone, of course, just not her husband. 'None of them are dated – they could be years old.'

'Then why keep them?' he asks. 'If she knew what she was going to do. . .' his words tail off. 'She must have known I would find them at some point, mustn't she? Do you think I should tell the police?'

I'm pretty sure Evie wouldn't want the police finding those letters. I'm not even sure myself why she kept them – did she not think about the fact that Richard would have to go through her things at some point? Or maybe she thought life here would just carry on exactly the same, her house, her bedroom, only an Evie-shaped hole torn out of the picture.

'No,' I say. 'The police think she killed herself. These letters don't really contradict that, do they? Either they're nothing, in which case you're wasting their time, or Evie was being blackmailed, in which case perhaps she did what she did because of whatever these letters are referring to.'

Maybe it's a good thing he's found these. Perhaps now he'll stop going on about murd—

'Or maybe she was killed because of it.'

43

Evie

There was one thing that made her exile from Wareham bearable, or rather, one person. Evie had thrown herself into university life, accruing one casual acquaintance after the other, avoiding any kind of meaningful relationship – and who could blame her after the humiliation she'd suffered from the last time she let herself fall in love? Finally she could see what her mother had been running from all of these years – the unbearable pain of loving a man who didn't love you in the same way. It could either make you guarded with your heart or reckless, desperate for someone to take it in exchange for their own. Evie had swapped hers with Rebecca.

She and Rebecca had been fused at the hip ever since the morning she had followed her into the greasy spoon and Evie had shown her the photographs she had taken. Evie had been desperate to see the girl again, intrigued by someone who had acted with such indifference when the boy she was seeing had betrayed her so easily. Evie hadn't known when she met the guitarist that he had a girlfriend, although she'd hardly been surprised when Rebecca had shown up clutching her bacon sandwiches. Her experiences of the unfair sex had

165

hardened her to betrayal, and here was a girl who was either used to being treated so callously or had at least been expecting it. A girl who would understand, as Evie did, that a soulmate didn't have to have a penis. And Rebecca had felt the connection too. There had been that one awkward moment when Evie's father had made a surprise appearance and Becky had felt as though she had been used as a distraction; which Evie supposed was only fair and partly true after all. It was entirely possible that her father may have mentioned that he would be coming to see her – it was *even* possible she had dropped some hints that she had wanted him to come. And when he had announced that his week-long visit had to be cut short to only one night she'd been bloody furious. She wasn't her mother – to be picked up for photo opportunities and discarded – and she intended to prove that to him, although she'd never intended to hurt Becky's feelings in the process. She had apologised profusely to Rebecca for the scene that had ensued and her new best friend hadn't been able to stay mad at her for long.

Since then they had spent nearly every day in each other's company, meeting after lessons, staying at each other's houses. For Evie, Rebecca was like the sister she had always wanted. She was funny and interesting, and the best part was she didn't even know it. It was nothing like being with Harriet and Jessica who only listened to you because they were waiting for their turn to speak. Her old friends seemed more like accessories now, something that looked good on your arm but had no more value to your life than a handbag or a bracelet. And she had been the same to them. She had meant nothing to these girls, nothing more than a sounding board for their boasting and benchmark for their common competitions – what she had with Rebecca was the closest she had experienced to a real friendship in her entire life. In fact, it felt exactly the same as what she had had with James.

It still hurt to think of him, living life in *her* hometown with Camille while she was so far away, practically alone and still dealing with the emotional repercussions of their brief affair. That he could move on so easily stung, and that he had done it with the one girl he knew she couldn't stand was like a blatant *fuck you*. She wondered sometimes whether they were even still together – a question that was answered for her one evening when she opened the door to her apartment.

It had been a good day. She had been away from the classroom and on site finishing one of her projects, the title of which was 'Light and Shade'. While most people in her class were focusing on the physical aspects of the brief, Evie had been looking at the socio-political slant on the topic, looking at issues of race in positions of power, the idea that so many people of colour were still in the 'shade' as it were, even in such a developed country as Britain. She had managed to set up interviews with some of the prominent black members of parliament to discuss the barriers they had faced in a political arena and intended to use her research to guide her photography, each picture telling a story of the underrepresented minorities in such a multi-cultural society. It was the kind of story she had longed to tell, the real reason she had taken up photography in the first place. The one and only time she had thought of James that day was to hear her own words to him: *I want people to see the world through my eyes.* She had discovered that showing the world through her own eyes wasn't enough for her any more, she wanted to show it through the eyes of anyone who hadn't had a voice, or who'd had their voice drowned out by the powerful majority. Her work was growing and her views on the world being tested – she thought he would be proud.

Exhausted after spending much of the day absorbing the plights of others, as well as travelling around what felt like a small country – London was so big! – she had cancelled her plans with Rebecca and fallen through the door of her apartment, cringing as she did so at the hypocrisy of her longing for her comfy king-sized bed. So deep was her fatigue that she almost didn't notice the letter underfoot. Reaching to pick it up, Evie's eye was drawn to the handwritten address, which made her carry it through to the bedroom rather than deposit it next to the other unopened 'To the Occupier' letters in the post rack. Throwing herself onto her bed she tore the top off, hoping for a letter from Yasmin or maybe even her mother – if she was writing then that usually meant her mood was improving – but instead pulled out a page torn from a newspaper.

The headline hit her like a punch to the stomach, but it was the photograph that made nausea rise in her throat. A couple, smiling happily for the cameras, him handsome in a suit and tie, her plain and small-looking next to the striking businessman, but beaming nonetheless. And why wouldn't she be? For Camille, it seemed, had won again. She was to become Mrs James Addlington.

44

Rebecca

When we arrive at the café I order us a sausage and egg sandwich each, already used to speaking for Richard as if we are a couple. I also ask the young girl who takes the order to instruct the chef to put on just the yolk of the egg in Richard's sandwich, because I know he'll only take the white off himself. That's how well I know him, and for a split second I wonder if Evie would have known the same, if she would have bothered to make the special request to save the snotty bit of the fried egg touching his bread – he really hates that. I also do this knowing how futile it is: the state he's in at the moment he'll probably barely touch it anyway.

I've noticed in the last few weeks that, when tragedy touches your life, one of the hardest things is knowing how to act, what is right and proper. Everyone expects you to be a certain way when your wife goes missing, for example, but when pushed the same people would say, 'Oh gosh, I just don't know how I'd react if it happened to me.'

One thing they do not want you to do, is smile. Or laugh. What could you possibly have to smile about, when someone you love is in Mortal Peril? People don't seem to realise that there might be whole minutes in an entire day, sixty seconds, when you almost forget that life is normal – but that's when they will see you smile and they will know, irrefutably, that you don't care that your wife/best friend/daughter/sister is missing. Maybe you even had something to do with it – especially if you can do something as normal as eat a sausage sandwich in a café, with another woman. Never mind that the other woman is the only person in the world who knows what you are going through, or the only person you can sit in silence with and not feel like you have to make conversation with, or even be particularly nice to.

Not that Richard would be smiling or laughing right now anyway. Once he'd found those bloody letters in Evie's wardrobe it was all I could do to drag him out of the house before he pulled the rest of it apart to find out what else she's been hiding. Now he glances around us, as though he expects at any minute to be besieged by journalists waiting to make a headline out of his 'intimate breakfast with another woman only six weeks after wife goes missing'. And I'm not surprised that he only picks at his sandwich, or doesn't notice the trouble I went to with the snotty fried egg thing.

'You look like shit,' I tell him and he raises his eyebrows.

'Cheers. What do you think—'

'I don't know, bloody hell, Richard, I'm as in the dark with all this as you are.'

I wonder if I told him now, that Evie was having an affair, if he'd be able to get over her easier? If I told him the baby she was carrying probably wasn't his? Would tomorrow bring a new man, freshly showered and shaven? Would he reclaim his life with the knowledge that Evie didn't care enough about him to stay faithful? I could say the words now – I could change his life for the second time in six weeks. But would it be for better, or for worse?

Instead I take the coward's way out.

'Will you tell the police about the blackmail letters?'

If Richard goes to the police of his own accord they might tell him about Evie's affair, absolving me of the responsibility. I know, I know, cowardly. Evie would hate me for throwing her under the bus like this but I know that if I'm the one who tells him then he will associate the news with me, maybe even blame me. He'd almost definitely want to know how I knew, and Thomas told me days ago – even if I hadn't known before then I've still had plenty of time to be truthful. That's been my problem all along, never knowing when to tell the truth or keep my mouth shut.

'We don't even know *why* she was being blackmailed.' He loses interest in the barely touched sandwich but does pick up the tea I've poured him. Tea is an acceptable outlet for grief – everyone knows that.

'I think I can help with that.'

The voice from behind me is now instantly recognisable, and I close my eyes and let out a breath. Like an angel of death this man always seems to turn up when I least want him to. Hasn't he got bigger cases to work on than following the husband of a suicidal woman?

'Detective Thomas,' Richard frowns but nods to the empty seat. 'Please, sit down. What do you mean, you can help?'

'I think I know why your wife was being blackmailed, although I didn't know she was. Why didn't you tell the police about the letters?'

'I just found them about half an hour ago,' Richard's face is stony – he doesn't like the police officer, and I can't say I blame him. He's brought us no answers, only suspicion and more questions. 'Why do you care? It's just more evidence for your suicide theory.'

'I'd appreciate if you brought those letters into the station. Try not to handle them any more than you already have, put them into a plastic bag if you have one. If Evie was being blackmailed then that person could be charged with manslaughter.'

'Will you DNA test them?' I ask.

Thomas shrugs. 'Not my call, I'm afraid. DNA testing is expensive and it might not be thought to be in the public interest if the letters aren't seen as malicious. I'll know more once I've shown them to the DCI.'

'You said you knew why she got the letters?' Richard says.

Thomas nods. 'I think so. When I got back to the station after seeing you in Lulworth I ran Evie's name through the police computer. Her father's name, not her mother's, which I understand she went by at university.'

'Why?' I could have answered Richard's question myself. Thomas was looking for domestic violence reports, to see if Evie had ever reported her husband for anything. I stay silent and Thomas is more diplomatic.

'It's a formality, and in murder cases would be the first thing we did. It actually *was* the first thing we did, but only a cursory search was done under her maiden name, White. The search I did included Rousseau, a name I'm told she went by before she moved to London. I take it you weren't aware that Evie was visited by police a few months ago with regard to a closed case from a few years ago?'

'No,' Richard looks at me. 'Did you know this?'

'No. Of course not,' I lie. 'Why would they visit Evie?'

'There was an anonymous tip-off to the local police that Evie had information about a fire that killed a man during a party years ago. It was deemed an accident – Evie's name wasn't even in the initial witness statements and there was no evidence she'd been at the party. To tell you the truth, we only followed up on the call because of the recent Newland case.'

Richard nodded. The case he was referring to was a young man who had been shot six months ago – apparently there had been a call to the police station to say he was involved in something that was going to get him hurt which had been put down to a crank call due to lack of resources. Now, it seemed, local police followed up every call – a well-known fact.

'According to the officer who visited she got very upset, was visibly shaken, but had no new information and denied ever being in the area before the fire – although she admitted that her father had driven her there when she'd had a message from a friend to say there was a fire. Apparently she knew the couple who were getting engaged that evening. As far as our records go there was no further action taken.'

'But you think that may be the reason she was being blackmailed? That she knew more about this fire than she let on?'

Thomas looks at me. He knows I haven't told Richard his theory about Evie having an affair and is probably wondering why, although I'd have thought it obvious for a man of his intelligence. Is he going to tell him now?

'Can you think of any other reason?'

Obviously not. Why doesn't he just tell Richard what he thinks he knows? That there is more than one reason my best friend, his wife, might have received letters saying 'I hope you didn't think you'd got away with it.' Maybe he has no proof of this supposed affair, maybe it was a bluff to get me to admit that I knew, a stab in the dark.

Richard shakes his head. 'She never said a word to me, about the letters, about the police visit, about this fire. Why wouldn't she tell me if there was nothing in it? Why wouldn't she tell you?'

He directs this at me, almost an accusation, as if it's my fault that Evie didn't entrust me with the information.

'Because it didn't mean anything,' I lie. 'Did you ever find out the source of the tip-off?'

Thomas shakes his head. 'I got the impression that they thought it was probably a member of the deceased's family, trying to give them a reason to reopen the case. Someone who didn't like the original accidental verdict clutching at straws.'

'There you are then,' I say, as though that closes the matter. 'Evie wouldn't have given it a second thought, I'm sure. And if there is no question of her involvement then it can't have anything to do with why she. . .'

'Why she killed herself?' Thomas asks. He looks at me as though he can see inside my mind, as if he is taking every thought out and flicking through them like a case file. '*If* she killed herself, that is. Did you find her passport, by the way?'

Richard screws up his nose. 'That's what I was looking for but when I found the letters they shoved it right out of my mind. I'll get on it when I get home.'

He looks like he'd rather chew the detective's toenails than start rifling through Evie's things again. Thomas just nods. I'd give anything to know what he's thinking at this very moment.

45

Evie

The text she'd sent Rebecca was inadequate, and Evie had known she'd either have to give her friend a better explanation of her disappearance or turn her phone off. She chose to switch it off – she'd told Becky that her mum was ill and she'd had to return home for the weekend, perhaps longer and she'd text her soon.

It would have been enough for some people, but she knew her friend better than that. She'd want to know if Evie needed anything, if she should come with her, if she should let her tutors know she wouldn't be in, and on it would go. Evie simply didn't concern herself with all the things Becky did – God, if she had to think so far ahead all the time, map out every eventuality, plan for everything that might go wrong, her head would explode. She knew the only difference between her and Becky was confidence. Evie didn't have to plan so far ahead because she had perfect confidence in her ability to think on her feet – she knew that if something in life went wrong she could deal with it there and then, instead of mapping out possible problems and their solutions in advance.

Which was why she hadn't given a second thought to

packing a suitcase and jumping in a taxi to the train station when she'd seen the news of James and Camille's engagement. Did she know exactly why she was going home? No. Did she intend to speak to James, confess her undying love to him and beg him not to marry the only girl she had ever hated? Probably not. That sort of thing happened in the movies. Much more likely she would bump into him in the town or the supermarket when she had no make-up on and was wearing a tracksuit.

She'd texted Harriet to ask if she could stay over – instinct told her not to go home and to alert as few people as possible to her presence in Wareham. If she turned up at home there would have to be a meal, probably a ridiculous fuss because she'd been away a whole six months – although given she'd spent the last seven years boarding you'd think they'd be used to it.

Evie scanned the departures board for the next train to get her anywhere near Dorset. Another thirty-five minutes to the next one, for a journey that would take her over two hours. Then she'd have to get a taxi from the station – it was times like this she wished she could just call Phillip to come and pick her up.

She dragged her suitcase over to the café, stopping to slip her headphones in on the way. Music filled her ears, which would likely be enough to stop her brain from spending the next two hours telling her she was making a big mistake.

46

Evie

'Thank God your hair grew back,' was the first thing Harriet said when she opened the door to her over two hours later.

'Seriously?' Evie snapped, hauling her suitcase over the front step and dropping it unceremoniously at her friend's feet. 'Six months away and a long train journey suffocating in other people's body odour and all you have to comment on is my hair?'

'Well, obviously it's good to see you,' Harriet grinned and wrapped her arms around Evie. 'Jesus,' she wrinkled up her nose and pushed her at arm's length. 'You smell like public transport. I've set you up in the main guest bedroom, there's an en-suite. Once you smell civilised again I'll be in my room waiting for you to tell me that it's pure chance that your secret visit coincides with James and Camille's engagement party.'

Evie emerged from Harriet's guest room showered and wrapped in a dressing gown that would make a sheep jealous and threw herself on her best friend's bed.

'Party?' she said, her eyebrows raised.

'Oh, don't tell me you didn't know,' Harriet grinned. 'You

turn up here on some secret squirrel mission and expect me to believe you aren't here to put a spanner in the works? Come on, Evie, I know you better than that.'

'Honestly, I didn't know there was a party. Where is it?'

Harriet snorted. 'Okay, I'll bite. They're throwing an engagement party at Casa Addlington tomorrow night. Our invites got lost in the post.'

'Since when did you ever need an invite?'

Harriet smiled. 'I wish I was going now, just to see Camille's face when you turn up. You *are* going, aren't you?'

Evie bit her lip and nodded. 'Wouldn't miss it.'

47

Rebecca

The news of the police's visit to Evie has hit Richard harder than I'd expected, and I'm not sure whether it's because it's yet another betrayal – that he had to find out more about his wife's life from a police officer – or if it is Thomas' parting words: *If she killed herself.*

It is obvious he thinks she didn't jump off that cliff voluntarily now, and it's equally as clear that he suspects Richard is hiding something – which he is, I suppose. Richard didn't tell Thomas that Evie was pregnant, and if the detective hadn't overheard us I'm pretty sure he wouldn't have told him about the letters he found. I can understand his explanation about the letters: he wouldn't want the police to think that they were a reason for her to commit suicide. But her being pregnant? Well, didn't a baby give her everything to live for? Didn't that argue against suicide?

We leave the café moments after Thomas, Richard's uneaten sandwich and still warm cup of tea discarded. I drive us in silence back to his house and don't get out of the car when I pull up outside.

Richard gets out and looks at me expectantly. 'Aren't you coming in?'

'I've got some work to finish, and I was going to go for a run.'

He pulls his best puppy dog face. 'I was hoping you'd look for Evie's passport for me. I don't think I can face that office after this morning.'

I know the passport isn't in there so agreeing to go and search for it seems like a fool's errand, but I suppose it's a good chance for me to weed out any other surprises she might have left behind, like a box of love letters or a bloody diary. Had she been thinking about anything but herself when she'd set off for Lulworth? Obviously she had no way of knowing that Richard would ask for her medical records, or that her solicitor would be able to get hold of them while she was still legally alive, but leaving the letters lying around was shoddy.

'Fine,' I say, thinking I'd have a look then 'remember' that Evie had sent it away to be renewed. I park up and by the time I get into the house Richard is already on the laptop.

'Study's unlocked,' he says without looking up.

The room loosely termed 'the study' is basically a desk, a filing cabinet, three sets of bookshelves and a lower set of shelves filled with box files. In all the years I've known them I've never known either Evie or Richard to actually work in here, or study anything, so essentially it's a paperwork storage room. Cabinet drawers marked 'Richard Work' are locked and I don't bother asking for the key. Evie needn't have bothered jumping off a cliff if she'd just opened one of those drawers; she'd have been bored to death.

On the desk there's a notepad and I have a flip through, mainly appointments scrawled hastily before being transferred onto the main calendar. There's a note to 'CALL ANNA' and I figure it must be someone from Richard's work. In the unmarked filing drawers is a pile of bills – not one of them filed in any order. Another drawer is home to takeaway leaflets, screws and batteries. How long is reasonable to pretend to look for a passport? There's nothing interesting in here. Well, except Evie's impressive book collection.

I turn my attention to the bookshelves. Evie read, from time to time, although she was never what I would class as a bookworm, or an avid reader. These bookshelves and their contents were Evie's attempt at being a homemaker. The study had all the elements it should, just as the kitchen had a coffee maker even though Evie and Richard both drank tea. This was the way she would be normal. The photograph on the wall – that was the only hint of the real Evie in the room. It's a young girl, naked, only her head and shoulders visible, her hair and eyes wild. She looks over her shoulder at the camera with a haunting expression. The name at the bottom reads 'Sally Mann'.

A memory shoves its way into my mind of Evie slamming the door and when I don't react she opens it up and slams it again.

'Something wrong?' I ask, not looking up from my battered old copy of *The Secret History*.

'That fat old bastard,' she grumbles. 'He does a session on the influential photographers of the nineties and the first thing he says about Mann is how good she looks for fifty-something. As if that's what she has to offer the decade! Twat.'

I hadn't known who Mann was then, although after an hour of Evie's lecture on her controversial use of children in her work and the disparity between the beauty in the world and the uncomfortable truths I felt like I knew her intimately. Smiling at the memory of my friend's passion, I turn my attention back to the bookshelves. Richard won't mind if I borrow one of these, surely? Evie isn't coming back for them, and I'm certainly entitled to take back the books she borrowed from me. When I pull out my copy of *The Secret History* something falls – not hidden but not in plain sight. Evie's passport.

When I go downstairs, passport and book in hand, Richard is on the computer. I'm confused about what this means – I hadn't expected to find it here at all, but I say, 'Got it,' and Richard barely looks up.

'Oh good,' he says – he was expecting nothing less. He sees no reason why Evie's passport wouldn't be in the house, and I can see no way it can be. Did she have two? A fake?

'What are you doing?' I ask. He glances at the notepad he has at the side of him, the words 'Addlington fire' scrawled at the top.

'I'm looking for details about the fire Thomas told us about,' he brings the laptop over to the sofa and I sit next to him. 'Here.'

He slides a printout of a news article towards me. 'This is everything I could get about the fire from the articles. It was an engagement party for Camille and James Addlington at the family home about a mile from Wareham. I've heard that name before. Somewhere recent.'

'The Evelyn Bradley profile on Facebook,' I remind him. 'The only friend they had, since I blocked it anyway.'

Richard nods, deep in thought. 'So do you think it might be her behind the profile? Pretty obvious, don't you think? To only "friend" her own profile.'

That's exactly what I'd been thinking, far too obvious if it were Camille behind the profile. Unless she wanted me to know it was her – which also didn't make any sense. Why not 'friend' Richard, if she wanted him to know the truth about Evie? And why not just send him a message and tell him what she knew?

'She was living in London at the time of the fire,' I say, steering the conversation onto safer ground. I make a circle around the date of the fire and write next to it the year Evie started university. 'We were already friends and yet she didn't mention anything to me at the time. I don't even remember her mentioning this event specifically but she was always going to parties when she visited home so—'

'Wait,' Richard makes a noise like a strangled dog and puts his head in his hands.

'What? What is it?'

'Look at the date again,' he says, without looking up. 'And think.'

48

Evie

'You are not serious?'

Evie raised an innocent eyebrow. She'd anticipated Harriet's reaction perfectly. 'What?'

'You can't go dressed like that! It's a real party – not one of your grimy student raves.'

'Seriously, Harriet, don't ever say rave again,' Evie laughed, opening up her backpack. 'Drink? Fine, I'll drink it myself then.'

She twisted the top off the cheap vodka she'd picked up from the off-licence outside the train station and swigged it neat. The liquid stung her throat and she screwed up her face in disgust.

'Besides, I'm not going to party, am I? I'm not even sure what I'm going *for*. Just to say hello, and congratulations.'

Harriet raised her eyebrows. 'You're going in the hope that James will see you and realise that that bitch Camille doesn't hold a candle to his darling Evie and call off the engagement. Which he's not going to do if you turn up looking like Cinderella before she meets the fairy godmother.'

Evie glanced down at her light blue jeans and baggy white vest.

'I didn't bring anything else. I wasn't prepared for a party. I'm not even staying long – I don't want to stand out.'

'What, and you won't stand out looking like you're going to the beach in a crowd of evening dresses? At least stick this on,' Harriet rooted through her wardrobe and tossed her a black blazer. 'And some heels. Here.'

'Fine.' Evie shrugged on the blazer. It was a size too small but luckily not designed to do up over her larger-than-Harriet's breasts. The silver Louboutins fit perfectly. 'Okay now?'

Harriet gave her an appraising look. 'Perfect for a shopping trip, but it'll have to do. None of my dresses will fit you and it's too late for the shops. We could always call Jessica. . .?'

'No,' Evie's voice was firm. The last thing she needed was her father turning up at the party to escort her home. 'I told you – the fewer people that know I'm here the better. I'm just going to sneak in, tell them how happy I am for them, and leave.'

She took another swig from the bottle. As always, this one didn't burn quite as much. By the fourth swig it would be almost like drinking squash.

'Yeah.' Harriet sounded as if what she'd said couldn't have been further from the truth. 'You keep telling yourself that.'

49

Rebecca

It wasn't unusual, back in our uni days, for me not to see my best friend for a week or two. Long lonely days of real life drenched in sepia tones, my life at the age of eighteen was divided into two: With Evie and Without. If I'm making it sound as though my best friend was my first, last, and everything then I'm exaggerating – memories tilted by the slant of hindsight. Because although that's how it feels when I look back – that Evie hit the pause button on my existence every time she left my student digs – my life plodded on without her there. So much so that during one of her absences I met a boy, and fell in love.

I suppose I have Evie to thank for that too, despite her not having replied to any of my calls or messages all week. She may have been physically AWOL but her presence was there in the form of her semi-nude photographs of survivors of life-threatening illnesses, some permanently disfigured, others forced to amputate limbs to stay alive. I'd been hanging the photographs around the Student Union after spending hours searching for the perfect frames and was in the process of re-ordering them for the third time when a voice behind me dragged me from my work.

'I thought they looked better the first time.'

My shoulders sagged, crestfallen. I'd known as I was tinkering that I should have stuck to the original placement, now I couldn't even remember what it was.

'Can you remem—' As I turned to see who had spoken, I registered the boy's grin. 'Oh, funny.'

'It doesn't matter what order you hang them in; they're beautiful.'

I looked back at the picture I'd been hanging. He was right – Evie's work could have been hanging in a toilet stall and it would still be breathtaking. It continued to amazed me every time I looked at this series and saw the pain, anguish and hope all emanating from one subject. Emotions played out in her art as keenly as if the words were scrawled on them with black marker.

'You're right, it doesn't matter. I just wanted to get it perfect.'

'It's an artist's prerogative.'

My cheeks burned at his mistake. 'Oh, no, I'm not. . . these aren't *my* photos. I'm just hanging them for a friend.'

The boy smiled and I looked at him properly for the first time. He wasn't tall, just a little taller than I was, and his hair was floppy – a style that hadn't been 'in' for years – and a sandy brown colour. He had dark eyes which were just like the rest of him, unremarkable, but he looked kind and his dress sense – blue polo shirt and jeans that were just shy of fashionable – suggested that he didn't just walk up to random girls and hit on them. He felt. . . *safe*.

'Well your friend is lucky to have someone who takes such care with her work.'

I laughed at that, at the idea that Evie was lucky to have me rather than the other way around.

'Yes, I suppose she is.'

'I'm sorry to have disturbed you anyway,' he took a few

steps back but didn't turn to leave. 'I just couldn't help myself. Tell your friend good luck with the art.'

'Wait.' I'm still not sure why I stopped him – I didn't feel any instant attraction, none of that 'spark' you read about in books or see in films. All I knew in that moment was that I didn't want him to walk away. Maybe I should have let him. Maybe everything would have been different. Maybe Evie would still be alive.

'I was just about to get a drink,' I told him, motioning to a free table. It was mid-afternoon and the Union was practically empty, I had nothing to do and suddenly the idea of returning to my twelve-by-twelve cell of a room seemed beyond depressing. And what did it matter to me if he said no? In a university this big I'd probably never have to see him again anyway. 'Would you like to join me?'

He hesitated and for a second I thought he was going to leg it, regretting ever speaking to me. Instead he smiled again, the third time in a few minutes, and this time I realised it made his whole face more attractive.

'Sure, why not?' He held out his hand in an awkward yet endearing way. 'I'm Richard. Richard Bradley.'

50

Evie

Evie tipped the taxi driver generously, squeezed the empty vodka bottle down the side of the seat and swallowed hard as she pushed open the taxi door and climbed out, wincing at the slam it made when it closed. The Addlingtons' house loomed before her, every bit as vast as her own, but whereas Evie's family home was a sprawling old country manor, James lived in what her mother would call a modern monstrosity, all glass and cladding, plonked on the landscape rather than grown from it. Tonight the huge iron gates were open, security abandoned in favour of convenience.

Taking a deep breath, she stumbled towards the house on unsteady legs and unfamiliar heels, noting the deluge of sports cars scattered across the driveway and on the grass. *Quite the turnout for the happy couple.*

As she rounded the garden to the back of the house – there was no way she was about to ring the doorbell knowing she would be turned away – Evie's heart began to thump. In her head she hadn't got any further than this, and now she was here she had no idea what she was going to say to James when she saw him. It suddenly all felt so idiotic, turning up here based on a brief fling between a couple of kids. What if it really had meant as little to him as he'd said when he'd found out about the baby?

The baby. It still hurt as much now as it had then, that he'd been so callous. But he had been scared, probably under pressure from his father. She needed to give him a chance to explain – to draw a line under the past and move on. Anything else. . . she didn't let herself dare to hope.

The back garden was bathed in the glow of solar lights and outdoor heaters. There was already a smattering of people on the lawn, smoking and chatting. Evie pushed past them and through the open patio doors as though she was perfectly entitled to be there. The alcohol in her system was giving her confidence now, and she knew from her mother that if you acted like you belonged no one would ever question you.

The kitchen was an open-plan oasis of sleek silver appliances and marble worktops. More people in here, most of them in matching black T-shirts and trousers – catering. The Addlingtons had pulled out all the stops for this soiree and it stung.

Evie moved beyond the kitchen into the hallway, pausing when she came to the doorway of what was clearly the heart of the party, a large reception room full of people. A string quartet was playing in the corner of the room, and everywhere was decorated with crystal and white roses. In the centre of the room, talking to a group of men old enough to be his father, was James.

Still the sight of him took her breath away. She could practically feel the warmth of his lips on hers – the only boy she had ever loved. Evie watched as he was joined by a familiar face, a floor-length black sequined dress hanging from Camille's emaciated figure. She'd lost weight – it didn't look good on her. Evie allowed herself a thrill of satisfaction before her heart plummeted as she saw James beam and lean over to kiss his wife-to-be. Camille practically purred. One of the men made a comment and the group laughed good-naturedly as James put an arm around her shoulder. He didn't look miserable – trapped in a loveless engagement because he had let the real love of his life slip through his fingers. He looked. . . happy.

Evie blinked back tears. What was she doing here? What had she expected? That she was so wonderful, so irresistible that James would dump his fiancée and declare his undying love for her? Did she really think that she was so much better than her rival?

Taking a deep breath she turned to leave, but not before Camille looked straight at her, her face contorting into a scowl.

51

Rebecca

'Richard,' I say. 'Stop being a dick and just. . .'

'That,' he says, pointing to the date of the party on his pad, 'was a couple of weeks after me and you, um, after we met.'

When we started going out, I want to say. When we were sleeping together. But I let go of that a long time ago – we'd barely been together a couple of weeks when Evie. . .

'That's when she tried to kill herself,' I say, looking at the date. 'Two and a half weeks after you and I met. Which means that this week,' I point to the week before, 'was the one she went home, without telling me. She'd already been away from uni two weeks, remember? That's why she'd never met you, why she didn't know who you were that day.'

Picking up my notes, I checked both dates. 'She was supposed to go back to lessons on the Thursday, then on Friday I got a text to say her mother was ill and she had to go and see her. If you're right about the date we met, of course.'

'I am,' Richard says, not looking at me. 'I remember because the day I went to the Union was the anniversary of my dad's death.'

'God, Richard, I'm sorry. Why didn't you say at the time?'

'I just met you that day, it's hardly the best chat-up line, is it? Then the day was over and there didn't seem much point in talking about it.'

I don't know why but it hurts that I'd never known that that day was a difficult one for him. My memory of my short relationship with Richard is clouded; it's almost as if he was someone else, or as if my mind has made him someone else, so that seeing him fall in love with my best friend wasn't so hard. Then something will happen to remind me that once I almost fell in love with him, and he hadn't been even close to loving me.

'Something happened that weekend that made her want to die. I saw her when she got back, she was practically catatonic.'

A memory occurs to me. 'I called Dominic that day, I was so worried about her. He told me that she'd split up with her boyfriend in Wareham, a boyfriend I never even knew about. Why wouldn't he mention if he died? He had no reason to keep it from me, and neither did Evie for that matter. And why would she come home at all if her boyfriend had just been killed in a fire?'

'If anyone died at a party she was at it's hardly surprising that she was upset.'

'But upset enough to try to kill herself? And for Dominic not to tell me that anyone had even died? That only makes sense if. . .' I leave the sentence to trail off, but Richard finishes it for me.

'If she was involved, or knew what really happened.' His brow furrows in that way I always find endearing, as though he is trying to work out a really difficult maths problem in his head. 'What was the name of the man who died?'

I pretend to scan the article, even though I already know all of this. 'It says here it was James Addlington.'

52

Evie

She had reached the kitchen and was pouring wine into a glass so quickly it splashed up over the sides when she heard Camille's voice call her name.

'Evie?' She turned to see her rival, a slow smile spreading over her angular face. What James saw in her Evie would never know. 'I thought it was you. It's been a while.'

'Camille,' Evie forced a smile onto her face but her voice was laced with acid. Just the sight of her reminded Evie how much they had hated one another at school. 'I was passing by, I popped in to say congratulations. I didn't realise you were having a party, my apologies.'

'Not at all,' Camille replied graciously. 'Come, I'd like to speak to you.'

'Oh, I was just going—'

'I insist.'

Evie followed Camille into a side room. Long pillar candles sat on an oak desk next to more large glass doors and Camille moved to light them. The walls were lined with bookshelves, mahogany furniture and heavy scarlet curtains out of keeping with the modern décor in the rest of the house – this must be James' father's study.

'Look,' Evie started. 'I didn't come here for any trouble.'

'And yet here you are. You disappear mysteriously from school, no one sees you for nearly a year and you turn up days after James and I announce our engagement. *What a coincidence.*'

Hearing the words 'James and I' coming from Camille was like a punch to the stomach. There was no denying it now, she had seen it with her own eyes. Camille had won, Evie had lost and it stung like a bitch. Anger surged through her and alcohol loosened her tongue. She took a swig of the wine she was holding and practically slammed it back down on the desk.

'Yes, your engagement. How does it feel to have my sloppy seconds, Camille? Does he ever whisper my name when he fucks you?'

Camille wrinkled up her nose. 'You're drunk.'

'You're ugly,' Evie retorted. 'At least I'll be sober tomorrow.'

'Very mature,' Camille spat. 'Look at the state of you. Just like your mother. At least Monique managed to trap your father when she got knocked up. How did that plan work out for you?'

The words were like a slap to the face and the smirk died on Evie's lips.

'I don't know what you think you know. . .'

'I don't think,' Camille replied. 'I *know*. James told me all about it. Poor deluded Evelyn Rousseau, thinking that her and her bastard child can trap an Addlington. You must have been desperate.'

Furious tears pricked at the corners of her eyes but she blinked them back. She would not cry in front of Camille, not even angry tears, but for once in her life she didn't have a comeback. Here she was, spending hours on a train, travelling hours to see a man who had mocked her, described her as desperate. Suddenly she longed to be back in London, in Rebecca's poky student digs, both of them lying on her single bed watching *Porky's* for the millionth time, or dipping their feet in the memorial fountain while eating huge ice-creams and making fun of men's paper-white legs. What was she doing here, in a place that had always made her feel like she wasn't good enough?

Camille smirked. 'What, no witty comeback? Why don't you go and get yourself another drink? Maybe that will make everything better.'

Evie clutched at the desk behind her as stinging hot bile rose in her throat. Her hand flew to her mouth but she knew she couldn't hold it back for long. She turned, looking desperately for something to be sick in, and dropped to her knees next to a plant pot. Camille made a disgusted noise in her throat.

'Oh God,' she said, her face a picture of contempt. 'Look at you! You're a pathetic, disgusting mess. Go back to London, Evie. No one misses you here.'

Without another word, Camille gave a satisfied smile and left Evie on her knees.

53

Rebecca

'Addlington,' Richard repeats. 'This can't be a coincidence, right? The fact that the fake Evie profile was friends with Camille Addlington, and here she is again, in connection with a fire that Evie was under investigation for.'

'Well, Thomas never exactly said she was under investigation. . .'

He ignores me. 'Do you think she's the one who sent the blackmail letters?'

'I think it's possible,' I say slowly. 'But those letters you found, well they weren't blackmailing her, were they? I mean, they said *I hope you didn't think you'd got away with it* but they never asked for anything. Money or otherwise.'

'It doesn't sound like Camille needed money though,' Richard says. 'She would have inherited all Addlington's money, the house probably too.'

'So what was the point of the letters?'

'To scare her, maybe? I don't know,' Richard rubs his face. 'It doesn't make any sense. None of it. If Evie hadn't done anything wrong, then why was she such a mess when she came back to uni? But if she had. . .'

He tails off and I notice the box that Evie's letters had been in.

'What's the box?'

'It's the box to Evie's camera – the one she stored away and never used. It's empty, I can't find the camera up there anywhere but the letters were in there. What do you think that means?'

'It's just a camera, and an old crappy one at that. Maybe she threw it away?'

'She wouldn't, I asked her if she still needed it when we moved our stuff here and she said she'd never throw it out, even though it didn't work any more. She was so cagey about it I didn't ask again.'

'Maybe she sent it to be repaired or cleaned and never picked it up. Maybe she lent it to someone – you know how generous she could be with her things. Or maybe it's in the loft, or the shed, or one of the other hundred places she would put things down and not away. I don't know, I can't see how it has any relevance to anything.'

Richard sighed. 'You're right, it's got to be here somewhere. And even if it isn't, she wasn't holding it when she jumped off that cliff so I don't suppose it makes much difference.' He looks like he might cry.

'Perhaps we should get in touch with Camille,' he suggests after a silence.

'No,' I snap, then when he looks at me sharply I add: 'You heard Thomas. If she was the one sending the letters she could be charged with manslaughter. She's not going to just admit it was her, is she?'

Even though Richard nods his agreement I know this isn't the end of it. The snowball started rolling down the hill the minute Richard found out about the man Evie was arguing with, her pregnancy and all this, the blackmail letters, the fire, it's just gathering size and pace. But I know that when we speak to Camille Addlington there will be no going back. Because she knows almost as much about what happened in Evie's past as me – maybe more.

54

Evie

Evie pulled herself to her feet and wiped her mouth on the sleeve of Harriet's jacket. Alone in the candle-lit study she just wanted to get out of this house and as far away from the Addlington family as she could. Looking up she saw a figure standing in the doorway. James.

But this man – although bearing an uncanny resemblance to James – was older, Evie realised. Was this his father? She tried to bring to mind the image of the man she had met when she was just nine years old but she could remember nothing of what he looked like. This man was smartly dressed in expensive grey suit trousers and a navy shirt, he looked around the same age as her own father. Was this who Dominic Rousseau hated so much? Before she could begin her explanation of what she was doing in his study he took a couple of unsteady steps towards her and she realised he was just as drunk as she was – in fact he looked worse.

He looked her up and down, a sore thumb in her jeans and blazer, yet he looked unfazed by her presence.

'Well, this party just got a lot more interesting,' his voice was thick with alcohol, his words slurring into one another. 'Who are you?'

'I was just leaving,' Evie said, ignoring the question. He took a step closer than was comfortable and she put a hand on his chest to ease him to one side. James Sr stood firm.

'So soon?' he lifted his own hand to hers and removed it from his chest, but he didn't let go. A dangerous tension buzzed between them. 'I could use some cheering up and don't you look just the type of woman who knows how to cheer a man up.'

He didn't know who she was, and why would he? The last time he had seen her she'd been a nine-year-old girl at the home of a former friend. Plus he'd been sober then. She'd never admit it to anyone afterwards but the thought of having sex with James' father briefly crossed her mind. Yes, he was older but he was attractive, rich, powerful – and wouldn't that be the ultimate revenge? Sex was no longer anything special to Evie, memories of her first time forever tarnished by what had come next. Now sex was a weapon, to be given out or withheld on her terms.

'Oh yes?' she asked, tilting her chin to meet his eyes. 'And why would you need cheering up? This is your party, isn't it? Your son is engaged, it's a happy day.'

James Sr scowled. 'It might be, if it weren't for the manipulative shrew he's chosen to marry. She's a real bitch. Wait,' his eyes sparkled mischievously and Evie's stomach leapt at how much he reminded her of his son. 'She's not your cousin, is she?'

Evie smiled. 'No, she's not. We don't exactly see eye to eye.'

James Sr moved over to the desk where he poured himself a glass of whisky, the candles swaying dangerously as he returned the decanter to the tray a tad too heavily.

'I can imagine you don't,' he replied, taking a swig. Evie wondered if he would be as loving and tender as his son. Doubtful. She'd met men like him since starting university

– his type either liked it rough or wanted to be dominated. Either way she was probably going to give him what he wanted. 'She wouldn't like you at all. I don't see what James sees in her at all. Far too bony for my liking.'

'And what is your liking?' He was coming towards her again and she wished he'd stop swaying. Or was that her? She blinked a couple of times; no, she was definitely standing still.

'Not some money-grabbing tent pole. Saying that, she's a lot less problematic than the last one.'

Evie froze. 'The last one?'

'Yeah, you wouldn't believe me if I told you. Then she went and got herself—'

'Okay, so I have to go.' If he said the words she might vomit again. She turned to leave but he grabbed her arm.

'Where are you going? Did I say something? I thought we were going to have some fun.' He ran his other hand up her arm, cupping a hand around the back of her neck. Evie smelt the whisky on his breath and her stomach turned. 'You are very beautiful,' he murmured.

'But problematic,' she replied, trying to wriggle free of his grip. James Sr didn't appreciate the reference.

'I could make this the best party you've ever been to,' his lips were so close now that his breath was warm on hers. 'I'll lock the door and I'm yours all night. No one will notice, the amount of free alcohol they've all been guzzling.'

'I tell you what,' Evie replied, moving another half an inch closer. She couldn't see the look in his eyes but she could feel his arousal elsewhere. 'How about I go and freshen up while you make yourself comfortable and I'll be yours all night.'

James Sr raised his eyebrows. It was a mark of how used to getting his own way he was that he didn't question the willingness of a girl half his age to throw herself at his erection.

'That sounds like a perfect idea. And to think, I came in here for a nap.'

'Sounds like your lucky night,' Evie muttered as she broke away from his grasp. She watched him slide onto the leather two-seater. 'Don't go anywhere, I'll be right back.'

'I'll be waiting.'

'Damn right you will.' Evie closed the door behind her and turned the key in the lock as quietly as she could. She slipped it into her pocket and grinned. 'Now *that's* what you call problematic, asshole.'

55

Rebecca

That first afternoon Richard and I talked for hours. Him about his course, and his ambitions – he was going to start his own business, something to do with computers that I didn't really understand – and me about Evie. I didn't even realise I'd been doing it, *Evie says this, Evie thinks that*, until about an hour after we first met he sat back in his chair and looked at me as though I was growing an extra head.

'What? What is it?'

'I was just wondering. . . I'm not treading on any toes here, am I? I mean, if you and this Evie are an item I don't want to. . .' he let the sentence trail off and I felt my cheeks burn as his words sank in.

'Oh God, no, it's nothing like that, I mean we're not *together*,' I sighed. 'Have I really been talking about her that much?'

Richard gave me a regretful nod, his mouth a thin line, but I could tell he was amused.

'Afraid so. At one point I thought Evie was the name of your car and you were trying to sell it to me.'

I laughed a little too loud, desperate to mask my discomfort. Inside I was mortified. Was Evie all I had that I felt was interesting enough to talk about? I'd always joked about her being the 'better half' but was it true? Was Evie the best thing about me?

It couldn't be true. I'd made friends before her, I'd had a life and made conversation and kept boyfriends before I'd ever met Evelyn White. So why couldn't I start a conversation without the words 'Evie says'?

'How about we start over?' Richard said, rising out of his chair. 'I'll get us another drink and you can tell me about who you are when Evie is nowhere to be found.'

I nodded, mentally kicking myself for sounding like such a total weirdo. *That's it, Rebecca*, I told myself. *No more of the whole cling-on routine. Be you.*

And yet it was still Evie's voice that pushed my own to one side, always with something cooler, some better advice to offer.

Yes darling, Evie said in the fake Parisian luvvie voice she used when she was imitating her mother. *Be you, only more faaaabulous.*

We sat in the Student Union until the music increased in volume and the DJ began to set up his equipment. Richard blinked and looked at his watch.

'Christ, did you know it was gone eight?'

I shook my head. In the empty gloom of the badly lit canteen it could have been the middle of the night and we'd never have realised.

'Give it a couple of hours and this place will start filling up with pissheads. Are you hungry?'

I hadn't been, but right on cue my stomach gurgled. 'Apparently so.'

'What do you fancy?'

Right from the start Richard Bradley was completely at ease in my company, and after just a few short hours, I in his. He told me afterwards that he'd never once in his life just started talking to a pretty girl – his words – and ended up spending the entire evening in her company. Things like that just didn't happen to a computer programmer slightly shy of 5'9 and with a wonky nose. I told him his nose wasn't wonky, even though it was a bit but that didn't matter to me in the slightest. Every minute we spent together over the next week he became more attractive to me until, when I looked at him, I was amazed I hadn't fallen for him instantly and I realised that – oh Christ – I was falling in love.

It was funny though, I'd never been in love before, unless you count Steve the bass guitarist, which by this time I firmly did not. In fact I only ever remembered Steve as being the reason I had Evie. (Predictably, without my notes to copy from, he had dropped out after our first set of exams.) I didn't have the worldly experience that Evie did when it came to the opposite sex – her first lover had been an older boy she had once told me when we were stoned, and he'd taught her everything there was to know about pleasure – and yet I knew that Richard was going to fall in love with me too. The way everything seemed to progress so easily from that very first afternoon, to meeting me after my classes, to spending the night. Within two days we were a couple, within a week we were inseparable.

When I couldn't stand not talking to anyone about my new boyfriend I sent her a text in what I thought was an ironic girly way.

I met a boy. He's not cool or hip or irresistible but I think I like him.

I hadn't expected her to reply but she'd texted back a few hours later.

Sounds perfect (???) Don't get married until I get back x

I promise. How are things at home?

Mainly zzzzz. Cant wait to hear about your uncool unhip boyfriend ;-)

Cant wait to hear your boring home stories :-) Sucks here without u x

Sounds like it

I cringed at her tone. Surely she didn't begrudge me a life without her? Then my phone buzzed again and I smiled at her follow-up text.

;-) Don't do anything I wouldnt do xx

I couldn't wait for her to get back and meet Richard. And yet there was a nagging feeling in the back of my mind. What if they didn't like one another? How would Richard fit in with Evie's bohemian lifestyle, the weekends we spent flitting from downtrodden flats in the East End to fancy bars in the city? However hard I tried to picture it, I just couldn't see them hitting it off and the thought of having to choose between them – even after knowing Richard for less than a fortnight – made me feel slightly sick.

56

Evie

She couldn't face going back to Harriet's, her humiliation written all over her face as her friend waited expectantly to hear how she had foiled the engagement of the year and won back her prince. No, she would go home, let herself in through the back door and hope that her parents were out, that way she could go to bed and face them in the morning.

The minute she pushed open the back door she knew she would have no such luck. Freezing cold from waiting half an hour for a taxi, and sober but emotionally exhausted, she shoved open the door and practically into her father who was pouring himself a drink in the kitchen.

'Evelyn?' His face contorted first in confusion, then concern. 'What's happened?'

'Papa,' Evie sniffed and fell into her father's outstretched arms.

'Has someone hurt you? What are you doing here?'

As he led her into the sitting room and waited expectantly for her to explain her sudden appearance, Evie's phone beeped. It was Harriet.

Are you okay? Did you get out safely? CALL ME WHEN YOU GET THIS.

Evie frowned. *Get out safely?*

'Just a minute, Papa.' Her father grunted impatiently as she clicked Harriet's number.

'Thank God!' Harriet said after only one ring. 'I was so worried. What the hell happened? Where are you?'

'What are you talking about?' Evie asked. 'I'm at home, I just got in. I was going to come back to yours but—'

'You don't know,' Harriet interrupted, saving Evie from making an excuse as to why she'd come home instead of going back to her friend's house. 'The Addlingtons' house is on fire.'

57

Rebecca

When I left yesterday Richard had promised not to contact Camille, but I'm desperate to know whether a night alone with nothing to think about but fake Facebook profiles and people dying in fires might have changed his mind. If he had spoken to her surely he would have called me – who else does he have to talk to these days? But it doesn't stop me trying his number, and when he ignores my second call of the day I'll admit to going round there to 'check' on him.

'You can't just not answer your phone,' I snap when he answers the door. 'I thought, well, what if you were. . .'

Richard looks embarrassed, and rightly so. 'Sorry, Becky,' he says, and he steps aside and gestures for me to go in. 'I didn't think.'

'I don't have to stay,' I say, walking past him anyway and kicking off my shoes. I still expect to see Evie standing at the bottom of the stairs, welcoming smile on her face.

'No it's fine,' he says, walking past me and into the kitchen. He doesn't mention Camille, so maybe he's kept to his promise.

'Did you sleep?' I ask, knowing the answer because it would be the same as mine. I wonder if he has the same nightmares.

'A bit,' he says, but I know he's lying. Is he still in the spare room? I can't ask him that, it's too soon, too personal.

'Can I use the bathroom?'

In the bathroom the disintegration of Richard's life in the last week is ever more apparent. Wet towels are draped over the edge of the bath, one has fallen onto the floor and the toilet has the unmistakable sharp odour of stale urine. When I think back to how well he was doing before I convinced him to go and meet his friends at the pub that day I could kick myself.

The door to the spare room is shut and I ease it open as slowly as possible in case it creaks and lets Richard know I'm snooping. The curtains are closed, leaving the room sheathed in darkness, but I can just make out the duvet slumped in the middle of the bed. It's more than likely that Richard has slept in here since his return to the house. Pulling the door closed, I move slowly to the master bedroom and open the door, taking one small step inside. The bed is made, the curtains wide open, the room is light and airy and basically tidy.

As I step back again something pierces my heel and I hiss out 'Shit!' Water soaks into my socks – the carpet here is saturated – but looking up I can't see a leak in the roof. Scooping up the silver necklace that jabbed me in the foot, I go back to the bathroom, flush the toilet and head back downstairs.

In the hallway I let the silver chain dangle through my fingers. The silver knotted pendant on the end is instantly recognisable as the one Evie wore every day of her life – a gift from her father that had cost less than five pounds. That's why she'd liked it. She said he'd bought it because he thought she'd like it, not because the sales assistant handed him the thing with the most diamonds.

'It's complex,' he'd said, 'like you.'

Evie had been wearing it the day she disappeared.

58

Evie

It had taken ten minutes of tears and begging but eventually Evie's father agreed to take her back to James' house, with a promise she would tell him what the hell was going on as he drove. She told him everything, sensing his growing annoyance as she got to the part about her sneaking back to Wareham to confront James and Camille. She edited down the party – merely telling her father that she'd seen how happy they were and decided against speaking to James.

Blue lights cut through the darkness on the approach to the Addlingtons' property. People were standing on the lawn, still dressed in their finery and shivering against the cold – women wrapped in men's suit jackets, many of them in tears. Hoses wielded by firefighters were trained on the house where flames were visible through the smashed-out windows. Where was James? Had he escaped the blaze, or was he trapped in the furnace?

'You stay here,' her father instructed, giving her a look that told her it was an instruction, not a request. Evie watched as he worked his way into the crowd to find a familiar face, and she scanned the crowd for signs of James, or even Camille. She could see faces of old school friends streaked with tears, holding one another, and she wanted to get out of the car and scream at them to tell her what happened here, but more importantly, was James safe?

She couldn't see her father any more and was about to risk getting out when a face appeared at the window. Camille. Evie pressed the button and the glass slid down.

'Where's James?' she said, without preamble.

'I don't know,' Camille's face was red and tear-streaked, mascara and eyeliner ringing puffy eyes. 'I've looked everywhere. You need to get out of here, you shouldn't have come back. I thought I told you to stay away from us, we don't need you here.'

'Oh fuck off, Camille,' Evie snapped, tired of the other girl's superiority all of a sudden. 'I just wanted to check James was okay, and I have every right to do that. You're his fiancée, not his mother.'

'Mr Rousseau,' Camille's tear-stained face turned to where Evie's father was getting back into the car.

'Camille,' he spoke through the open window. 'You need to go to the operations vehicle – the Land Rover over there. I'm very sorry for your loss.'

'My loss?' Camille looked confused. 'Why. . . who?'

Dominic's face clouded – he'd spoken out of turn and now he knew it.

'You should go,' he replied, putting the car into gear and pulling away.

59

Rebecca

The necklace is burning a hole in my pocket as I re-enter the kitchen. Richard is sitting at the table and he smiles at me as he looks up from his phone.

'Becky – look, I'm sorry about when you first arrived, I—'

'Did you spill something upstairs?' My heart is thumping, I don't know what to do. Do I tell him about the necklace? How sure am I that Evie was wearing it at her wedding? I have to know. *I need to know.*

'Upstairs?' he looks confused, at my interruption, my question, the sharpness of my tone, I don't know. 'No, I don't think so. Why?'

'There's water, all over the hall carpet. And—'

'And what?'

'And there's no leak,' I finish.

He sighs impatiently. 'I'll go and have a look.'

As soon as he leaves the room I pull the necklace from my pocket and study the pendant in the palm of my hand. I've seen this necklace so many times – I should be able to identify it perfectly. And yet I know it can't be the one she was wearing, because the necklace Evie was wearing went over the cliff with her.

I slip it back into my pocket as I hear Richard coming back down the stairs. It's a replica – it has to be. Either that or someone found it on the clifftop. *What, and brought it into Evie's house and dropped it into a puddle on the floor?* Who would do that? Thomas? Is he fucking with me? Or most likely fucking with Richard – after all, if he'd been the one to go into his own bedroom he'd have found the necklace.

'It's soaking,' Richard says as he re-enters the kitchen. 'I don't know how. I probably spilt something without realising,' he gestures around the kitchen. 'I'm not the tidiest at the moment.'

'Probably that,' I say, feeling the necklace in my pocket burn white-hot against my leg. 'It's probably nothing.'

He's got papers out on the desk and I realise they are the notes he made yesterday on the fire at the Addlingtons' house. Over the timeline he's written:

WHY DID SHE WANT TO DIE?

It's a question I asked myself the first time Evie tried to kill herself, a question I found out the answer to before she did it the second time.

60

Evie

'Who is it? Is it James? Papa!'

Dominic spoke to his daughter in French for the first time in years and pushed the button for the electric windows, waiting until they were all the way up – even though they were back on the main road now and there was no one here to hear them.

'It's James Sr,' he said, his face tight. 'They were working on him on the grass by the front of the house but it was no good. He's had heart problems in the past – if he even had a heart to begin with.'

Evie's gut clenched as she thought of the key to the office that she'd thrown in a plant pot as she left the Addlingtons' house. Was that why James Sr hadn't made it out of the house? Surely he'd have been able to get out of a window. She pictured him waiting for her, lying down to take a nap and passing out on the couch as smoke filled the room. Had he even woken up?

'Do they know how it started?' Evie asked. Dominic shook his head.

'They're concentrating on making sure everyone is out,'

he replied. 'The investigation will come later. Why were you there tonight, Evelyn?'

'I told you, I wanted to send my congratulations.'

'Did you see him? James Jr? Did you tell him about the baby?'

Evie processed the words slowly. 'Why would I need to tell him about the baby, Papa? He knows already – you told him.'

'Your French is rusty, Evelyn,' her father reprimanded in English. 'I asked if you spoke to him about the child. I thought maybe you argued. . .'

'And set his house on fire? You think I did this?'

Dominic hesitated, then shook his head. 'Of course not.'

'I didn't even see him. Only Camille,' Evie lied. Now was not the time to tell her father the truth. Now was not the time to tell anyone the truth. 'She knew about the baby. She said James told her.'

Dominic frowned. 'Camille knows?'

Evie nodded. 'Yes, but I don't think she'll tell anyone.'

'And now Addlington Sr is gone,' Dominic shook his head. 'And you are lucky you weren't in that house when it happened.'

Evie shuddered. If she hadn't got so angry at James' father when he made his little joke about her being 'problematic', would he still be alive? Was she a murderer?

61

Rebecca

I want to ask Richard about the necklace – did he drop it there? What does it mean? Where did the water come from? But he's caught up in his notes and paperwork, he doesn't need more questions. It's nothing, I tell myself. Nothing.

'I was just writing this,' Richard points to the PC, where there's a Facebook message on the screen. A message to Camille Addlington. So much for promises.

'I thought we'd agreed it was best not to contact her,' I start. Richard looks bashful and is about to launch into a detailed explanation of all the reasons he ignored my advice when my phone buzzes.

MAKE HIM STOP.

The text message comes as a shock – I've heard nothing from 'the wife' in days, and before I realise it I've let out a strangled noise from my throat.

Richard looks up. 'What is it?'

'Oh, nothing,' I say, looking back at the message and clicking 'delete'. Make him stop what? Contacting Camille?

How does she even know that's what he's doing? Another coincidence? 'My phone is playing up. Virus, I think.'

'Here, let me see,' he says, and takes the phone before I can object. Thanks God I deleted Camille's messages in time. He taps away at the phone looking for a virus that doesn't exist, so you can imagine my shock when he says: 'Here, it's this tracker you've installed.'

'The what?' I ask, peering over his shoulder, hoping he can't feel the pounding of my heart.

'This Cerbus thing. The anti-theft device. You've hidden it on the phone but if you call your security number you can make it visible again.'

'Cerbus?' I've never even heard of it, but I don't want to admit that to Richard.

'Yeah, it tracks your phone if it's lost or stolen. Good bit of kit – you can find the location – even take screenshots of the person holding it, all on your computer. You did install this – right?'

'Oh yes, ages ago now, I remember. Bugger, I've forgotten the security number. How do I recover it?'

'You have to call the number you set up – or the default number if you didn't change it. Here, I'll Google it.'

He turns back to his own computer and closes Facebook – at least Camille has her own way for now. Is this how she knew where I was the day at the supermarket? And when I was at Richard's house? How long has she been tracking me?

'Here you go,' he says, and shows me the screen, placing an arm around my back and pulling me closer. Trying not to let him see my face burn red, I dial the number and, sure enough, a bright red Cerbus logo appears on my phone.

'Can you get it off?' I say, handing him the phone back and stepping away quickly before he can touch me again. 'It's draining my battery and causing me all sorts of problems.'

'Just log in,' he says, and I feign embarrassment.

'It's been so long – I can't remember any of my details.'

'Give it here,' he takes the phone back and messes around with it for so long I wonder if I'm going to have to throw the damn thing away. Eventually he says, 'There, done it.' He looks triumphant. 'You're not supposed to be able to do that – so the thief can't just uninstall it. But that's one of the perks of being an IT geek, I suppose.'

'Indeed,' I murmur, thinking of how little I really know about Camille Addlington. Her Facebook profile is private and, apart from some grainy pictures in some old internet news articles, I barely know what she looks like. When did she put this onto my phone? Was she at the wedding? My mobile would have been in my clutch bag on the table for ages – at a wedding you tend to trust the guests not to steal from you. Was Camille there without us even knowing? And why is she doing this at all?

62

Evie

When she woke the next day Evie's head pounded rhythmically and her eyes were tight and raw from the tears. She wasn't sure whether she had been crying for James, for the loss of his father, or her loss of hope, or the loss of their baby, but it was grief all the same. When she plugged in her phone to charge messages chimed through, one after another. Three from Harriet, then a number she didn't know.

Did anyone see u here last night? C.
Don't ignore me. In big trouble if any1 finds out u were here.
Txt me back.

Evie thought back to the key she had discarded. There was no way Camille could know – could she?
Leave me alone, she texted back. U don't scare me.
The reply was almost instant, as if Camille had been on pause, waiting for Evie to reply.

The fire started in the study. The door was locked. I have the key with your fingerprints on. Scared yet?

Evie's stomach lurched. A vision of the study as she left, her fingers turning the key, Camille watching from the shadows. If that was true Camille had known James' father had been locked in there. Why didn't she tell anyone?

Her fingers hitting all the wrong keys, eventually firing back a message to Camille.

Doesn't mean anything. Leave me alone.

But Camille wasn't so easily deterred.

I saw u lock the door. Didn't know James was inside until the firefighters knocked down the door to search. You killed him because he made James deny the baby was his.

Evie sucked in a breath, dropping the phone onto her bedroom carpet and covering her cheek with her hand. It was her fault. She had locked a man away to burn to death. But how was she to know there would be a fire? It wasn't her fault! And yet Evie could see the beauty of the situation, from Camille's point of view. Evie wasn't supposed to be there, and although she and James had strived to keep their relationship under wraps for the sake of their parents, plenty of people knew about it, or at least suspected. If Camille told anyone Evie had been at the house on the night of the engagement party they would believe exactly what Camille was saying – that Evie had started the fire in anger and locked James Sr in his study as revenge for her baby. Why would they doubt Camille's word?

What do u want?

She knew the answer before the text even arrived.

Stay away from James. Leave us alone or I will tell him u killed his dad as revenge for the baby. If you go near him again I will tell police everything. I still have the key.

63

Evie

It won't stop playing through her mind, a screaming reel of macabre images, her turning the key to the study, James Addlington Sr engulfed in flames. She doesn't know how she'll ever sleep again – not when she knew she was a murderer, even if she had never meant him to die.

She hadn't shown her father the text messages – Evie couldn't bear for him to think of her as anything less than his little girl. Telling him about the baby had been difficult enough. Telling him she was a murderer, saying the words out loud, well that would make it real. And after today she would go home to London and forget all this ever happened.

According to her father there had been whisperings already that the fire may have been started deliberately. Apparently James Addlington Sr was involved in everything from dodgy dealings to fraternisation with lonely housewives, blackmail and extortion, rumours that it seemed his family were desperate to play down. They had got away with it, he said.

'Got away with what?' Evie replied, her throat in her mouth. 'I didn't do anything.'

'No,' Dominic murmured. 'No, of course not. But it wouldn't look good for you to have been there, Evelyn. I've heard nothing to suggest anyone saw you – best if no one knows.'

It was as close to a warning as he'd come, and they had never mentioned her presence at the party again. Evie wondered, as Phillip drove her back to London, if her father truly believed that she'd had nothing to do with the fire, or if he now thought he was protecting his vengeful murderess daughter.

By one pm the day after the fire she was back in London.

64

Rebecca

When Evie had arrived back in London after her trip I'd expected her to be refreshed and ready to hit the party scene as hard as ever. Instead, the girl who came back to me was a shadow of the one who had left. It worried me so much that, after two days of her barely speaking, not leaving my apartment or answering the phone – I saw it ring several times and she just clicked 'reject' or let it ring until the answerphone kicked in – I decided to take drastic measures and call her father. It wasn't difficult to get hold of her phone and write down his number – if she wasn't asleep on my sofa she was staring at a black TV screen as though it held the meaning of life.

'I'm just going to go and get us some food and we're out of loo roll,' I told her, kissing her on the forehead. She looked up at me and smiled, not a real smile but it was the most I'd had in two days.

'Thanks, Becks, I really love you, you know? I just, I want you to know that.'

'I know that, idiot,' I said, ruffling her hair. 'Will you be okay here?'

'I'm fine,' Evie's eyes welled up with tears, stopping me in my tracks.

'What is it, Evie, what's wrong with you? Is it your mother? Ever since you got back from home you've been. . .'

'I'm just exhausted,' she replied, giving me a tired smile. 'I don't want anyone meeting me for the first time like this. Honestly, Becks, go and do your shopping, I'll be fine. Love you.'

'Love you too,' I replied, dropping a kiss on the top of her head.

I waited until I was a good ten minutes away from the flat before I dialled Dominic Rousseau's number. I knew she'd said that there had been a change in her plans and that she'd had to dash home because her mother was ill, but everything about it felt wrong. I'd been distracted at the time, I'd wanted to spend the weekend with Richard, but now, the way she was acting since arriving home – it wasn't right.

So I did the only thing I could. With my heart thumping in my chest, I pressed 'call'.

'Hello?'

With Evie's English being perfect and her accent barely noticable, I had almost forgotten that her father would sound so French. It threw me so much that when I didn't reply for a couple of seconds he spoke again.

'Hello? *Bonjour?* Who is this?'

'Hello, Mr, I mean Monsieur Rousseau? My name's Rebecca Thompson, I'm a friend of Evie's.'

'Is Evelyn okay?' he asked instantly, his tone sharp.

'She's fine, I mean, she's not fine, that's why I'm calling you but she's not hurt or anything,' I cringed at how stupid I sounded, blathering like some kind of idiot. 'Did something happen while she was away, do you know? I'm not trying to pry but she's so different, I. . .'

There was a sigh at the other end of the line and I thought I heard Monsieur Rousseau swear quietly under his breath.

'I knew I shouldn't have let her go home. Has she said anything?'

'Nothing,' I replied. 'She's barely spoken, except to say that she's tired. But I've seen her tired before and I know when something's wrong.'

'It's very kind of you to call me, Rebecca, I'm glad Evelyn has a friend like you looking out for her. Are you with her now?'

'God no,' I said, 'I dread to think. . . She'd go mad if she knew I was calling you. I just didn't know what else to do.'

'No, of course. I probably shouldn't tell you this, Rebecca, if Evelyn hasn't, but she had a break-up while she was at home, from a boy she was seeing before she left for London.'

I'll admit, that threw me. Evie had talked about boys from home, but never one specific one, and she'd never let on that she'd still been seeing someone. True, she hadn't been involved with anyone since I met her in Steve's flat, but what was she doing sleeping with Steve if she was involved with someone back home anyway?

'Oh, okay, well—'

'Is there something else?'

'Um, no, no, sorry. As long as you think it's just this guy, I guess she'll be fine. I'm sorry to disturb you.'

'Not at all,' Dominic replied easily. His deep voice and his thick French accent was very sexy and I remembered the tall handsome man I'd met at Evie's apartment. 'I appreciate your concern for my daughter. I don't doubt she can be, um, how do you say. . . *difficult* at times, but having a friend like you in London is good for her. Thank you.'

Despite the fact that he couldn't see me, I felt my cheeks redden. I imagined that his charm was part of what had made him so successful.

'You don't have to worry about her, sir,' I promised. 'I'll look after her. I'm just heading into town to get us some food and I'll stay with her until she feels better.'

'You're very kind, Rebecca. Monique and I would love to have you visit us when Evie is feeling up to coming again.'

'I'd really like that, thank you.'

We said our goodbyes after Dominic had made me promise once again to keep an eye on Evie and to call him if I felt things with her weren't improving. When I got off the phone I felt better, although admittedly confused. Why hadn't she mentioned the boy she felt strongly enough about to go into a two-day depression over when they broke up? I had almost finished the food shopping and was trying to decide whether to confront her about the break-up, swinging between letting it go because she obviously didn't want to talk about it, and trying to sneakily get it out of her because a problem shared was a problem halved, when my phone rang. Expecting it to be Evie asking me to pick up some Ben & Jerry's, I was surprised to see Richard's name on the display – I'd thought he was busy this weekend.

'Hey baby,' I answered with a smile. We were still in the stage where an unexpected phone call from my new boyfriend gave me butterflies.

'You need to get here asap,' he spluttered into the phone. Was this a booty call? Because if it was he wasn't very good at it – he sounded petrified.

'Sorry, no can do' I grinned. 'I'm afraid we'll have to skip the session, Evie's at mine and she's in a bad way.'

'I know, that's what I mean,' he said, his voice urgent. 'I'm at yours now. The girl on your sofa, I think she's dead.'

65

Evie

When Evie woke, there were a few moments where she could barely remember who she was, let alone where or why. Her brain felt as though it was on fire, blood pounded in her ears and her eyelids were too heavy to open so she didn't bother trying. Words ran through her mind – *I have proof* – and she remembered now. She had wanted to die. There had seemed, at that moment at least, like there was no other way out of her own head – however hard she had tried she couldn't forget the image of James' father engulfed in flames.

She had been at Rebecca's, she remembered now, but she must have misjudged the timing. Rebecca had found her too soon and now she was in a bed, a sharp scratching pain in her hand and noise, too much noise to be alone in the flat. She must be in hospital. She gave a groan at having woken up at all – she was still alive and it wasn't all over. And yet she felt something else, relief maybe? Had she really wanted to die? She hadn't taken the time to think it through before she had taken the pills, pills the doctor had prescribed her mother to help her sleep and that Evie had slipped in her bag before leaving Wareham. Had her mind been planning it all along, without her even being conscious of it?

She opened her eyes tentatively, like a newborn testing them out for the first time. The bright lights forced them closed again but not before she sensed movement at the side of the bed.

'Evie?' a voice, male and concerned but too young to be her father, said.

'James?' she croaked, but her throat wouldn't form the word fully, it was as though she had forgotten how to speak. Opening her eyes again, letting them adjust to the light, she looked over to the seat, expecting to see her. . . her what? Her lover? Her friend? What was he to her now? Nothing.

But it wasn't him who sat in the chair, elbows on his knees, leaning forward in anticipation of her waking. She didn't recognise this man, didn't think she'd ever seen him before.

'Doctor?' she tried her voice again but the pain was almost unbearable. 'Water.'

The man moved quickly to the bedside table and picked up a plastic cup. 'The doctor said ice chips would be better – can you manage that? There, here, let me.'

And even though she'd never seen him before, and she was fairly certain from his jeans and polo T-shirt and the fact that he'd said 'the doctor' that he wasn't one, Evie let him take a chip from the cup and place it gently on her outstretched tongue. His movements were slow and tender and he had a kind face; somehow she knew she could trust him. As the ice soothed her tongue and the cool water slid down her throat, she still didn't have the energy to ask who he was. As if he had read her mind, he spoke.

'I'm Richard, a friend of Rebecca,' he said, quietly, as though speaking to a young child or a frightened animal. 'I came to visit her and I found you on the sofa. I saw the pills and I thought you were. . . I couldn't wake you so I called an ambulance. Rebecca came straight here but she went back to get you some things while you were having your stomach pumped, and your dad, he's just arrived and he's talking to the doctors.'

It was a lot of information to take in considering the insides of her head felt like they had swelled to double their usual size. But as she couldn't ask any questions due to the red-hot poker that was lodged in her throat, she laid her head back on the pillow and tried to digest what the man – she had already forgotten his name – had told her. *Her father was here.* That was the first piece of information that sank in and lodged itself in her mind. He was going to be fucking livid. After everything he had been through with Mama, the times she had seen him go with her in the ambulance, coming home with his eyes red raw from crying at her bedside. His voice hoarse from promises that he'd be a better man. If there was anything more horrific than seeing a grown man you idolise more than Leonardo DiCaprio reduced to a sobbing mess then Evie was yet to experience it. No – her mind slipped to the image of fire licking up a pair of curtains, spreading like a sheet across the ceiling, snaking itself around the father of the only boy she'd ever loved – she *had* experienced it. It was the image that had accompanied her into a sleep she had hoped never to wake up from.

Her stomach had been pumped. She wondered at this – how did they do it? She'd heard of people having it done when they'd drunk too much or taken one too many drugs but she'd never actually thought about the details. She imagined it was something to do with tubes, and the reason the back of her throat felt like it had been scraped with a rusty spoon.

'I'll get the doctor,' the man said, rising from his chair.

'No,' Evie lifted an arm filled with lead. 'Don't go.'

She didn't know who this man was, or why he'd been in Rebecca's flat. All she knew was that he'd saved her life and for now she didn't want him to leave.

66

Rebecca

When I awaken it is in the middle of the night, and to the sound of dripping. My blackout curtains have succeeded in sinking the room into perfect darkness, yet I know there is something wrong, there is danger here, in my home, in my bedroom. I push myself into a sitting position but my hands slide against the sheets and when I look down at them, my eyes adjusting to the darkness slightly, they are black and I realise they are wet. I wipe them furiously against my duvet, leaving smears of thick, black liquid everywhere. Blood. My hands are covered in blood and no matter how hysterically I wipe them, still more remains.

It is then that I realise I am not alone.

She stands at the end of the bed and I can see her now, even in the darkness I can see her clearly and I wonder how I did not see her before. She is soaked through, as though she has only a moment ago climbed from the very water that should have stolen her life. She is the source of the dripping sound – water seems to ooze from her, spilling out of her grotesquely parted lips, which are swollen and bruised, her nose, her eye sockets. Her hair is plastered sodden to her head, the right side thick with the same black liquid that still won't come off my hands. It oozes from a fist-size hole in her skull where her head bounced off the rocks at the foot of the cliff from which she fell. I try to move but I am frozen in terror. What is she doing here? Why has she come for me?

But when she speaks, then I know. Her voice – yet not her voice at all – is the rasp of a creature that has dragged itself from the depths of hell and it doesn't just spew from her broken mouth, it comes from all around me and I know I will hear those words for as long as I live.

You could have saved me.

My eyes fly open as I wake to the sound of screaming and realise it is my own. My heart thuds in my chest so fast that I think for a minute I am having a heart attack. I can't catch my breath and sweat pours down my back, welding my T-shirt to my skin. As I scan the empty room and realise that the horrific apparition was only a dream, my breathing calms but my heartbeat doesn't slow. Already though, she is fading from memory, her accusing eyes, the broken, battered and bruised face. Like tendrils of smoke the vision is impossible to grasp and by the time I have glanced at my hands – they are clean and so are my bedsheets – I can barely remember what my best friend looked like at all. The feeling though, that slightly sick feeling when you know something is wrong, that everything looks normal but there is something so very *wrong* here, that remains. And the voice. I can still hear her voice.

I feel foolish now, and glad for once that I don't share my bed with anyone else. God only knows what an idiot I might have made of myself – what I might have screamed into the darkness.

The dawn light filters in through a gap in the curtains; the day has made enough inroads for me to get up. There's no way I can sleep any longer now, but still that childish part of me, the part I thought was buried much deeper, urges me not to slide my legs out of the covers, not to put my feet on the floor. *You're okay as long as your feet aren't on the floor*, she whispers. *No one can get you in bed*. Such a childish thought to have – of course grown-up Rebecca knows you're no safer in your bed than you are anywhere else. It is not the dead you should be afraid of, after all, it's the living. And the living don't respect the rules like the bogeyman does.

Still, when I do make the transition from bed to floor, I make sure not to get too close to the edge, lest those cold wet fingers clasp around my ankle.

All throughout the day I can't shake that feeling of wrongness. I'm jumping at my own reflection and getting out seems like the only option to take my mind off the dream. The house is too quiet, her voice too loud inside my head.

Youcouldhavesavedmeyoucouldhavesavedme.

67

Evie

His name was Richard, and it seemed as though he might have been sent from heaven at exactly the moment she had needed him. He was attractive enough, if a bit plain-looking, and wouldn't have turned her head in any other circumstance. But this wasn't any other circumstance. She had wanted to die. And it was because of Richard she was still alive.

He'd left her room eventually, when her father had stormed in without even a glance or a thank you for the man who had saved his daughter's life. She found out afterwards that he'd sent Richard a cheque for a thousand pounds – she didn't know whether she should be insulted but it was so incredibly Papa that she didn't bother wasting the energy figuring it out.

Her father had swung between furious and worried, exploding into a tirade of 'how could you's and 'so selfish. . . your poor mother, your friend finding you like that. . .' until finally he had sat down next to her, picked up her hand and looked at her, imploring.

'Did you really want to die?'

'Of course I did,' she replied, feeling a pang of guilt at the way her father shuddered when she said this. 'Why else would I do it?'

Her father hesitated and Evie understood. Mama. Her mother, who had for years been using threats of taking her own life to attempt to control her family. She remembered finding her, as a child, lying dead on the sofa – her father's anger at her mama which had confused and frightened her.

'I'm sorry,' she said quietly. She had done what she'd done because she could see no way of carrying on day after day with the terrible secret of what had happened hanging over her. A man's life, taken, and the responsibility hers. But her father had no way of knowing that, of course.

'What happened on Saturday night,' her father leaned in close, his eyes flicking to the door to make sure it was closed properly. 'It wasn't your fault. You aren't responsible for what happened, it was an overcrowded party in the Addlingtons' monstrosity of a fire-trap. And when I said it was better no one knew you were there I wasn't implying that. . .'

'It's okay, Papa,' Evie said, gently covering his hand with her other. 'I know you weren't saying the fire was my fault.' She searched his face for a clue that he might know the truth about the fire. 'I think it was just seeing James and Camille together, knowing that they are going to be married, after the baby and. . .'

Dominic sighed. 'Oh Evie. I wish you would forget about all this. Your friend Rebecca is getting you some clothes to wear and as soon as you've had your evaluation you are coming back home with me.'

'No!'

Evie couldn't think of anything worse. What if she were to run into James? What if Harriet wanted to talk to her about Saturday night? About what had happened? What if

Camille heard she was back and thought she was making an attempt to see James? No, she would stay here.

'No, I have things to do here. Classes to go to. I'll be fine, honestly.'

'And who is going to look after you here? Make sure you don't pull this kind of stunt again?'

'I will,' a voice came from the doorway and Dominic turned to see who it had come from. Rebecca stood in the doorway, a duffle bag and an overnight bag in her hands. She lifted both. 'I got your things. I'll look after her, Mr Rousseau, I promise.'

68

Rebecca

Richard had been sitting outside the hospital room when I arrived, laden down with everything I could think Evie might need. The doctors had said she would be staying at least forty-eight hours while they arranged a psychiatric evaluation and for Evie that meant at least four outfits, with accessories.

He stood when he saw me. 'Her father's in there,' he said, gesturing at the window where I could see Dominic Rousseau sitting next to his daughter's bedside holding her hand. 'She woke up about twenty-five minutes ago.'

'You okay?' I moved forward to take his hand and inexplicably Richard flinched.

'I'm fine, thanks. Just a bit of a shock, you know?'

He hadn't taken his eyes off the window – off Evie. That's when it dawned on me, the flinch, the weirdness in his voice. . . it had all happened exactly the same to me the first time I'd met her, and I hadn't saved her life. Richard was in love with Evie. Of course it wasn't love yet – right at that moment in time it was a weird kind of instant infatuation, the inability to tear your eyes from her, the urge to put out a hand and touch her light brown skin, to make those lips twitch upwards in a smile that you knew would be the most beautiful thing you would see that day. I didn't believe in instalove, but I believed in the knowledge that one day he would love her. It started like this, like a tickle in your throat that you knew without a doubt would be a full bout of flu in a week's time. And I could either try and hold onto him, fight my best friend for a man I'd known two weeks and inevitably lose or give in gracefully. Of course, if Evie knew that Richard was the boyfriend I'd been so keen to introduce her to she'd never go near him in a million years anyway, but the relationship would be fractured in a way that could only be repaired by cutting one of them loose. Evie or Richard. It was a choice that I had to make now, before this could go any further.

'Richard,' I said, my heart splintering a little as I watched him tear his eyes from my best friend. 'This thing, between us? I don't think it's going to work.'

69

Evie

Although she'd been waiting for it for months, she hadn't looked for it – somehow she just knew the news would find her.

The three of them, Evie, Richard and Rebecca, had been out all day in what had felt like the first ray of sunlight all year, breaking free of the fug of indoors like daffodils breaking free of the ground. Evie had been awake at the crack of dawn – sleep didn't come as easily for her these days – and, vowing for today not to let the black thoughts pin her to her duvet, she got up, leaving images of a house engulfed in flames and the sound of screams in the bed behind her. She glanced at the empty bottle of wine on her kitchen countertop but didn't open the cupboard to look for a full one. Today would be a good day. Downstairs in the street the smell of warm bread and bubbling jam drew her into the deli like she was a child following the Pied Piper.

'*Salut*, Claude!' Evie greeted the old man behind the counter in his native tongue and he rewarded her with a grunt and a lift of his hand. Claude had been running the deli for as long as Evie had lived in London, but she suspected it was actually since time began, he was that old and crabby.

He had never smiled at her and it had taken him a year of her regular appearances to lift his hand when she entered, and yet she was exceedingly fond of the old man and she could tell he was of her. For a start she had never seen him converse with anyone except her – he would give her snippets of conversation every now and then, but only ever in French, and she thought that once she'd seen a flash of a smile when she entered, although it was gone in an instant. He had a daughter her age who had stayed in France and she wondered if she reminded him of her.

'I got new cheese,' Claude spoke in French as he wrapped up a block of creamy white cheese speckled with red. 'Strawberries and champagne. Stupid if you ask me but Verity says it's popular in La Dordogne so I give it to you. What else you want?'

Evie smiled. 'Careful, Claude, that was almost a nice gesture. I'll have some of that bread you gave me last time and the brie, some grapes and do you have the pâté with the wild mushroom? I'm taking my friends on a picnic.'

'It will probably rain,' Claude grunted and Evie laughed.

'It might even snow, Claude, but what is the point in worrying about what might happen?'

Neither Richard or Rebecca had been particularly happy about being dragged from their (separate) beds so early in the morning to go on a road trip but neither had put up much of a fight. Evie had hoped that they would have got together by now. Of course she knew Richard had his sights on her but she'd made it clear that a relationship between them wasn't going to happen. Why couldn't he see that he and Rebecca had more in common anyway? Evie had seen the way Rebecca looked at him when she thought no one was looking, and things with the new boyfriend she'd texted Evie about seemed to have fizzled out, possibly because of the appearance of Richard himself. But if they were going to get together it would happen eventually, Evie just had to let them take baby steps and step aside when it was time for it to happen. The thought of her two best friends moving forwards without her made her a bit sad but Rebecca deserved some happiness – and she did not.

Stonehenge was three and a half hours away by train and when Evie got back to her apartment that evening, exhausted but exhilarated, it was nearly ten pm and the envelope was the first thing she saw. She'd been expecting it, waiting for it even, but seeing it still sent a punch to her stomach. She lifted the magazine article out and smoothed it down on the coffee table. James looked as breathtaking as ever, just as she had imagined him at their wedding. His bride looked beautiful, and triumphant.

Evie screwed up the article and tossed it into the bin, picked up the phone.

'Richard, it's me. I was wondering if you'd come over, please? No, Rebecca's not here. It would just be you and me.'

Evie put down the phone and sighed. She just needed some company for tonight. Was there really anything so wrong with that? She wouldn't let it go too far, she didn't want anyone getting hurt.

Four months before the wedding

70

Evie

'Stop being a grade A bitch and answer the question.'

'Yes. You know it's yes. But honestly, Eves. . .'

'Eeeeee!' Evie squealed. 'Honestly Harriet, we're so happy and I want you to be happy for us too.'

'What, all three of you?'

'Don't be mean.'

'Well seriously, I'm surprised you ever got any time to yourselves to get engaged. Was she there when he popped the question? Will she be there when you conceive your first child?'

'Ten seconds.'

'What?'

'Ten seconds you managed to stop being a bitch,' Evie grinned. 'Becky is a good friend. My best friend.'

'Oh sod off. I'm your best friend and you know it. She's got this weird thing about *knowing you the bestest* in the whole wide world. I've only met her twice in God knows how many years and both times she looked like she was sucking a lemon whenever I mentioned anything from our past. Like she thinks you came into being when you met her.'

'I called to ask if you'd be a bridesmaid – not to slag off my maid of honour.'

'Oh God, she'll be frigging unbearable. Fine. I'll toe the line and be nice to single white female. Four months? You're lucky I'm not already booked, who arranges a wedding in four months? DM me the details and I'll have my assistant respond accordingly.'

Evie laughed. 'You are unbearable. I don't know how Penny puts up with you. Speak soon. Love you.'

When the phone rang again Evie grabbed it off the cradle. 'Morning, Penny.'

'Who's Penny? Are you cheating on me?'

'Anna! Sorry, I thought you were my friend's assistant. How are you?'

'Perfect, sweetheart. Even better when you agree to come on board with the biggest project OnBrand has ever had.'

'No, Anna, listen,' Evie took the phone through to the kitchen and lowered her voice. 'I told you I don't plan on taking any more jobs. It was fun, honestly it was, and I'm grateful for the experience,' *and the break from the tedium*, she thought, 'but it's not really something I want to do.'

'But you're so good at it, darling woman!' Anna's voice went to her London luvvie that only ever came out when she was trying to get someone to do what she wanted. 'And this client, he asked for you specifically.'

'Me?' Annoyingly she felt the exact prickling of pride that Anna had intended. Damn, the woman was good.

Which Evie had known from the day she met Anna at the gallery. She had taken the position when her university degree was over, intended at first as a stopgap while she built her own portfolio, but apparently her camera had other ideas. Evie had scarcely taken a decent set since the fire, barely scraping through her degree with her backlist and some not-totally-shit project pieces, but she and her tutor both knew that the passion she'd had when she started the course had waned and eventually fizzled out completely.

Anna had seen something in her, though. Evie had come back from grabbing a lunchtime bagel to find a ridiculously tall woman, all bottle-red hair and patterned shrugs over skintight leather leggings, poring over one of her old portfolios she'd left behind the counter.

'Oh, those pictures aren't for sale, sorry,' Evie had said, slightly annoyed that the woman had let herself behind the counter, and also that Gareth had done another disappearing act.

'I don't want the photographs,' the woman had smiled and Evie had instantly forgiven her transgression. 'I want the person who took them.'

It transpired that Anna was from a marketing agency that worked with clients to produce and reinforce brand awareness, and after stumbling across Evie's portfolio she had immediately asked her to do some work for OnBrand. Evie had refused initially – that was not what her photography was about, she had no intention of using her talents to benefit multi-national corporations. But Anna had been persuasive. It was a small, family-owned business she would be working with – who paid their taxes in full, she added – and Evie's work would be helping them build something to pass on to their children, and their children's children. Evie had agreed, secretly excited about the chance to develop a new set of skills, and had risen to the challenge admirably – if she did say so herself. Now though, Anna was back, as Evie should have anticipated.

'He saw your name on the campaign website and was very impressed. He's offered to double your asking fee and wants to come and meet you face to face – it's a huge client from an IT consultancy based in Wareham.'

An IT consultant from Wareham. A coincidence, surely? And yet Evie found herself saying yes, she would meet with the director of the company, at four pm on Tuesday, leaving Anna thinking she'd worked her persuasive magic once again.

She hadn't told anyone about the work she'd done for OnBrand so it had been a stupid mistake to allow them to put her byline on the campaign. For some reason, she didn't want to admit to her friends, colleagues at the gallery, or even Richard or Rebecca, that she had 'sold out' – even though she knew Richard would be proud of the work she'd done. After everything she'd demanded her work had stood for in the past, after the difference she was supposed to be making in the world. She didn't allow herself to wonder what James thought of headstrong Evelyn Rousseau, whose photography was going to change the world, working the desk hanging other people's pictures on the walls. For a start, it was unlikely to be him – she was still going by her mother's maiden name these days and James Addlington had never met Evie White. In fact, it was more likely to be her father asking for her by name, although why he'd do such a thing when he barely bothered to call her on the number he had for her was beyond her.

So, as she prepared to leave the gallery on Tuesday in a new black shift dress and heels, she told herself that she wasn't deceiving Richard because of the possibility that it was *him* she might be meeting, that this job was no different to the last. She was meeting a potential client, nothing more. So why, as she approached the OnBrand offices, did her mouth dry up and her palms begin to tingle?

'He's in there already,' Anna hissed, as Evie approached her desk, and she noticed that her boss had applied a full face of make-up more colourful than usual.

'Come on, Anna, enough of the air of mystery. Give me a name.'

She had asked more than once for the name of this mystery director, or even the company, but Anna had said that he wished everything to remain a closed secret until the deal was done – adding further fuel to the fire of Evie's suspicions. Now, Anna screwed up her nose in contemplation.

'I suppose it can't hurt now – it's Addlington Consultancy. Don't keep him waiting.'

Evie had known, since the first phone call, that James had finally made contact. She'd been preparing for this meeting with the knowledge that she was about to face the man who made her abort her child, the man who took her virginity, the first man she ever loved, and the man whose father she killed. Still, when she pushed open the door to the conference room, she realised how underprepared she had been to see the face she'd imagined so many times.

71

Evie

'James Addlington,' Evie cleared her throat and crossed the room to greet him. 'What a lovely surprise.'

He gave her that deep, appraising look he had had since he was nine. So confident, and yet she was the one who had been able to tease out his insecurities, the fears he had that he would never live up to his father, the thoughts that maybe he didn't even want to. Obviously his wife had convinced him that he should, otherwise he wouldn't be here. He was every bit as alluring as he had been the night she last saw him across the room with his fiancée the night his father died. The thought made her stomach contract.

'Evelyn Rousseau,' he said, drawing her name out as though it tasted good on his lips. 'It's been so long.'

He leaned forwards and she offered him her cheek. James moved his lips to hers and kissed her, his lips lingering on hers a second too long to be professional. Oh God, even after all these years she longed to let herself fall into him, feel his body against hers. It had been nine years; it felt like two hours.

She pulled away first, her cheeks burning.

'How's business?' she asked, willing her face to return to its normal colour.

'Booming. Although we could always use some help from someone of your considerable skill. I saw the campaign you did for Travis Bolton – it was amazing. Imagine my shock when I saw your name on the byline.'

The barb may or may not have been intended but Evie felt it anyway, her temper flaring, a temper she had barely felt since she was seven years old and being told she couldn't join a party because her mother worked in the kitchens.

'And your marriage?' Evie shot at him. 'Could that use some help also?'

But instead of taking offence James laughed. 'Still the same spiky Evelyn, I see.'

How wrong he was. She hadn't been the same Evelyn since the day she left Wareham, her womb as empty as her heart. She sighed.

'Why are you here, James? You could have your pick of marketing experts – you had no need to come here, after all this time.'

'I've never stopped thinking about you – do you know that? Even after what you did.'

'What I. . .?' *Getting pregnant? The fire?* Evie shook her head. She couldn't deal with this – if James knew anything of what she'd done he wouldn't be standing there looking at her as though he was struggling not to pull her into his arms.

'It's in the past,' he said abruptly, breaking the silence. 'I came here to see if your marketing is as good as your photography was. I'd really like to spend some time with you, Evie. Will you accept the job?'

She knew she should say no, just as she knew she wasn't going to. She could tell herself that Anna's business was relying on a client this big, or that it was a brilliant opportunity. But the truth was that she would work with James Addlington because, although their lives had been running

251

on separate tracks all these years, she had known that one day they would have to collide.

Fine, she would do this. Put on a show, act like she didn't care. And she could act as well as anyone she knew, she'd been doing it since the day she killed his father.

72

Evie

Wednesdays couldn't roll around soon enough any more, and keeping her excitement from everyone around her was getting harder and harder. As far as Richard was aware she was at the gallery, as far as the gallery was aware she was taking one day's leave a week to work on her photography. If Richard happened to pop into the gallery she would tell him that she had wanted to surprise him with a new portfolio. She thought she had it all figured out.

Unlike James Addlington – there was a man she couldn't figure out at all. He claimed he had come all this way just to see her again, but what did that mean for his marriage to Camille? She had spent three whole weeks playing him at his own game, feeling like a giddy teenager again, each trying to prove that they were in control of the relationship. He would arrange last-minute meetings, she would bring along junior employees from OnBrand, citing training needs and note-taking. James would call her specifically when he knew she would be with Richard and ask her what she was wearing and Evie would remain unflustered as she politely informed him that she'd claimed all of her payment protection insurance but thank you for asking. Once he sent a bunch of flowers to her home and she had redirected the delivery to Anna's address – James had been apologetic when Anna had thanked him profusely for them the next day but warned him that it wasn't really acceptable to send a dozen red roses to a person's home address – especially when one's husband was at home.

'You can't avoid me forever,' he muttered to her as they filled their mugs, backs to everyone in the room. 'One of these times you will have to be alone with me.'

'The campaign will be closing in two weeks' time,' Evie smiled, her voice low and measured. 'I hope it was money well spent.'

Despite his assurances that they would be alone together, most of the work for the campaign was completed from home. There were only so many reasons James could come up with for arranging face-to-face meetings, and in two weeks the campaign was launched successfully – this time without Evie's name on the website. When James emailed her to ask her to dinner to celebrate she forwarded the email to the entire team, headed with 'Mr Addlington asked me to pass on his thanks and extend a dinner invitation to you all in celebration.' For the first time in years her heart was racing every time her phone made a sound, she was having to think on her feet to stay one step ahead and she felt more like herself than she had in a very long time.

'I suppose you think yourself very clever,' Evie was standing at the bar ordering another orange juice when his voice startled her. She turned around and raised her empty glass to him.

'Congratulations on a very successful campaign, Mr Addlington,' she said evenly. 'The meal was very generous of you. The team worked very hard, I'm sure you'll admit.'

'They would have had less work to do if you hadn't dragged them to every single meeting,' he replied with a wry smile.

The smell of his aftershave and the closeness of him made her heart thump furiously in her chest. His blue eyes studied her face intently. 'You always were an obstinate pain in the ass.'

'And you never did like not getting your own way.'

The bartender passed Evie her drink and James leaned over her to say, 'Put it on my tab. And before you order drinks for the entire restaurant, or give it away to your rather over-friendly boss, you will take that drink and you will drink it, as a thank you for the hard work you've done,' he screwed up his nose. 'Even if it is only orange juice. I know your passion was always photography but you have a real eye for marketing, you know. I'm very impressed with your work.'

'That's it?' Evie asked incredulously. 'You're "impressed"? No attempt to lure me back to your hotel room, or offer to throw me down on the table and show me what I'm missing? Just a compliment?'

'You flatter yourself, Evelyn,' James said, that smile playing on his lips. 'It has been a pleasure working with you.'

He placed a kiss on her cheek and walked back over to the table full of people, where Evie could see him shaking hands with the rest of the team, kissing the women as he had her, slapping the men on the shoulder. Then, without a backwards glance, he left the restaurant.

'He's gone then?' Evie asked Anna, taking a sip of her juice.

'He's travelling first thing tomorrow, said he needs his beauty sleep. Although God knows how long my Tom would have to sleep to look that beautiful.' Anna raised her eyebrows.

So that was that. She had won. All of her game-playing had got her exactly what she wanted. Once again, James Addlington was out of her life – she was safe. And now she could carry on in her perfectly ordinary, uneventful life while he returned to Camille. It didn't feel like much of a victory.

73

Evie

It had taken just a couple of hours in the company of James Addlington for Evie to order her first glass of wine in what felt like forever. After everything that had happened at university she had slowly stopped reaching for the bottle in order to drown her feelings, but it was remarkable how easily old habits could resurface and before long she was stumbling to the bar to order a third bottle of Chardonnay.

'Sweetheart,' Anna placed a hand on her back. 'We're going to make a move. Are you going to be okay getting back?'

'Oh, I'll be fine,' Evie gave a wave of her hand. 'I can't believe you're going so soon! It's only,' she attempted to focus on her watch but it was jumping around all over the place and she couldn't get a fix on the hands.

'It's ten thirty and we have work in the morning,' Anna lowered her voice. 'I think you should forget that bottle and go home to your fiancé. He'll be worried.'

'Yes, it doesn't take much to worry Richard,' Evie snorted. She handed over her bank card and picked up the bottle of wine. 'I'll take this with me.'

'Should I call you a taxi?'

'No, honestly, Anna, I'll be fine. Thanks so much for the opportunity with this account.'

'You've done an amazing job,' Anna kissed her on the cheek. 'You really should think about a permanent career change.'

Outside the fresh air hit her and Evie's head swam. She put a hand out and grasped at the windowsill of the bar to steady herself, grasping at the pack of cigarettes in her handbag. Pulling one out triumphantly, she lit up and took a drag, leaning against the cold stone wall with her eyes closed.

'It's bad for you.'

Evie opened one eye, even though she knew exactly who she would find standing in front of her.

'I thought you'd left.'

'I meant to.'

'Yet here you are.' Evie stood up straight and took another drag on her cigarette, her fingers shaking.

'Here,' James handed her a bottle of water which she took without comment. 'And these.' He dropped two Nurofen into her palm. 'To stop the hangover.'

'I'd say my mother told me never to accept drugs from strangers but she was never really fussy about where she got her temporary highs.'

'How is she?'

Evie's face crumpled and James reached out to put a hand on her arm.

'She's not well. Not enough blood in her alcohol system.'

'I'm really sorry.'

She wanted to say she was sorry about his dad too but she couldn't bear to bring up the subject. This was why he was so dangerous to be around: looking at that face was like looking at a piece of home. It was so easy for her to drop her guard around him.

She pushed off from the wall. 'I have to go.'

'Let me walk you home.'

'I live in Kensington,' Evie smiled, looking at his sharp suit and uncomfortable-looking shoes. 'You're not dressed for a jog.'

'Then let me get you a taxi.'

'I'm fine. . .' Evie pulled off her heels and began walking in what she hoped was the right direction for Victoria tube station.

'Just what is your problem with me?' James demanded.

'My problem?' Evie swung around, anger rearing up inside her. Suddenly she felt as though she was seventeen years old again, banging on the Addlington family's door after a skinful, demanding to have her say. Well now she was getting it and it felt just as good as she'd hoped it would. '*I* don't have a problem. You stopped being my problem nine years ago when you told me I was as easy as I was stupid, you arrogant asshole.'

'I never said that to you,' James replied quickly. 'I wouldn't say that to anyone, let alone you.'

'No,' Evie spat. 'You didn't. You didn't even have the balls to say it to me – you sent me a text message. My father tells you I'm having your baby and—'

'My what?' James stepped back, brow furrowed. 'My *baby*?'

For a second Evie thought he was going to be sick. Her mind might be on a time lag from the alcohol but even in her state she could see that he had no idea what she was talking about. Had he forgotten so easily?

'You said you wanted a DNA test. You told my father I was sleeping around and the baby could have been anyone's.'

'Really? Does that sound like me? How could you believe I'd say that?'

Evie threw the cigarette to the floor and ground it out with her shoe.

259

'Easily. You sent me the text messages. You wouldn't answer your phone. What was I supposed to believe? Are you telling me now that someone else sent me those messages?'

'I'm telling you that I didn't. And I tried calling you when I got your letter, your number was out of service.'

Evie took a deep breath. The cold air hit her lungs and she struggled to concentrate. This wasn't making any sense. She hadn't changed her number, how could it have been out of service? These lies, they were all part of his plan to get her into bed, screw her and fly back to Camille, just like he had the first time.

'My father wouldn't do that to me,' Evie's voice was firm and unyielding. All these years of believing James hadn't wanted to be with her or their baby – she had come to terms with that now. To have to acknowledge that it was her father who had betrayed her, that these last few years could have been so different. . . that was too much to ask.

'I'm telling you, I didn't know about the baby. You can choose to believe me or not.'

'Oh fuck off, James. If you didn't know then how did your precious Camille know?'

'Camille knows?' James scowled. 'I might have known. She knows everything about everyone. She probably knows more about the truth of how our relationship ended than we do.'

'You married her.'

'I loved you.'

'You *married* her.'

'I love you,' he grabbed her arm and Evie stopped short. These last few weeks, seeing him and not being able to be anything more than professional had been hard enough. But now they were alone and he was saying the words she'd wanted him to say ever since she'd found out she was having his baby. He put a hand behind her neck to draw her in for a kiss but she pulled away.

'I can't go through the same thing I went through last time you claimed to love me,' she started walking again, her stockinged feet cold against the pavement. 'I nearly got kicked out of school. I spent four years drinking myself into oblivion to forget what happened between us and you show up and here I am,' she gestured to her bag where the unopened bottle of wine poked out of the top. 'Drinking to forget you again. After everything I've done to forget. Why is it so hard to move on from you? What's so special about you?'

'No idea,' James smiled. 'I thought I was a bastard.'

Evie suppressed a smile. She didn't even remember calling him a bastard now, but it had been a running joke between them, something that would have been told to their children – you know, the first time Mummy met Daddy. . . Well, maybe not until they were old enough to know what a bastard was.

'Look,' James handed her his phone. 'I kept your number. Sometimes I call it – although I never know what I'd say if you answered – but you never do. It's been out of service ever since you sent me the letter.'

'I didn't send you any letter, and that's not my number,' Evie said. The water and ibuprofen had cleared her mind enough to see that the middle three digits of the number he was showing her were wrong.

'Yes it is. It ends in 693.'

'Yeah, that bit's right, it's the middle that's wrong. When did you say it went out of service?'

'I can't remember the exact date, but it was the night Dad gave me your letter. I went out with my friends, got drunk and must have left my phone at home because it wasn't in my jacket when I got to the pub. When I got home I drunk-dialled you and you'd changed your number.'

'And you left it at that? Anyone could have written that letter, anyone could have changed my number in your phone.'

'And anyone could have sent you those texts,' James pointed out. 'But you believed them.'

'I came to see you,' Evie countered. 'I at least tried. But you were out and your mother called my dad, who dragged me away and sent me to study in London.'

'I don't understand why they would go to so much trouble,' James cursed under his breath. 'Okay, we were young but was avoiding a scandal really worth lying to us both?'

'Dominic Rousseau lies on a daily basis,' Evie said. 'I'm not at all surprised he lied to me. In fact I remember thinking how surprised I was that he'd taken it so well, given what he thought of your dad. Did your father ever tell you why they fell out?'

James shook his head. 'Not properly. He said Dominic accused him of stealing from him and it cost him, but he didn't say what.'

'Stealing? Like IP or something? Perhaps that's why Dad was reluctant to go into business with him, if they'd fallen out over idea theft before. They didn't trust one another.'

'It doesn't explain why they would be so against our relationship,' James replied.

'I'm not sure whether it was just our relationship, or if it would have been any boy,' Evie chewed on her bottom lip. 'Papa has always been protective of me, he's always acted as though someone is waiting to steal me away. He's been horrid to Richard. Maybe they just thought we were too young to be as serious as we were.'

'They lied to us,' James' jaw was set in a hard line. 'Things could have been so different.'

'And then you got married,' she said, straining to keep the bitterness from her voice. 'To Camille, of all people.'

'The biggest mistake I've ever made.'

As much as Evie had wanted to hear those words so many times in the past, hearing them now just made her feel hollow. If he wasn't even happy then what had it all been for? Her moving to London, the fire, his father's death. All for James to end up in a loveless marriage and her to have nearly killed herself.

'I'm sure all married men trying to get laid say that,' Evie snorted. 'Let me guess, she doesn't understand you.'

'To be honest, Camille didn't want me from the moment she'd got me. Almost straight after the wedding she began having affairs, and no, I'm not trying to justify coming here to find you but I don't even think she'd care if I started seeing someone else. Although she'd go ape-shit if she found out I was with *you*. Sometimes I wonder if the only reason she went after me in the first place was how much she enjoyed getting one over on you.'

'So why are you still together?'

James shrugged and Evie saw in his face how miserable he was, how much their fathers' lies had cost them both. Their baby, their love, James Sr's life – it had all been lost over some stupid feud that should never have involved James and Evie at all.

'She can't bear for anything to fail. It's like she hates me for keeping her tied down but it's her who desperately doesn't want to be divorced after less than four years of marriage.'

Evie thought of how quickly Camille had made her move on James after news of their split had hit the grapevine, and how delighted she'd been to tell Evie all about it. Had she known the whole truth all along? She must have known that James had been in the dark about the baby.

No matter, it was clear the ball was in her court now. They both knew the truth.

But not the whole truth, that niggling voice inside her whispered. *You haven't told him everything. Do you still think you will get your Happy Ever After when he finds out what you did to his father?*

74

Evie

Evie lay in his arms, knowing she should check the time, at least message Richard with an excuse as to why she was out so late, but not wanting to break the spell she felt under. The grass was damp underneath her, and she was certain her chinos were covered in mud stains, but every second had been worth it.

'You know, I've never been to St James's Park before,' James said, pushing himself up onto one elbow. Evie sat up, pulling her top straight. 'It's nice.'

'Will you come again?' Evie asked, grinning.

'If you insist.' He grabbed her waist and pulled her down to kiss him again. 'Actually, I'm not sure I could manage it again yet. I'm not eighteen any more.'

'We're hardly old fogies,' Evie glanced at her watch. 'Although it is past my bedtime. I need to get back.'

'Don't go back,' James wrapped his arms around her waist, his full weight against her. 'Stay with me. Tell whatshisname you're staying with a friend.'

Evie felt her stomach flip at hearing James dismiss Richard so casually. How could she treat him like this? He'd been there for her through so much, she'd never even looked at another man, and yet an hour in James Addlington's company and she was having sex in St James's Park. And it wasn't even a weekend. She felt like a reckless teenager – she should go home right now and forget this ever happened.

Except the minute she left that would be it, it would all be over. She couldn't risk an affair; if Camille ever found out she would tell James about his father and he would hate her. She would rather never see him again than have him know the truth.

'What are you thinking?' he asked, stroking her hair.

'Let's do it,' she said, looking up into his clear blue eyes. 'Just one night.'

75

Evie

James had wanted them to confront Dominic, to find out which of the two fathers, his or Evie's, had written the letter that had allegedly come from Evie; whose idea it had been to use his phone to send the text messages that had led her to the clinic. But Evie knew they couldn't, not if they wanted to keep things between them a secret. Besides, they were both equally to blame. It was ironic that two men who couldn't stand to be in a room together could join forces to execute a plan so well – James Addlington Sr had been right to think that they would have been formidable business partners.

She wanted to be mad at her father but her mother was so ill these days – finally both her liver and her mind were rebelling from years of abuse – and Evie couldn't bring herself to add to his heartbreak. Things could have been so different if the two men hadn't done what they had done – one of them would still be alive – and she would confront that with Dominic one day, but for now she had to support him through her mother's illness. There would be time for angry confrontation another day.

As for Evie and James, what she thought would be a

one-night stand was never going to be enough. Despite her begging him to let her go, James had contacted her almost as soon as he got back to Wareham, and ever since they had talked whenever they could, though not enough to make Camille suspicious, and nowhere near enough for Evie's liking.

James hated it when she asked him about his marriage to Camille, especially as she refused to speak about Richard whatsoever – to do so almost seemed like a double betrayal – but she managed to glean that their marriage had never been a happy one. Despite what he had told Evie at their engagement party, it had been James Sr who had pushed their relationship forward at every opportunity, and Evie couldn't work out why. Why he'd push his son together with a woman he couldn't stand – was it just to keep him away from Evie? When she pushed James further, he admitted that Camille hadn't been right for him from the start, but she hadn't always been awful and he'd allowed himself to get swept along with the relationship, a few dates at first, then family holidays. It wasn't until after they were married that Camille had shown her true colours. These days they were married in name only – they barely spoke to one another.

'I stay with her now because I feel guilty,' he admitted one night when he'd been late calling because Camille had got drunk and smashed all their crockery. 'She's always known that I was only with her because I thought I couldn't have you. She hates you, you know. Her invisible adversary. She knows she can't stop me thinking about you and it drives her crazy that she can't control my thoughts. God knows she controls everything else.'

'What do you have to feel guilty about?' Evie asked. 'You married her, she got what she wanted.'

'Yes, but I never loved her, not like I loved you. Imagine

knowing the person you were with was only with you because they couldn't have someone else. It would drive you crazy too, I bet.'

'What a mess we're in,' Evie sighed. 'What are we going to do?'

'I'm going to tell her,' James replied. 'Now we know we want to be together nothing has ever seemed simpler. She can have half of everything, I don't care. We have no children, thank God that was one thing we agreed on. Bringing children into a relationship like ours would have been a disaster.'

If only it was that simple. If James told Camille about them, who knew what surprises she would reveal in turn?

'Wait a while,' Evie found herself saying. 'We've managed apart for this long – let's make sure nothing goes wrong this time.'

76

Evie

The first letter came on a Tuesday morning, as she was preparing to leave for the gallery. Richard usually worked from home on a Tuesday, but he was out of the house for an unexpected meeting, so it was Evie who found the small white envelope on the mat.

I know what you did, it read.

At first she thought it was referring to her night with James – but how could anyone know? Then she unfolded the second piece of paper that had been in the envelope, and dropped it to the floor.

Her hands shaking, she picked it back up, hastily shoving it inside the envelope. The picture on the second sheet – a printout from the internet – burned fierce in her mind. An article about the Addlington fire. So Camille knew about her night with James, and was reminding her of the promise she had made to stay away from her husband. What would she do now?

She was contemplating calling Camille, or perhaps James, when the phone rang, a sharp voice at the other end when she picked up.

'Were you there that night?' It was James.

There was only one night he could be referring to. So he had told Camille about them then, and this was her last-ditch attempt to keep them apart.

'Yes,' she admitted. 'I came to tell you I loved you, and ask you not to marry Camille. She was there, she told me you'd told her about the baby and you hated me so I left without speaking to you. I should have said but I didn't know how.'

James groaned. 'She's saying you locked Dad in that study.'

Evie let out a tiny gasp, but loud enough that James heard.

'So it's true. Why would you do that?'

'I'd been drinking,' Evie admitted. 'He was coming on to me, he didn't know who I was. So I told him to wait for me and I'd be back to give him what he wanted, then I locked the door on my way out. I thought it was funny – I had no idea he was going to set the house on fire.'

'And you couldn't have told me before now?' James demanded. 'These last few weeks, we've told each other everything – at least I've told you everything. Now I don't know what to think.'

'Please,' Evie whispered. 'It was an accident. I'm so sorry.'

'Camille is threatening to go to the police if I ever go near you again,' James sighed. 'I don't know what to do.'

The letters came with alarming frequency after that, and Evie waited and waited for the phone call from James that never came. And then the police arrived.

77

Evie

She took a sip of her tea and flipped the page of the novel balanced on her knees. Richard was at the football for the afternoon – a fact that she hadn't mentioned to Rebecca – and a lazy Saturday afternoon stretched out before her. She'd stayed in bed late after Richard had left, watching a drama on Netflix cuddled up under her covers, even falling back asleep for an hour. When Richard was there they both felt obliged to do something, feeling that to stay in bed or read a book was wasting the weekend, so as soon as she had the place to herself all she wanted to do was waste time.

She was so deeply engrossed in her book that she didn't hear the knock at the door. After a persistent and louder second knock, Evie frowned and went to answer it.

Her first thought, when she saw the two police officers standing on the doorstep, was that something terrible had happened. She'd watched enough TV shows to know that this was how they delivered bad news – in pairs – so that one could comfort her while the other one watched to see if her reaction made her a psychopath.

'Is it Richard?' she asked automatically, her mind running through all of the things that could have happened to him.

Car crash? Stabbed in the midst of a fight between rival football teams? Heart attack?

The police officer shook his head. He was young, she thought, too young to be doing a job like this, where you never knew where the danger lay. Where you never knew if the person you were talking to was a killer.

'No, ma'am, no one's hurt. Are you Evelyn Rousseau?'

At the mention of her former name a different picture formed in her mind. A life in Wareham where Evelyn Rousseau was her only name. A picture of the letters burning a hole in her cupboard surfaced.

'Yes. I mean, I don't go by that name any more, I use my mother's maiden name, White.'

'Yes,' the police officer replied. Of course they knew that – otherwise how would they have found her? 'May we come in, Miss White?'

Evie stepped to one side in silence, waving them through to the sitting room where her book and blanket lay discarded on the sofa. She moved them to one side to allow the officers to sit down and picked up her mug.

'Would you like a cup of tea?' she asked, not really knowing what the etiquette was when the police turned up on a Saturday afternoon.

'No, thank you. Have a seat, please.'

Evie sat down on the edge of the single-seater and looked at them in expectation. The second officer, who had yet to speak, looked at the first. Despite his youth, Evie assumed he was the senior in this relationship – he got all the speaking parts.

'I'm PC Hollis, this is PC Gallow. We've been asked to speak to you, Miss White, regarding a party you attended six years ago.'

'Well,' Evie struggled to look casual. 'I've been to a lot of parties and that's a long time ago.'

'This was an engagement party, one that resulted in a fire.'

'Oh, you're talking about the Addlington fire? That was horrible.'

Evie's heart was pounding. Was she overplaying the dumb blonde schtick? *Cool it, Evie, don't give them the rope to hang you.*

'The police force in Dorset received a call from someone who suggested that you may have been at the party, although you weren't on the list of guests.'

Evie tried her best to look puzzled, rather than petrified.

'I don't know why anyone would say that,' she told them. 'I wouldn't have been at the party. James was an ex-boyfriend of mine, I would hardly celebrate his engagement to someone else.'

Hollis nodded sympathetically and Evie could have cried with relief. Camille was crazy to think that anyone would look at Evie and think her capable of setting fire to a house.

'Can you think of why anyone might have remembered seeing you there?'

Evie nodded, as though something had just come to mind.

'Yes – I went straight there after I heard about the fire. A lot of my friends were at the party and I wanted to see what was going on. A lot of people did the same. Someone might have seen me there afterwards and assumed I'd been to the party.'

The officer nodded and Evie's shoulders sagged as the tension ebbed away.

'I'm sure that's it,' he said. 'Thank you for your time.'

Evie sat on the floor of the empty house, her back slumped against the sofa and her hands over her face. The minute the police had left the house she'd started shaking uncontrollably, she was cold and her chest was tight, as though an elastic band had been wrapped around her ribcage. She wondered if she was going into shock. Wrapping her arms around her knees, she leaned forwards and started taking slow deep breaths until the shaking stopped and she began to calm.

It was fine – James would sort this out. She thought of the pregnancy test in her bag and said a silent prayer that his anger at what she'd done would subside. She couldn't lose him again – not when she was carrying his baby for a second time.

78

James

'You still want her, don't you? After everything I told you.'

James turned, cringing to see Camille leaning against the doorframe, her cheeks red and her eyes glassy. He could see straight away she was drunk.

'Even knowing she's responsible for your father's death, she's still a better prospect than me. So shall I just wait it out? Or you think you're going to leave me for her, is that it?'

She moved towards him, stumbling slightly.

'Millie, please, you've had too much to drink. Let's discuss this in the morning.'

He didn't want to do it like this, not when she was drunk. There was a side to drunk Camille that James neither liked nor trusted. She could be quick-tongued and cruel, especially where Evie was involved.

'There's nothing to discuss. You aren't leaving, James, there's no way you can.'

'You can move on, you can find someone who loves you the way I love Evie.'

Camille laughed. 'Look at you! Look at you, all pathetic because you think you're in love. You say you've never loved me like you love *her* but I bet you've never hated anyone as much as I hate the pair of you. I should have told you this years ago but I thought she was going to stay away, after I told her I knew the truth about what she did to your father. But that girl's like a bad smell, just when you think you've got rid of it there it is again.'

'I think you should go to bed. You're too drunk to know what you're saying and—'

'Know what I'm saying?'

She leaned in so close that her face was inches from his. He could smell the expensive perfume he had bought her as a birthday gift, mingled with the smell of white wine. Far too much of it. She swayed slightly in front of him.

'I'm saying what should have been said years ago,' she spat. 'You and Evelyn Rousseau won't ever be together and *I know why.*'

79

Evie

The call came in the middle of the night. Evie was to return to Wareham – her mother was ill and this time it was serious. Richard had dropped everything to come with her, despite her father's apathy towards him on the few occasions they had met. Evie could tell he had wanted more for his only daughter, but if James hadn't been good enough, who on earth would be?

The room already smelt like death when she walked in. Even though her mother was still alive, breathing noisily through her mouth, as though every breath was a struggle; she sucked in air as though it was heroin.

Evie could hardly bear to look at her, her beautiful young mother now aged twenty years in just a few months. Her skin was sallow and paper-thin; there was barely any flesh underneath and the effect was of looking at a living, breathing skeleton. Monique's teeth were black and her mouth hung open, her glassy eyes barely seeing her daughter.

'Oh Mama,' Evie breathed, sitting in the chair next to the bed and taking her mother's hand in her own. It was cold and had no weight to it, like the hand of a child.

It hurt more than she could express to see her mother this

way. She had been ill before, Evie's whole life in fact, but her bouts of depression had kept her away from the family, locking herself in her room for days on end, refusing to see anyone except Yasmin; or gripped by mania, dressing in elaborate cocktail outfits for breakfast and calling everyone 'daaarling'.

It had even been funny when Evie was very young, she would hide her giggles behind her hand while Mama seized Papa's hand at the dinner table and tried to make him dance with her. If he caught her laughing he would look at her sternly, then give her a secret smile – he must have known how funny they looked, waltzing around the dining room with no music save for that in Mama's head, but Mama was ill and you weren't allowed to laugh when people were ill. And now laughter was the furthest thing from Evie's mind and she thought she would give anything to go back to the times when she would watch her mother and father dance to imagined music.

'I brought you some audiobooks,' Evie said, pulling CDs from a plastic bag and stacking them by the bed. 'The nurse can put them in your CD player for you.'

Her mother squeezed her hand and Evie smiled.

'I knew you'd like that. Do you remember, Mama, when you used to read to me? Stories about heroic girls who were stronger than all of the boys around them. I used to think it so strange, that you loved these stories about girls who didn't need any help from boys so much when it was clear that all you wanted in life was for Papa to love you and only you,' she lowered her voice, even though she was certain that none of the nurses were listening. 'But now I understand. You can still be a strong woman, even if you crave the love of a man above all else. I understand, Mama, because I am in love.'

Her mother turned her head slowly to look at her, and the corners of her mouth attempted a smile.

'Richard,' she said, even that one word a struggle in her breathlessness.

Evie shook her head. She did love her fiancé. Only she loved him in the way she might have loved a brother, if she'd ever had one, in the same way she had loved Rebecca, only probably less still than that. But he had made her feel safe, like he would never abandon her, or cheat on her. Like she would always be his number one, never his bit on the side, never his *mistress*. She had thought she would marry him, and be perfectly happy, have a family, a nice house. Maybe she would own her own gallery one day, just like she'd always dreamed.

Then James had agreed to leave Camille. They had tried to stay away from one another and that hadn't worked. And now she was having his baby, and the truth wouldn't change that.

'No, Mama,' Evie whispered. 'It's not Richard. It's James, James is the man I love. I always have. And now he's going to ask Camille for a divorce and we are going to be together. There are a few things to sort out but he loves me and he always has.'

She watched her mother's face intensely, waiting for her to smile, to tell her how delighted she was, even if it wasn't in so many words. And when she did Evie would tell her about the baby. Instead, her mother's face contorted into a frown, her brow bone, now completely hairless, furrowing.

'James?' the word came out a croak. 'James?'

'Yes, James. James Addlington. Do you remember him?'

Her mother's fingers tightened on the thin sheets that were pulled up around her.

'Your father,' she whispered. 'Your father.'

'I know, Papa never liked James. Tell me why, Mama. Tell me the reason why Dominic hated James' father so much.'

Evie's mother was in a state of full agitation now. She

swiped her hands in front of her face as though fighting imaginary bugs and her breathing was ragged and even more laboured than before.

'Mama!' Evie gasped. 'Nurse! Nurse!'

She grabbed for the button beside the bed to call for help. Was this it? Was her mother dying? Evie had known this moment was coming but still she felt completely unprepared. Before the nurse could arrive her mother reached out and clasped Evie's wrist in her ice-cold bony fingers.

'Your father,' she gulped in air as the door swung open and a nurse ran to her bedside. As the carer filled a syringe with morphine and eased her back onto the pillow, Monique made one last lunge for her daughter and finally managed to speak.

Now

80

Rebecca

I wander through the park, my fingers clasped around a cup of coffee to keep them warm. The day is mild but the wind is biting, not enough though to keep the hordes of children from the swings and climbing frames. Groups of mothers huddle together, thumbing through their phones and trying to look delighted as their offspring fly down the slide for the sixteenth time. I stand and watch as a young girl commands the attention of a group of six-year-olds gathered around a pair of trampolines set into the floor. She is bouncing enthusiastically, apparently unaware of the commotion her scissor kicks and forward flips are causing. Her build is slight, her jet-black hair pulled into a pair of perfect French plaits that knock against each other as she bounces.

On the second trampoline another girl bounces up and down, watching the first girl from the corner of her eye. She is heavier, although only slightly, her dishwater blonde hair pulled carelessly into a ponytail. There seems nothing dislike-able about her, and yet not one of the children are watching her, their attention commanded by the smaller, prettier, more watchable girl. *Look at her*, I feel like demanding. *Just because she's not showing off, putting herself on display, doesn't mean she's not worth watching.*

Just as I'm about to turn and walk away, the first girl bounces off the trampoline and goes over to the second girl. She grasps her hand and pulls her off and the girl looks as though the sun has just been turned on. Adulation is written on her plain, unassuming face and the pair of them walk off together, ignoring the crowd of children who groan and shout for more. *More jumps*, they shout, but they may as well be saying, *Give us more of you. We don't know why but we want to watch you, we love you.* But this girl knows that one true friend is worth more than all of those spectators put together, and that what she has done is to cement that girl's utter devotion for as long as she wants it.

It makes me think of another duo, in another time, hand in hand as they walked through another park, one of them talking about her mother, a beautiful woman who loved her father with the fire of a thousand suns, but also a troubled woman who had her own demons to extinguish.

'It never helped,' Evie said to me, her eyes dark, 'that he wasn't entirely discreet about his "extra-marital interests". But then,' she said with a sigh. 'Mama is really so difficult to live with sometimes. She's so impulsive, and nothing she seems to do makes any sense. It's like her brain is wired differently to you and me – things she sees as perfectly reasonable that a normal person would consider absolutely bonkers.'

She opened her mouth as though she was about to elaborate and thought better of it.

'Like what?' I pushed. I remember the warmth of that day, the sunlight pressing down on us, smothering us. It was the height of summer in London and the too high buildings and streets gave off a whiff of garbage every time the slightest breeze got up. Today, to combat the smell and the heat rising from the pavements, Evie had dragged me to Hyde Park where she now lay draped along the Princess Diana Memorial Fountain, her feet dangling in the water.

'Nothing,' she replied, closing the conversation. Her camera, as always, was attached to her hand, and she rolled over onto her front and began to shoot the others at the memorial. 'Tell me about your family again.'

Sometimes Evie would tell me stories of her growing up, the kinds of parties her parents would throw and the exquisite beauty and grace of the people who attended them. But other times she would listen rapt to my stories of how I'd grown up, my parents' council house full of children – not just my two brothers and one sister (I was the youngest by nine years, clearly an accident and resented by every last one of them) but all their friends, girlfriends and boyfriends. Saturday mornings in front of *Live & Kicking* where we would all fight over the comfy bean-bag so much that Mum put an egg timer on the side and rotated us every three minutes – until it got to my turn and she forgot to kick me off. Begging my sister to let me borrow her make-up, or play with her and her cool friends while they pretended to record talk shows and put on fashion parades. It was just boring everyday life for me, but for Evelyn Rousseau of the big house and the nursemaid and the glitzy parties and ten-thousand-pound-a-year schooling, my overcrowded, underfunded lifestyle was like a fairy tale.

'What I would have given for people,' she groaned once, all of a sudden sounding very French. For the most part her accent had blended in so seamlessly with ours that it became barely noticeable; so much so that I found it hard to believe she had ever lived in another country. But every now and then a word or two would make her sound uncannily like her father and remind me that she hadn't just been conjured into existence the day I met her. 'Someone to talk to, to argue with. To share my secrets and fears. You don't know how lucky you've been, Becky.'

Which was probably why, the entire time I knew her, Evie was surrounded by people. Evenings were spent at poetry readings in trendy cafés, or in a tiny room of a sweeping Victorian house, where dozens of students seemed to inhabit five bedrooms. Always the smell of incense or something stronger in the air, but more noticeably, always the incessant noise, chatter, music. The nights we spent alone, just the two of us, would be to a background of the radio or at the cinema, alone but still surrounded. Now I was just alone. Tears pricking at the edges of my eyes, I blink them away to see that the girls have gone and I wonder if their future holds the same as ours.

81

Rebecca

We'd been at a house party the night I got confirmation of what people really thought of me, and of Evie. She and Richard had been together less than a month and we'd only gone to the party because it was Philippa's birthday. Ever since the incident with the pills Evie had tried her best to stay sober, and Richard was hardly the party-going type anyway, so we'd fallen into a natural rhythm of evenings on the sofa watching a film, or one or another of us cramming for a final exam. But Pippa had begged Evie to go, and naturally we had gone with her.

It was funny how, in just a couple of short years, the lifestyle I'd thought of as wildly exotic and bohemian, lunging from one party to another, smoking weed and sleeping on bare floorboards, now seemed repellent to me. Although Evie didn't seem to mind reverting to her old ways and had been debating the elections with a group of politics students with a vigour that had been conspicuously absent of late.

I was in the en-suite of the master bedroom when I heard the girls come in. Preparing to give up my refuge so they could all cram in and hold each other's hair back in turn, I froze when I heard Evie's name.

'I see Evie came. Pips didn't know if she was going to, she said she's basically dropped everyone in the last few months.' There was a sound as if they were undressing – perhaps I was in one of their bathrooms.

'Well,' a second voice said. Who are they? 'I'm not surprised. Boring Becky had to rub off on her sooner or later. And what's with that new boyfriend? He looks like an extra from the *IT Crowd*.'

There was an explosion of giggles as my face burned red. Evie would have burst out of the toilet at this moment, she'd have loved watching them squirm as they backtracked and wondered how much she'd heard, but I stayed rooted to the spot.

'You're such a bitch,' a third voice said, one that was vaguely familiar but I still couldn't name. 'I thought he seemed nice.'

'Oh well, if he's *nice*, then he's perfect for Evie, isn't he?' said the second girl. 'I mean, don't you just picture her with someone *nice*, all settled down in a pinny with four *nice* kids? Not. She'll ditch him for someone more exciting – you wait and see. People like Evie don't stick with IT losers for long.'

'I think Becky will get with him instead.' The third voice spoke again. 'You know, I heard they had a thing before he fell head over heels for E. And they're much better suited.'

I couldn't have been more humiliated at that moment if I'd been forced to walk down the stairs naked with 'SECOND BEST' scrawled on my tits. So everyone knew? Were they all whispering when they saw us, about how, obviously, given the choice, he chose her? About how insecure and desperate for her friendship I must have been to step aside so easily? Which I had, hadn't I? I'd known that if it came to it there would be no contest, I hadn't even wanted one. I'd finished with Richard before he could dump me for my best friend – I'd taken the classic coward's way out because

I'd known that I'd never win. These witches were right – I was pathetic.

'When all's said and done, Evie will get what she wants in the end. Girls like her always do,' the first girl to speak announced, and I breathed out as I heard the door open and close again and the room fall into silence.

When all's said and done, Evie will get what she wants in the end.

Hadn't she already? What more could she want?

82

Rebecca

She's everywhere I look now, wherever I go. When I move around the house – her house – I sense her in every shadow, around every corner, behind every door. I see her in my dreams most nights, a ghostly spectre that won't let me rest, besieging me to confess. But what good is that now? Evie is gone, dead, and confessing my part in her 'suicide' won't change that. I tell her this, in my sleep when she comes to me, but she says nothing – just looks at me in that way she has, that way that makes you feel as though she is inside your thoughts.

Richard is starting to worry about me now, but it makes a change from him thinking about her. I'm spending more and more time at the house, and less of our time together is spent worrying about Evie, trying to uncover her past or find out why she did this to him. I think he's coming to the kind of acceptance that I hoped he would – it doesn't matter why she betrayed him, only that she did. Detective Michelle called him – six weeks after the wedding night – to tell him that they could find no evidence of foul play and the case was being closed. There would be an inquest on the following Wednesday where he should prepare himself for a verdict of suicide.

That was that then. I should feel relieved but somehow I feel empty.

I'm making us lunch in the kitchen, lost in the actions of chopping tomatoes, washing lettuce leaves, bright sunlight streaming through onto the worktop, when I hear a vibration from my phone in the front room. Popping through to grab it I realise that Richard is on the front doorstep talking to someone. Funny, I didn't hear the door. Pausing to listen, I recognise the impatient tones of his brother, Martin. Urgh, what's he doing here? Funnily enough, his next question is exactly that – about me.

'Is she here again? Is that why you're keeping me on the doorstep? Bloody hell, Richard, that girl is like a bad smell, you need to get rid of her.'

How fucking dare he. I knew he never liked me, he was a FOE (fan of Evie) and was often sharp to the point of rude when we all socialised together.

'Don't be so mean. Becky has been a godsend these past few weeks – I don't know how I'd have held it together without her.'

I feel a rush of warmth towards Richard – so he does appreciate all I've done for him. I know at first he wished it had been me on that cliff instead of his wife, but I also knew that, given time, he'd realise that what he needed in his life was solid dependability. Someone who might be less glamorous than Evie White but ultimately less selfish and unpredictable. That was the only reason I'd agreed to all this, agreed to losing Evie.

'Besides,' I hear him continue. 'I'm worried about her. She's held it together so long for me that I think she might be having a delayed reaction to Evie's death. She's acting strange, talking in her sleep and stuff.'

'You're *sleeping* with her?' I imagine Martin all red and blustery, in his Ralph Lauren polo shirt and straight-leg jeans that he wore so often I'd sometimes wondered if he just owned a wardrobe full of the same clothes.

'No, of course not,' Richard replies a little too quickly. 'She stays over sometimes, if we've had a drink. On the sofa. God, Martin – what kind of person do you think I am?'

'I think you're lonely, and vulnerable, and to be honest, Rich, I just don't trust her. She was always hanging around you and Evie, always sat between you or diverting one of your attention away from the other. God knows how you ever had enough time alone to propose. And don't think I don't know who she is.'

'What do you mean, who she is?'

Yeah, Martin, what do you mean?

'You think I don't remember, but I do. Before you fell head over heels for Eves you called me talking about a girl you'd met. Really nice, you said. The kind of person you can just chat to for hours. Rebecca, her name was. It's the same girl – isn't it?'

I don't hear Richard's reply but I can picture him nodding solemnly and I know he's confirmed Martin's suspicions when I hear his brother saying, 'I knew it! And here she is, a couple of months after Evie. . . after she's gone, practically living in your house. It's weird, mate.'

That's it. I'm not going to stand here while he puts doubt in Richard's mind and makes him scared to open up to me for fear that other people will feel the same as this cynical piece of shit. I'll do the only thing I can do, go on the charm offensive. I'll put in the work to get Martin onside. I can't lose Richard the way I have Evie. But his next words floor me.

'Don't be ridiculous, Martin. You know that Evie is my absolute world. I'll never stop loving her, and there's no way anything will ever happen between Becky and me. Not while there's still a chance that Evie might walk through that door.

294

She's my wife and nothing that has happened at the wedding or since will change that.'

So there it is. Until Evie's body is found there is no chance of Richard and I ever moving forward. We will stay trapped in this limbo, living with her ghost. Unless I can convince Richard that his wife isn't worth waiting for, that she didn't love him – the way only I know she didn't. It's a betrayal, I promised her I'd look after him and never let him find out the truth, but it's for the best, otherwise how will he ever move on?

There is another man, one who knows everything about the extent of Evie's betrayal. It is time Richard found out about James.

83

Rebecca

I drop some bits into the office and on my way back I stop in at the EE shop and buy a pay as you go SIM card. Back in my car, I shove the SIM card into my phone and tap out a text message to my own number.

You should speak to James Addlington.

That's enough for now. When I show Richard he recognises the name immediately.

'Wasn't he killed in the fire? The one Evie. . .'

'He had a son,' I interrupt. 'Also called James. It might mean him.'

'Right,' Richard nods. 'Is this the same number as before? The one Camille was texting you from?'

'Yes,' I lie. 'She's his wife. Weird. Shall I delete it?'

'But why would she be saying we should speak to him? Does she think he knows something about why she. . .' even after over two months he can't say the words. 'Or maybe he knows who she was arguing with.'

'Maybe he is who she was arguing with,' I suggest, trying not to speak slowly as if talking to a child.

Richard frowns. 'Can you get me his address?'

84

Rebecca

The door opens and before us stands the man I've heard so much about, the man who stole Evie's heart at nine years old and never gave it back. I'd thought Richard looked in a bad way, but finding James Addlington is a hell of a shock. Compared to this guy, Richard looks like he's spent the last few weeks on an all-inclusive holiday. *Oh Evie, what a wicked web we weave.*

The photographs of James I'd seen had shown a confident-looking man adorned in razor-sharp suits, looking more like a Calvin Klein model than a businessman. When I remarked that he looked like he should have been on *Made in Chelsea* Richard muttered something disparaging about being too busy spending his father's money. Already I could sense he was not a fan. And why would he be? From what he was about to learn, this was the man who had held Evie's affections for over a decade and was most likely to be the last person to have seen her alive, the man she was arguing with on the clifftop. The only one who knew the full story. I was curious to know myself how much Evie had told him. Did he know the whole plan? Was I walking into the lion's den? At this point I was confident that I could handle what was coming. At this point I thought myself invincible.

Pride comes before a fall.

'I wondered how long it would be,' James says, standing aside to let us pass through.

'You were expecting us?' I ask, shooting a glance at Richard. His expression is blank, unreadable. How must this feel for him, coming face to face with a man he had never even known he was in competition with? At least I had known about my competitor, I'd had a fighting chance.

'No,' he replies, following us through into the apartment. It is a thing of beauty: wide open space, sheer glass front, white leather sofas that gleam in the sun and a long sleek glass coffee table, completely bare and pristine. He may not have been taking care of himself but he – or someone – is taking care of his home at least. There isn't a speck of dust or a cushion out of place. 'I was expecting Dominic, but he's been nowhere to be seen. I assume he sent you instead?'

Richard and I walk over to the sofa, expecting to be invited to sit down. Instead James shakes his head.

'Not here,' he said. 'I can't. . . I haven't. . . Come through here.'

We follow him again, through a corridor and into another room, smaller, darker, and suddenly things make sense.

This room is no immaculate haven. As soon as we are inside the stench of body odour and old food is overpowering. A bowl of half-eaten soup perches precariously on the flat arm of a grey sofa; some of the soup has dribbled down the side of the bowl and pooled around its base. When James moves the bowl onto the table he doesn't even seem to notice.

'Have you been sleeping in here?' I nod towards the pile of blankets and pillows that lie strewn on the floor. 'Three properties in this country alone and you're living in a room not much bigger than a prison cell?'

James raises an eyebrow. His face is devoid of the tan we

have seen in the pictures, so pale that his features barely stand out at all – he reminds me of Munch's *Scream* face. His hair is unbrushed and he's wearing a light grey T-shirt and jogging bottoms, stained with dark grey patches. He smells of stale tobacco and old man.

'You've done your research.' He gestures at the sofa and the single chair. Richard sits instantly in the chair, leaving me with the only other option, the sofa next to James. He must sense my hesitation because he pulls up a box and drags one of the blankets over it, sits down on that. I thank him silently. The smell in here is fading as I become accustomed to it, but I'm not sure I can become as nose-blind to the smell of him.

'What did you mean about Dominic sending us?' Richard asks. 'Why would he send us here?'

'I wouldn't have expected him to,' James replies, picking up a can of Coke from a pack on the floor and offering us each one. 'But here you are. Maybe I should have, Dominic was never one to do his own dirty work.'

'We're here because *my wife*,' Richard spits the words and James visibly flinches, 'threw herself off a cliff because she was being blackmailed by *your wife*. And I want to know why.'

I go to say something, to try and calm him down, stop him being so angry and combative before James throws us both out, but the fact is he's got every right to be angry and I've got no right to stop him. Here is this man, the man for whom Evie gave her life, even though Richard doesn't quite know it yet.

85

Rebecca

He tells us everything. Some things I know, and some I don't. How they met, how their fathers conspired to keep them apart – the only thing they could agree on, according to James. The letter his father forged for Evie to 'dump' him, the baby that Evie thought was unwanted, about the party, and the night that Evie was responsible for the death of his father.

'The last time I spoke to her she said she'd found a way for us to leave the past behind us. Camille had been blackmailing her about the fire and the police had been to see her. I said we could just go somewhere people wouldn't find us but she said she'd thought it through – that the only way to truly be free was if everyone thought she was dead.'

'So you paid someone to say they'd seen her jump.' I saw hope shine in Richard's eyes and for the first time I look at him and feel disgust. Doesn't it matter to him – any of what James has just told him? His wife betrayed him, lied to him about a new job, slept with another man, and still he would welcome her home with open arms. 'She's still alive, isn't she?'

'No,' James whispered. 'No, Richard, I'm sorry. I wish she

300

had paid them – that would have been easier, safer. As far as I knew she was only going to pretend to jump from the cliff and disappear for a while. The first time I realised she was actually going to jump was when I followed her that night.'

Richard frowned. 'She thought she would survive that?' he shakes his head. 'No, she was reckless and impulsive but she wasn't stupid.'

James frowns. 'She knew she could survive it. She was the strongest swimmer I've ever seen. Her parents had a swimming pool and when her mother was ill and her father was away and she couldn't stand being in the house she would swim lengths until late into the night. Once I snuck round to see her. I'd waited until I knew Dominic was away on business and her mother would never answer the door. Yasmin, their housekeeper, she had a soft spot for me and she would sneak me into the house and keep watch until Monsieur Rousseau was asleep so I could slip out. But this time when I went to the door Yasmin told me Evie wasn't there. She took me by the arm and led me to the pool where Evie was swimming lap after lap, touching the side and kicking off again. 'How long has she been doing that?' I asked, because it was late, nine pm at least. 'Four hours,' Yasmin replied. 'Madame Rousseau had one of her outbursts this afternoon.' When I pulled her out she was wrinkled as a prune and her arms and legs were shaking. She had no idea she had been in there that long – she asked me why it was so dark at seven at night.'

James gets to his feet and leaves the room. When he returns he is clutching a large storage box.

'Ah! Here,' he pulls out a small black book, six-by-four photograph size with a tatty, worn cover. When he flicks it open I can see that it's filled with old photographs, some faded and ripped around the edges, hastily shoved in and well thumbed. James finds the photograph he was looking for and passes it to Richard. I lean over his shoulder for a look.

It's her, a close-up of Evie. Except she doesn't look like our Evie, she looks different. Younger, yes, but something else. *Free.* Even though I'd been expecting it from the moment James had pulled out the photo album, seeing her there, alive and smiling – no, *beaming* – is like a punch in the stomach. This is the Evie I loved.

What have we done?

She is in the sea, holding onto the edge of a boat, at the foot of some cliffs, craggy rocks in the background, her smile wild and triumphant.

'This wasn't the first time she jumped from a cliff in front of me,' James says. 'She showed me up a treat in front of my mates, then pretended she was drowning so I'd jump in and save her. She had no fear back then.' He smiles at the memory. 'This one time,' he holds up the photo, 'when she was sixteen she didn't even tell me she was going to do it – told me to take the boat out and she'd meet me there. Next thing I heard a voice shout my name. I looked up and saw her dropping through the air like a stone. I remember screaming as she landed, thinking of all the ways I was going to tell Dominic that he was right, I hadn't managed to protect his daughter, I'd let her kill herself right under my fucking nose! I searched the sea where she'd broken the surface and was taking off my jacket to jump in when she popped up like a mermaid, gasping for breath but the most elated I'd ever seen her. The look on her face – it was phenomenal. She clung onto the side of the boat to recover, and before I could yell at her I had to take that,' he gestures to the photo. 'I had to capture it before I broke her good mood – which I did. I ripped into her, telling her how stupid and reckless and selfish she was, how she hadn't killed herself was a miracle, blah blah blah. When I was finished she just smiled. Pulled herself into the boat on arms that should have been jelly and told me that she'd been learning to cliff-dive properly since she was twelve and I shouldn't worry about her.'

'You're saying she could easily jump from that cliff, but why bother? If Evie wanted to be with you that badly why not just leave me?' Richard asks. 'Why this ridiculous charade?'

'Evie's mother died,' James replies. 'And she told Evie the one reason we couldn't be together. The reason our parents had forbidden us from seeing one another and insisted Evie get rid of our child. James Addlington Sr – my father – was Evie's father. Evie was my half-sister. And Camille knew.'

86

Rebecca

Richard is broken, and I need to get him home, but before we go we both need him to hear what happened next. Why he has to move on, why James is sitting here now talking to us instead of starting a new life abroad with his half-sister and their bastard child. Because until we both hear the words none of us will ever be sure. I know, I know Evie is gone forever, because there is something else I know. That, although Evie had planned the spot she would jump from to the last inch, on the night she jumped, the rock she had been using to mark her safe spot had been moved. I know this, and yet I need to hear James say the words. Richard is practically catatonic and we both need this to be over.

'If Evie jumped off that cliff expecting to live,' I say. 'And her body hasn't been found. . . if she's done it before she might be. . .'

'She's not alive,' James says. He blinks his eyes as though to push away tears. 'I know she's dead.'

Thank God for that.

The night of the wedding

87

Rebecca

I checked the time again and glanced around to see where my best friend was. We locked eyes across the grass and she gave a small nod. *Yes*, the nod said, *now is the time*.

She took a surreptitious look around, found where her new husband was standing surrounded by friends and family, unable to wipe the huge grin from his face. Richard looked so happy and I watched as Evie's expression fell, panic seizing me when I saw the hesitation cross her beautiful face. She was wondering if she should go through with the plan, she was having second thoughts. Not about her safety, which was what she should have been concerned with – no, Evie was too arrogant and sure of herself to imagine that anything might go wrong with the dangerous and near impossible plan I'd concocted – but about leaving the man who had dedicated the last few years to making her happy and breaking his heart. In that moment I almost became convinced that she was finally going to think of someone other than herself and abort the plan completely.

My face flushed red and my heart pounded a beat in my chest. She couldn't change her mind now! I began to rise from my seat, ready to go and convince her she was doing the right thing, but it turned out I needn't have worried. I saw her tear her eyes from her husband and give herself a small nod, yes, she was back to thinking of herself again.

I can't tell you the rush of satisfaction it gave me to watch her slip away from the party towards those cliffs. I know that probably makes me sound like a monster, but if I am it is only because that is what she made me. The years of living in her shadow I could have coped with – I gladly gave up Steve, I dedicated my every waking moment just to making her happy. We could have been best friends forever, I was the most loyal and loving friend she could ever have asked for – until she took Richard from me.

Even that I might have coped with, if she'd genuinely loved him. I wanted them both to be happy, and if that meant being together I would have found a way to be happy for them. But she never wanted Richard, he was a distraction, an easy option to heal her fractured soul. She was prepared to cheat on him, lie to him about the baby – she was going to ruin his life, either by forcing him to live a lie or by breaking his heart when she eventually grew bored of her loveless marriage and returned to her lover. I couldn't allow it to happen.

And so I watched her go without a doubt in my heart. So you can imagine the fear that gripped me when I saw who was following her out of the party, when I realised she had betrayed her promise and told someone else about our plan. And if James managed to convince her not to go through with it then everything was ruined.

88

Rebecca

Let me tell you about the first time I heard about the fire that killed James Addlington Sr.

To say my best friend had changed in the last six years was an understatement, and although now I know that the change in her was ignited by the fire that happened near the end of our first year at uni, at the time it had seemed natural progression. We grew up, we settled down, stopped the partying and concentrated on our degrees. The first year had been pass/fail but the second and third years actually counted towards our final grades. The idea that Freshers was a party year and then we would all knuckle down a bit more wasn't a new one – it was seen all over the university. Now though, I know that it was more than that for Evie. The fire inside her had begun to flicker and die away, which I suppose is what happens when you believe you have taken a man's life. How could her work be a commentary on society, how could she ask people to see through her eyes when she was a liar, a fraud, a murderer? The rest of her life would be spent trying to come to terms with the person she was versus the person she wanted to be.

I don't know whether she even remembered the night she

told me about what she'd done. Richard had been at a conference where he was to be the main speaker, and I was staying at the house so that we could drink and not worry about how I was getting back. The fire-pit in the back patio was roaring – I can remember wanting to suggest so badly that we let it die down a little, that Evie not lean so close to drop in little bits of wood that the flames almost licked the ends of her honey blonde hair, but as usual I said nothing, just pulled the blanket further around me and watched her.

She looked as beautiful as ever in the firelight, flame and shadow flickering around her like a Shakespearean fury. Fire burn and cauldron bubble. We drank wine until it tasted like juice, talked about current affairs, things we'd seen on the news – there was enough going on in the political world to keep us going for at least until the wine ran out. I'd been telling her about my sister's friend, whose husband had been accused of rape, when she said it.

'Becky, imagine if you found out one thing about someone you loved, one thing that redefined everything you knew about them. Could you forgive them?'

It might seem like an innocuous question, given the subject we were discussing, but if you could have seen the look in her eyes – as though my answer meant more than just a throwaway 'What would you do?' question.

'It depends what they'd done – if I found out my husband had raped someone? No, I couldn't forgive that, it would make them a person I couldn't dream of loving or trusting ever again. There's no possible excuse that could make that right.'

We were sitting on a wooden bench, the fire-pit our only light now, both wrapped in thick fleecy blankets, our feet up facing one another.

Evie nodded thoughtfully. 'What about murder?'

I started to say no, I could never forgive someone who

had murdered another person, but it was clear she didn't want an off-the-cuff response – she wanted me to think about the question.

'Murder's different,' I concluded, and seeing that this answer pleased her I continued. 'Because there are so many different situations where a person might kill another person. There's self-defence. . .' I leaned over and filled up our glasses, not too drunk to notice the hungry look in Evie's eyes. 'There's accidental – I mean, if my husband told me he'd been responsible for a car crash that killed someone it's a bit different than raping a woman, or killing someone because he's a psychopath. It's all about the context.'

'So an accident – that would be okay? What if they were a bad person anyway? What if they had done something awful – or they might do something bad in the future? Maybe you've done the world a favour.'

'Well, an accident is hardly okay, but maybe more acceptable. I mean, if you'd just been honest, and done your time. . . but you can't just go ahead and kill someone for being a bad person – otherwise the world's population would die out overnight. Although isn't that what God was doing? With that boat?'

Evie frowned. 'The Ark?'

'That's it!' I grinned. 'The Ark. But He's different, I think. I think He's allowed to make those kind of decisions. And thirdly – you can't kill someone because. . .'

'Because he might hurt someone in the future,' Evie murmured, but she suddenly looked like she didn't want to be part of this conversation any more.

'Like *Minority Report*,' I nodded. 'Yeah, but look what happened there because Tom Cruise changed his future and so, wait, actually – did he?' I shook my head. 'I can't remember but I'm sure the point was that you can't freeze someone for something they might do in case they don't do it. Right?'

'Right,' Evie muttered. She unfolded herself from the blanket and stood up, stumbling slightly.

'Whoa,' I put out my hand to steady her. 'Watch the fire.'

'I think I'm going to go to bed,' she said, pushing her hair from her face. 'I feel a bit ill.'

'Are you okay?' I asked, ever concerned. 'I'll get you some water, bring it in to you.'

'Thanks.'

When I took the water in to her Evie was already in bed, half asleep. As I placed the glass quietly on her bedside table she stirred, opened her eyes slightly and looked at me.

'I am sorry, you know. If that makes a difference,' her words were slurry and I wondered if she was still half dreaming. Did she mean sorry for Richard? Was this her finally acknowledging that she knew about my feelings for him? After all these years the last thing I wanted to do was to open that Pandora's box.

'It's okay, shhhh, go to sleep,' I pulled the covers tighter over her.

'I just wish I could tell them,' she said, more urgent this time. 'Tell his family I'm sorry. I didn't mean to kill him. If I could just tell James. . .'

'What?'

Evie's eyes were closed again now, she was drifting off. She was dreaming, obviously, the wine and the late hour – a silly dream.

'James Addlington,' she muttered, and then one last thing before she fell silent. 'His father. I loved him, you know? And I killed his father, but I'm sorry, I promise.'

89

Rebecca

Unable to sleep, I'd been haunted by Evie's words. Suddenly the conversation we'd had in the back garden took on a whole new meaning to me. Had we even been talking hypothetically? With the house swathed in darkness and Evie snoring gently, I'd gone back to the spare room and opened up my laptop, typed in the name 'James Addlington'.

James Addlington was the name of the owner of a multi-million-pound IT consultancy firm, which muddied the results a lot. When the initial search threw up LinkedIn and Facebook profiles, news articles and business reports for a man who was very much alive, I'd almost stopped straight away. What was I thinking? This James Addlington was a successful businessman and hadn't been murdered. Evie had obviously drunk too much and been in the middle of a vivid dream when I'd spoken to her – there was no way she had killed someone. Then I thought about the intensity in her face when she'd spoken about the reasons someone might kill another person and I'd added one more search – 'James Addlington fire'.

The results were the same as those I showed Richard, only that time I'd known what I was looking for and what I'd find. This time it took me much longer to piece together the details of the man killed in a house fire the night of his son's engagement party. I'd spent half of the night determining that the fire had taken place the weekend before Evie had made her now infamous suicide attempt, and that what she had said to me might not have been the ramblings of a drunken woman after all.

When morning came, after only a few hours of fitful sleep, I woke to hear Evie bumping around the kitchen. When she saw me standing in the doorway she started guiltily and I wondered how much she remembered, if anything, of what she'd said to me the night before.

'Sleep well?' I asked, scrutinising her reaction for any hint of a memory. She shook her head.

'Not really. I had the most horrible dreams – but I suppose that's what too much wine does to you. Gives you an over-active imagination.'

We'd spent breakfast in much the same way – both waiting to see if the other would mention the previous evening's conversation. Neither of us did. I'd seen enough from my research to tell me that Evie had got herself involved in something terrible, but not enough to figure out any specifics, such as why Evie had been at the engagement party of the man she'd told me she loved. Not for the first time, I began to wonder if I knew my best friend at all. The answer to that was still to come a few days later.

90

Rebecca

Did you ever love someone so much that you would have done anything to overlook their glaring flaws? That was me with Evie. Even when she and Richard got together I managed to tell myself that she had no idea that Richard was supposed to be mine, even though she must have known how strange it was to find a guy in my apartment – I'd never so much as mentioned any man other than my new boyfriend. But no, I'd given her the benefit of the doubt – she said she loved him and he was clearly smitten with her. It never occurred to me to confront her, to try and fight for my man. After all, what good would it have done? I like to think she'd have stood aside in a heartbeat but what kind of relationship would Richard and I have had, knowing he wanted her instead of me? So I was unselfish, I put two people's happiness ahead of my own.

I'd waited patiently for her to tell me about the fire at the Addlington residence. Even though a huge part of me was screaming to know what happened, I'd put it from my mind, told myself that if she had been involved she would have told me. It had been an accident, nothing more. I thought we told each other everything. I trusted that I was the one to have made a mistake. I was wrong.

When she came to me that day, her eyes puffy and red, I wondered if this was it. If this was when she told me about what had really happened the night of the fire. I folded her into my arms, took her over to the sofa and let her sob into my jumper sleeve. Eventually, when the sobs subsided, I held her away from me.

'What's happened?'

Evie pushed a balled fist into her eye to wipe away the tears.

'I'm pregnant.'

A baby? That was the last thing I was expecting to hear. I'd been expecting her to tell me about the fire that had killed a man but in that instant the fire was all but forgotten.

'But that's wonderful news,' I said. 'Why are you crying? Isn't Richard pleased? What did he say?'

'I haven't told him,' Evie sniffed. 'I can't. The baby. . . it's not his.'

Trying to explain the wave of emotions that hit me in that second is nearly impossible. She had the only man I'd really loved absolutely besotted with her, willing to do anything to make her happy, and she cared so little that she had got pregnant by someone else. How dare she treat him that way?

'Whose then?'

Evie shook her head. 'Some guy from back home. It doesn't matter. The point is, what am I going to do?'

'Do? Do you want to be with this guy?'

'I thought I did,' she said, her eyes welling up again. 'But that's not possible. There's too much. . . it's complicated.'

'You have to tell Richard.'

Evie looked shocked, her beautiful face knotted in a frown. It hadn't even occurred to her to tell him the truth. Of course it hadn't.

'Of course I can't tell him, Rebecca, are you completely

out of your mind? He'd never forgive me, and even if he did it would break his heart. No.'

She shook her head, her hands wringing. I saw that they were shaking, she desperately needed a drink and she couldn't have one now. That might have been the moment I really noticed how much of Evie's life had centred around being drunk to have fun.

'Well you can't get rid of it. . . you'd be devastated. You'd end up resenting Richard as completely as if it were his decision.'

'You're right,' she nodded, chewing on her lip. 'You're always right. I'm going to have to keep the baby. I couldn't do that. . .'

'So you're going to tell him?' I had a suspicion I knew what she was about to say, and the thought filled my stomach with lead.

'I could tell him it's his. We'll raise the baby as our own, and Richard will never have to know. He's going to be over the moon.'

91

Rebecca

He's going to be over the moon.
  Over the moon.

The words drifted around in my head all evening, alongside images of the two of them choosing baby names and putting up scan photos on Facebook, all the while Richard being completely in the dark about his happy family. How could this be happening? Could I let it happen? How could I stop it?

I could tell Richard, of course, but Evie was right, he'd be devastated and what if he stuck around to raise the baby as his anyway? All that would be achieved would be for me to be cast out of our little threesome – something they had probably been planning for a while anyway. I wouldn't be surprised if Evie had lied to me about the baby not being Richard's in the hopes I'd tell on her and she could pretend I was just trying to cause trouble. And if she wasn't lying, was she really expecting me to sit back and allow Richard to raise another man's child? Is that how little she thought of me, that I'd defend her actions, keep her secrets, no matter what?

If it was Richard's decision to break it off, then perhaps I could stay out of it, remain unscathed. I could even help with the baby once he had gone, it would be just the two of us again. Evie and Becky against the world.

But how?

That's when I thought of it, the great idea that led to where we are today. The fire. If I called the police anonymously to say Evie was involved, they would at least be obligated to look into the tip-off, wouldn't they? And if the police were involved Richard would have to take it seriously. It might be enough by itself to make him see sense, and while all the past secrets were coming out maybe she'd tell him the truth about the baby.

And if not I'd think of something else.

92

Rebecca

As it turned out, Richard didn't find out anything. She'd kept it all from him, not just the blackmail letters but the visit from the police – they had arrived while he was at football, which just demonstrates the difference in luck between Evie and I, doesn't it?

I watched her with him, wondering when she was going to tell him, waiting for the moment he announced he was going to be a father. And the more I watched her pretend to be normal, pretend to be in love with him, the more it ate away at me, gnawing at my conscience. I'd always thought of our relationship as an open book, a diary we shared of our hopes and fears, our visions for the future, our disappointments from the past. That was until I found out that Evie had rewritten huge chunks of it.

She hadn't even told me about the letters, or about the visit from the police, yet I knew she must be wondering where the next attack would come from. At this point I knew nothing of Camille, or who she thought was responsible for the letters. Did she suspect me at all?

She approached me one evening, coming to my flat rather than I to hers, which was unusual. I knew something was wrong the moment I saw her, she was jittery and flushed with anxiety. She picked at the skin around her thumbnail, causing angry red gouges in her skin.

'I'm going to tell him tonight,' she avoided looking directly at me. 'About the baby.'

'Oh.' That was it then. She'd decided to go ahead with the deception, and the police visit, the letters, none of them had worked. If I'd known more details of the affair perhaps I could have made sure Richard found out by himself, but I knew Evie was clever enough to cover her tracks. Hell, even I hadn't known until she'd confessed.

I don't even think I meant to say it. None of it was part of a grand plan, you have to understand that. It might look that way now, like I callously planned it all along, but at the time it seemed to sweep me away, like someone had left the tap running in my mind and my thoughts were drowning me, spilling from my mouth without warning.

'Are you going to tell him about the man you killed?'

If I'd been watching it on a movie I can imagine feeling a surge of triumph at this point, the point when the killer realises they are found out and their jaw slackens, the blood drains from their face. Instead I felt only the pounding of my own heart inside my chest, heat rising in my cheeks. I had no idea how this would end. Would she kill me now? Was my best friend such a cold-blooded killer that I had put myself in danger thinking I was so clever?

'What are you on about?' Her voice was shocked and indignant but her face didn't match the outrage. She remembered what she'd said that night, and now she knew I remembered it too.

'In the fire. The one you told me about, remember?'

Evie gave a fake little laugh that made me want to hit her. Still she was lying to me! After all I'd done for her, all the times I'd been there for her, she still couldn't be honest.

'Oh, you're talking about my drunken "confession",' she put fingers up for inverted commas. 'Of course, I should have explained the next morning but I was so embarrassed, then you didn't mention it and I thought. . .'

You thought you'd got away with it.

'What I'd meant to say, what I *thought* I'd said actually, until I woke up the next morning and replayed the conversation to myself, was that I felt responsible for the fire. Maybe if I'd been at the party I could have stopped it or—'

'Bollocks,' I said, and she jumped at my harsh tone. 'I know what you said, Evie. Perhaps you remember some of what you said but you clearly don't remember it all. You told me that you were at that party, and that you killed James Addlington. Did you start the fire? Was it on purpose because you were jealous of that woman – Camille? Your lover's fiancée?'

Evie's face was ashen. 'It wasn't me. I made a mistake but I didn't start the fire.'

'Then why the secrecy? If it wasn't you, you wouldn't be charged for it.'

She shrugged. 'Maybe, maybe not. I can't exactly ask our family solicitor for advice, can I? Maybe it's best if it does come out. I've felt guilty about it for years, maybe it's time I told the truth.'

'And have your baby in jail?' I said, and her eyes widened. Until then I didn't even realise I could be so cruel. Now though, I was on a roll. 'And this James, you're in love with him?'

Evie nodded. 'It sounds pathetic, I know, but I always have been,' she replied. 'But it's complicated. My father never approved of the two of us, our families hated each other. . .

'Never was there a tale of more woe,' I said sarcastically.

Evie gave a humourless smile. 'Someone else once said that to me. But it's all in the past now. We couldn't be together if we wanted to be.'

'Why not?'

If Evie was still in love with this James, if there was a way they could be together, Evie and her baby would be out of my life forever. And out of Richard's.

She told me everything then, or at least as close to everything as I know now. About locking James' father in his study, and Camille, who had seen her throw away the key, about James who, despite years of no contact whatso-ever, still managed to show up in her life and blow it to pieces once more, and about the last words her mother said to her, about James' father – her real father, the affair he'd had with her mother on a trip to England nine months before she was born and the reason she would throw herself off a cliff one month later. And that was how I got her to fake her death on the night of her wedding. That was how I killed my best friend.

93

Rebecca

When I found her the day of her mother's funeral, she was close to breaking. Her face was swollen and blotchy from crying and when she saw me she threw herself into my arms. I held her tight and let her cry. For a moment it was just the two of us, just as it had been before, and no one else mattered.

'I don't know what to do,' she sniffed, wiping her eyes on her sleeve. 'I can't stand carrying his baby and not being able to tell anyone, not even him.'

I stroked her hair, kissed her forehead.

'Are you sure it's his?' I whispered. She nodded.

'I'm pretty sure. I can't be certain, but the dates match the night we. . . What am I going to do? Camille is black-mailing me anyway. She must know about us. She called the police! And if she finds out James is my flesh and blood. . . She won't stop until I'm in prison or dead.'

'So let her think you're dead,' I said, in a moment of inspiration. And in that second I didn't think about the future about a life without her in it. 'Let them all think you're dead Then you and James can be together and without fear the police or papers or your father will ever find you. If you want a life, Evie, you have to die.'

Now

94

Rebecca

'How do you know?' I demand. James still hasn't said anything that can tie me to Evie's suicide but I need to be sure he doesn't know something I don't. 'Have you seen her body?'

'No,' he admits, 'but she's not here either, is she?'

'She was supposed to come to you,' Richard says. His fingers tighten on the photo book he's holding and I think for a moment it might crumple under his grip.

'Of course. What would be the point otherwise? She had it all arranged, she'd hidden some clothes and booked a hotel in a fake name, she would take a boat to shore and escape before the alarm had barely been raised. She would send me a text to tell me she was okay and then lie low for a couple of weeks, before making contact at a prearranged date and time, at which point I would do my own disappearing act. Mine didn't need to be so dramatic, she said, I've never jumped off a cliff in my life and there was very little chance of me learning now. All I needed to do was fold some clothes up neatly, leave my phone and shoes on a bridge somewhere in the night with a note telling my wife how sorry I was. No one would know there was any real connection between me and Evie after all these years.'

'Except your wife,' I say bluntly. *And me*. But he said *no one*. He doesn't know this was my idea, that he's relaying to me *my* plan. I don't know how the thought that Evie stayed loyal to me to the end makes me feel. She trusted me.

He nods.

'Yes, Camille knew we had been together, but after my "death" there would be no reason for her to make that public. It would just embarrass her. She would inherit everything except some money we'd both squirrelled away. Camille doesn't love me anyway, she loves the lifestyle I give her, the prestige. She could keep all that.'

'Evie didn't contact you.' Richard's quiet voice comes from the floor. James looks up, as though he's almost forgotten he's telling a story.

'No,' he says, his voice cracking. 'No, she never got in touch. I waited and waited for her to get in contact, to tell me she was okay. We weren't going to have much contact in those early days, in case Camille got wind of something, but she was supposed to send me a message from a pay as you go phone to confirm she was okay and then later details of where to meet her, disguised as a marketing email. At first I thought I had the date wrong, then perhaps that I was supposed to meet her somewhere and I'd forgotten where. I went to every place we'd ever visited together. But still, weeks after the fall and nothing. That's how I know she didn't survive. That's how I know she's dead. I'm so sorry, Richard, but she's not coming back.'

The night of the wedding

95

Evie

'What are you doing here, James?'

Her voice carried across the air and it stopped him in his tracks. He turned to face her and she was hit once again by just how beautiful he was. Even when his features were etched with pain.

'You know why I'm here, Evie. I came to ask you to reconsider.'

'The wedding? You're too late. It's done.' She was being deliberately obtuse – she knew he hadn't come here to stop her marrying Richard.

'Not the wedding. It's very nice, by the way,' he gestured to the hotel in the background, to the lawn where her guests were yet to miss her presence. 'And you look beautiful as ever. Your husband must be very proud.'

'He is,' Evie set her chin in defiance.

'He's a good man, Evie. He doesn't deserve this.'

Evie felt her frustration growing, but it was mingled with guilt. She knew Richard didn't deserve what she was about to do, but wasn't it better than the alternative?

'It's better this way,' she said softly. 'Richard will inherit everything now. If I hadn't married him he'd be left with nothing.'

'He'd have the truth. Don't you think he'd prefer that?'

'What, to know his wife was in love with someone else? What do you think? This way he will be sad for a while but his memories of our life together will be intact. He will get over me, in time he'll marry again. Maybe he'll settle down with Rebecca, like he should have done in the first place.'

James moved closer to her. 'Don't do it, Evie. There has to be another way.'

'There is no other way! Don't you see that by now? After all our fathers have done to keep us apart, you think Dominic would let us run away into the sunset now? And Camille? Do you think she would roll over and watch her husband walk away with his half-sister? No,' Evie shook her head. 'If they know that you and I have disappeared together they will never stop until they find us. And the press?' she gave a chuckle. 'The press would have a field day. Not only does one of the richest men in England desert his wife for his lover but his. . .' she stopped, unable to finish her sentence. 'And there's something else.'

'What?' James was thrown. 'What else can there be?'

'I'll tell you when I see you again,' she replied.

She couldn't tell him what else there was, or any more about what she had planned. She couldn't tell him about the people across the cliffs, or Becky, or the boat. It was better this way, better if he thought it was all real, if they all thought that. Evie put her hand on her stomach and knew that she'd been wrong all those years ago, when she'd made the vow never to love someone so much that it made her want to die. Because she would die for the child she was carrying. And that's exactly what she had to do.

Now

96

Rebecca

'I need to go back,' Richard grasps my arm as we reach the car. He looks as though he might fall over without my support and I pull him in close, wishing this could have been different for him. If only he could have grieved then moved on, like he was supposed to. Why did he have to start digging around?

'Why, did you forget something?' I turn to look back at the house. James has already closed the door behind us, retreated into his grief. I wonder if he feels better for telling the truth now, or worse. I think of him sitting in that tiny room, staring at the blank TV screen, watching his phone and waiting for Evie's call. A call that never came. At which point did he begin to panic? When she was a day late. . . two? How strange it must have been for him, to be waiting while we searched, while we mourned, and then for his grieving to begin weeks after the world had thought her dead.

'Not in there,' he looks at James' house in disgust. 'I need to go back to where she. . .' he doesn't finish his sentence. That spot – a beautiful place for weddings and picnics – will forever be, to us, *where she*. . . 'To the bottom.'

He believes every word, I can see that, and now he wants to see for himself. What does he think he will find? Her bag of clothes, abandoned and rotting, tucked into a crevice? I searched for them in the week we spent there after her death – kicking myself that I hadn't asked her where she'd put the bag. But if we find them then he has his proof, and maybe he can move on – with me. So I take his hand and agree to help him look.

The waves lap against the rocks, so calm and serene that I can barely imagine them taking the life of my best friend. Evie was far too alive for something this beautiful, this *ordinary*, to have robbed her of it. I can imagine her swimming in there now, her strong arms cutting powerfully through the water, pulling herself ashore, panting, exhausted but not beaten. Despite what James had said about knowing she had not survived the fall, it is standing here that I can feel her, now more than ever, alive.

'Look everywhere, for anything, anything at all.' Richard appears briefly over the rocks and then disappears again. Unlike me he can't feel her here, he can't even bring himself to look at the sea and will search the shore beyond. He isn't looking for Evie any more, he is looking for evidence of her death, and of her betrayal.

97

Rebecca

It is nearly a mile from the spot where Evie would have landed that I find it. It is smaller than I remember, maybe that's why I couldn't find it the first time I looked, or maybe I was so scared of being caught that I didn't look properly. A brown hessian knapsack inside a plastic carrier bag stuffed inside a hastily carved out hole and covered by a pile of rocks. This is the final confirmation I need: she never came back for it.

The brown jumper I'd chosen for her and a pair of denim jeggings, some socks folded inside. I lift them to my face and breathe in her scent – even after all this time in the rain-sodden earth they still retain her smell. A ziplock bag with a small wad of notes – these are the only things that Evie chose to take with her into her new life. There is one other thing – the only way I know this is not a decoy bag or a change of clothes left by a hitchhiker – and I know now that the owner isn't coming back for it. It too is wrapped in plastic to protect it from the elements, although it probably hasn't worked in years. Evie's first camera.

98

Rebecca

'Nothing,' Richard pants as he rounds back over the hill where I have been sitting, staring into the sea. 'I've walked over a mile, between us we've reached every rock and crevice on the entire coast and still, nothing. Do you think he was lying?'

'Maybe he was telling the truth,' I say quietly. I can't look him in the eye, maybe I won't ever again. 'Maybe she came back for it. Maybe someone else found it first and had no idea what it was.'

He grunts and sits down next to me. Together we look out across the deep blue water in silence.

'Would you want to know?' The crack in my voice makes Richard turn to me. 'Do you really want to know what happened to her? Or is it better if we can just keep going?'

I'll tell him about the bag, I have to if I want him to believe what James told him, which is, after all, mostly the truth. Evie had planned to survive the jump and start a new life in Paris, a life with her baby and the man she loved. What James hadn't mentioned was that she expected a boat to be waiting for her that night. A boat that she was certain to be there because it had been arranged by her best friend,

338

who she would never have believed would betray her – leave her in the freezing cold water with no way of getting ashore but to swim, in a wedding dress, in the darkness. Poor Evie. Poor, stupid Evie.

Eight months after the wedding

99

Richard

'Richard Bradley. I'm here to see—'

The nurse smiled kindly. She was thin and had too much skin for her face, it made her impossible to age. She had what Evie would call – would have called – 'resting bitch face', like she'd be more likely to give you a lecture for wasting NHS time before even taking your temperature. But when she smiled her face transformed and he could see why she was a nurse.

'Of course, Mr Bradley. Rebecca is doing fine now. Come with me.'

When she pulled the curtain back Rebecca was sitting with her feet on the hospital bed, her knees pulled up to her chin, arms wrapped around them protectively. She looked at him, her eyes brimming with confusion – he wondered for a moment if she even knew who he was, if she was expecting someone else. Was there anyone else in her life? Or was he her entire world now that Evie was gone?

'Richard,' she breathed sounding relieved. Had she thought he wouldn't come? She had given the nurses his name and phone number, she had asked them to call him here in the middle of the night.

'Becks, what happened to you? I get this call from the hospital saying I needed to come straight away because,' he lowered his voice. 'They said you were sleepwalking.'

'I don't remember. I, she. . . I followed her, she was there and I thought if I could catch her I could. . .'

The nurse placed a hand on Richard's shoulder. 'The paramedic who brought her in said she'd been sleepwalking, they thought. She was in the thinnest of T-shirts and some pyjama bottoms – looked frightened half to death. It was a taxi driver who called it in – didn't want to go near her in case she'd been attacked and lost it. When the paramedic got to her she started thrashing around, shouting and screaming. If she hadn't calmed down and gone with them willingly—'

'Thank you,' Richard moved towards the bed slowly, as though she might start screaming again at any moment.

'I'll leave you two to it. The doctor has said she's fine to go home whenever she's ready,' she gave Rebecca's shoulder a squeeze. 'Best of luck, Mrs Bradley.'

Richard cringed at the woman's mistake and glanced at Rebecca to see if she'd noticed but she was staring at her fingers so intently he wondered if she was willing them not to do something.

'The nurses asked me to bring you something to wear,' Richard reached into the bag and pulled out some jeans and an old jumper of Evie's. He wasn't even sure of the size difference between the two women but it was all he had access to in the middle of the night. 'I hope these are okay?'

Rebecca took them without comment and he turned his back so that she could change. He jumped at the feel of her hand on his shoulder and when he turned to face her again she was close enough to kiss. She'd lost weight, Evie's clothes seemed to swamp her and she looked so scared and. . . exhausted. Richard wrapped his arms around her and pulled her close, breathing in the scent of Evie's fabric conditioner that lingered after all this time on her jumper. Rebecca folded herself into him, little jumps every now and again telling him she was crying quietly.

How had he been so stupid, so blind, so naïve? While she was keeping him together, all the time since Evie's death she had been slowly falling apart and she'd had no one there for her.

'I'm so sorry, Becky,' he whispered into her hair. 'I'll be there for you now. I'll be better.'

100

Rebecca

I hear him say the words, even though he sounds like he's speaking underwater. It felt so real at the time, seeing her in my bedroom, following her out into the road. Then there were lights everywhere and people talking at me, telling me it was okay – and she was gone, or maybe she'd never been there in the first place, just like the other times.

But it's going to be okay, it was just another dream, one of the dreams that have plagued me these last months, but they will stop with time. And as I stand there in *her* clothes, smelling of *her* as the nurses fuss around me, calling me Mrs Bradley, I know that she's gone and she can't hurt me any more. I've won.

Epilogue

Nine months after the wedding

Curled up in a ball on the sofa, Richard lets out a gentle snore. I move around the house without waking him, switching off the Christmas lights on the tree and rearranging some of the decorations. Richard had wondered whether or not to put up a tree at all until I'd convinced him that Evie would never want him to ignore Christmas entirely. It will be our first one without her, although sometimes the ghost of her is so tangible it feels as though she's in the room with us. Slowly though, things are getting easier. Richard is starting to heal and I have been there every step of the way, patient and respectful.

I take out the glasses from the table, put them into the dishwasher and wipe my hands on the oversized T-shirt of Evie's I'd borrowed with the slogan *Ambition made me do it* on the front. It swamps me like a dwarfish thief in a giant's robe but it's comfortable and she won't be needing it. I go back through to where Richard is still sleeping soundly.

'Wake up, sleepy head,' I whisper, switching off the TV and shaking his arm. 'It's finished.'

He opens his eyes, looking confused at first, then grins at me. 'I wasn't asleep.'

'Oh right, you always snore when you're awake, do you? Don't worry, I won't post the pictures of you drooling on Facebook.'

'Okay, you got me. Did they catch the bad guy?'

'Come on, the bad guy always gets their comeuppance. What kind of film would it be if they just got away with it?'

I lean down to pick up the half-empty bowl of popcorn off the floor at the same time as Richard starts to sit up. Our faces are so close that they are almost touching. My heart is pounding and this time, nine months after Evie left us, neither of us moves away. There is the smallest moment's hesitation on his face before Richard leans in and kisses me. I respond automatically, my hand reaching around to run through the short soft hair on the back of his head. His hand rests in the small of my back, gently nudging me closer. It lasts no more than thirty seconds but it's everything I've been waiting for. When we pull apart I start to apologise – was it too soon? Have I ruined all that time planning and waiting by rushing things now? But Richard's face isn't angry or embarrassed.

'I should go,' I say, and start to stand. But he grabs my hand.

'Stay,' he says, and it's not a question. Like a nervous schoolchild I follow him upstairs and I see him hesitate at the door to the room he and Evie once shared. But the hesitation is fleeting and he pushes open the door.

'Oh damn, my phone is downstairs,' I say, not wanting to break the moment and bring us crashing back to reality but my contraceptive pill is in my purse and I can't risk missing it. Especially if tonight is going to end the way I hope it will.

Downstairs I flick on the living room light and my blood runs cold. On the coffee table, propped up against my handbag is an envelope that wasn't there five minutes ago.

THE NIGHT SHE DIED

I rip open the envelope and pull out a newspaper article. There is a photo of James Addlington smiling back at me in a smart suit and tie, and as I read the article my mouth dries up, the elation of moments ago evaporated.

> Sudden disappearance of business tycoon leads to suicide fears: wallet and wedding ring found on 'suicide bridge'

Fears are growing for missing business mogul James Addlington after a wallet and wedding ring believed to be that of the twenty-eight-year-old were found at a spot dubbed by locals as 'suicide bridge' yesterday. Addlington has been missing for three days now and a source close to the family say they are 'frantic with worry'. His father, James Addlington Sr, died in a house fire several years ago, leaving his business operations to his son, making him one of the richest men in Britain. His wife, Camille Addlington, was not available for comment.

Before I can even begin to wonder what it means and who left it here my phone buzzes inside my bag. I pull it out and look at the message from an unknown number.

It's a photograph, taken less than ten minutes ago in this very room. Richard and I are sharing our first kiss in years, his hand on my back, mine around his neck. The photographer is across the room – judging from the angle it has come from the computer that sits on the desk in the corner, where a webcam sits unassumingly. I think of the Cerbus software that had been on my phone, and now I know that it wasn't Camille who put it there. It was someone who had unfiltered access to my phone, and to her own home computer. Someone who obviously didn't trust me as much as I thought she did. My heart plummets as another text from the same number flashes on the screen. The words make my vision of my perfect future with Richard crash down around me.

Enjoying my life?

Now

Evie

I can't pinpoint the exact moment I realised that the person I'd grown to rely on like a sister had grown to hate me in return. Was it the way she would turn away when Richard and I kissed? Or the air of contempt rather than appreciation when I bought her gifts? She looked the way I felt when my father turned up with expensive trinkets, when once upon a time I'd been able to make her face light up with just a plastic ice drink maker. I should have known how she felt about Richard really, I mean look how intensely Rebecca fell for the people in her life. She doesn't do things by halves – she loves or she hates. She breathes life or she kills.

I'll admit, even I was shocked when she suggested I throw myself off a cliff. I watched her face as she said the words, as though it was the most logical thing, like she was suggesting we go to the cinema or for a curry. *Make them believe you're dead.*

And the more I thought about it, the better the idea seemed. Alive, things were messy: the truth about my affair with James, my part in the death of his father – *our* father. I'd never really been good at sticking around to face the music. But dead, I could walk away from every mistake I'd ever made, every wrong turn, every bad decision. The problem was, there was only one person I knew who had the power to make it happen.

Did I know then, that my best friend planned to betray me? That on the night of my wedding she would let me plunge to my death knowing there would be no boat waiting for me? I don't think it was until I saw the rock we'd placed to mark my safe spot had been moved that I knew for certain.

It was a week after Becky's suggestion and I'd thought of nothing but what I was going to do about the baby, and whether I could make my death work. There was no doubt I could fake a cliff jump but making a new life work after my death would take money and planning. That's what I would need my father for.

'How is he today?' I asked Yasmin as she ladled pasta into a bowl and placed it on a tray.

'I've never seen him like this,' she replied. 'He's not coping, Miss.'

Since my mother had passed away I'd begged Papa to leave the house and come and stay with Richard and I, but he'd been his usual obstinate self and refused. Offers for me to come and stay with him had been waved away with equal brevity. Hearing about his steady decline made me realise I should have tried harder.

Seeing my strong, handsome papa so pale and grey, black stubble unruly and dark circles shadowing his eyes, was painful, and I almost didn't say what I'd gone all that way to say. When I walked into the sitting room and saw him sitting there staring at my mother's empty chair I was certain that one more shock would kill him. But he looked up, saw me hovering in the doorway with the tray of pasta and smiled.

'Evelyn,' he started to rise but I waved him to sit back down.

'Yasmin says if you don't eat this she'll come in and feed you like a senile old man.'

Papa looked down at the pasta and grimaced. 'She thinks I need senile old man food. Maybe when she cooks a duck I'll eat. Come here, sit down. To what do I owe this visit? And don't tell me no reason because I can see in your face, you have something to tell me.'

I didn't move. Suddenly I was seventeen years old again, having to tell my father I was having a baby, only this time it was so much worse. This time I knew the reason my parents had tried so hard to keep us apart, why they had lied to convince me to abort our child.

'I'm having a baby, Papa,' I said, and before he could express joy at his first grandchild, before the news that he was going to be a grandpops could sink in, I added, 'And James is the father.'

Over the next hour we had talked together, my papa and me, more than we had in my whole life. He told me how my mother had got pregnant by him at sixteen and they had decided to terminate the pregnancy, how Mum had never really got over it, and how, when she had her affair with James Sr and found out she was pregnant again – this time with me – none of them had been able to go through the pain of losing a second child. I told him how I felt about James, and how I couldn't lose him or my baby again. I'd expected him to rage and shout, have me shipped off to Paris or Dubai, have James arrested or shot, but instead he nodded. We could never be together in public, he said. It would only ever be a shameful secret. Is that how I wanted to live?

No, I replied. *I want to die.*

That night my father had waited himself in the boat tethered to some rocks. I'd known he wouldn't be present at the ceremony, and also that people wouldn't be particularly surprised that he'd been held up by work. I'd never told Becky about Papa's involvement, and so she'll never know how many practice runs we made, how I knew my positioning off by heart without the need of any marker. How Papa had dropped me straight off with Phillip who had driven me the hundred miles to the ferry.

I was out of the country before the helicopters turned up to look for me. Once I was safely in France Phillip returned my passport to my father who used my key to get it into my old home when Richard was out. Yasmin joined me that evening, James had to wait – although my father called him the instant I was safe in the car. I understand that when I gave him the heads-up Richard and Becky were on their way he played the grieving lover part very well, practically emptying out a week's rubbish into his drawing room and having to clear it all up again before Camille returned.

Part of me had still hoped, as my arms cut through the water that night to reach my father's boat, that a second boat would be tethered to the rocks, one that had been left by my best friend so that I might escape into the darkness. Miles from shore with no boat – even if I had managed to make a lucky jump from the danger spot she'd marked, there would be no getting ashore. The most I could hope for would be to drag myself onto the rocks below and hope to be found before I froze to death. What a wicked web we weave.

It's been nine months since I 'died' and James is about to meet his untimely death. It's felt like an eternity but arrangements had to be made, and we didn't want Camille's suspicions aroused by playing our hand too soon. Monique is a month old as we await our first Christmas. Her doting grandpops has spent far too much money and the small flat we occupy in Paris looks like Santa's grotto.

And me? Well I've had my fun, thanks to the tracking software I installed on Richard's and Becky's phones, and our home computer. It was a bit of a blow when Becky discovered hers but since she was usually stuck to Richard's side I could guess where they would both be from his. I often check in on him – despite the awful way I treated him I do love him like a brother, although I understand that no one would ever believe that if they knew what I'd done. I even went home once, although that was stupid and careless of me, but I was getting bored and homesick, and I look so different these days with my short dark bob and brown contact lenses. I wanted to take my camera back – I hated leaving it but it was the only way I'd convince Becky that I was really dead. She knew the only way I'd leave that camera behind was if I never made it ashore and now she's keeping it for herself, just like the rest of my life. The necklace and the water was a spur of the moment thing, I wish I could have seen her face. I wonder if it was her who found it, or Richard? I regretted it afterwards, it was never my intention to upset him – I just wanted her to think she was going crazy. Thank goodness they never mentioned it to my father – he'd have hit the roof if he knew about my fun and games. On the whole though, I've been waiting. Waiting and watching as she tries on my life to see how it fits, making her think that poor, distraught Camille – who lost everything on the night I died – was spying on her, playing games with her. And just when she thinks she's safe, that I'm dead and gone – that's when I will make my move. Because dead women tell no tales. And dead women can't take revenge.

Acknowledgements

Thanks (again and always) to my wonderful agent, Laetitia Rutherford, who has been my constant champion in my publishing journey and kept me sane – without you I would have lost my mind long ago. Also to Megan and everyone else at Watson Little and The Marsh Agency who work tirelessly to get my books into the hands of readers all over the world.

To all of the gang at Headline, my lovely editor Kate Stephenson, Ella Gordon, Jenni Leech, Jo Liddiard and Jen Doyle in particular who always make me feel like part of the Headline family. I feel very lucky to be working with you all. Thanks also to Siobhan for allowing me to judge my books by their gorgeous covers.

Books are nothing without readers, so thanks will always go to the fabulous readers and bloggers who tirelessly promote my books. There are too many of you to mention by name but I am grateful to every single one of you.

And lastly, but never least, to my friends, fellow crime writers, family and particularly my husband Ash who always knows when a deadline is approaching by my mood and hasn't divorced me yet. Thanks love.